Mutton

Mutton

INDIA KNIGHT

FIG TREE
an imprint of
PENGUIN BOOKS

FIG TREE

Published by the Penguin Group
Penguin Books Ltd, 80 Strand, London WC2R ORL, England
Penguin Group (USA) Inc., 375 Hudson Street, New York, New York 10014, USA
Penguin Group (Canada), 90 Eglinton Avenue East, Suite 700, Toronto, Ontario, Canada M4P 2Y3
(a division of Pearson Penguin Canada Inc.)
Penguin Ireland, 25 St Stephen's Green, Dublin 2, Ireland (a division of Penguin Books Ltd)
Penguin Group (Australia), 707 Collins Street, Melbourne, Victoria 3008, Australia
(a division of Pearson Australia Group Pty Ltd)
Penguin Books India Pvt Ltd, 11 Community Centre, Panchsheel Park, New Delhi – 110 017, India
Penguin Group (NZ), 67 Apollo Drive, Rosedale, Auckland 0632, New Zealand
(a division of Pearson New Zealand Ltd)
Penguin Books (South Africa) (Pty) Ltd, Block D, Rosebank Office Park,
181 Jan Smuts Avenue, Parktown North, Gauteng 2193, South Africa

Penguin Books Ltd, Registered Offices: 80 Strand, London WC2R ORL, England

www.penguin.com

First published 2012
001

Copyright © India Knight, 2012

Set in 12.5/14.75pt Dante MT Std
Typeset by Jouve (UK), Milton Keynes
Printed in Great Britain by Clays Ltd, St Ives plc

A CIP catalogue record for this book is available from the British Library

ISBN: 978-1-905-49084-4

www.greenpenguin.co.uk

MIX
Paper from
responsible sources
FSC   FSC® C018179
www.fsc.org

Penguin Books is committed to a sustainable
future for our business, our readers and our planet.
This book is made from Forest Stewardship
Council™ certified paper.

ALWAYS LEARNING   **PEARSON**

For E

'One should never trust a woman who tells one her real age. A woman who would tell one that would tell one anything.'

Oscar Wilde

Prologue

Here are some of the things I have started doing due to age. I am forty-six years old.

a) Making sounds when I sit down or bend. The sound is often 'Oof', even though sitting or bending causes me no discomfort whatsoever. There is nothing physically the matter with me; in fact, I'm really bendy. Sometimes I put my hand in the small of my back, for emphasis. I also groan with pleasure, quite loudly – 'Wooaaarrrgh' – when entering either the bath or bed.

b) Asking, loudly and indignantly, 'Who *are* these people?' when I read a gossip magazine. Occasionally jabbing crossly at the photographs with my finger. A mere three years ago, I could have named every person in *Heat* and given you a potted bio – 'And that's Dyamondé, who got up the duff to the Loin, who was dating Pipette, you know, with the implants that went wrong. Keep up!'

c) In the rare instances when I do know who the people are, darkly muttering things such as, 'Heh, that won't end well,' Cassandra-like.

d) Going to new restaurants and saying, 'Ooh, dreadful acoustics,' as though I were hard of hearing, which I'm not. Leaning forward ostentatiously to emphasize the point. Talking extra loudly. Making exaggerated facial expressions and over-articulating to convey non-existent partial deafness.

e) Being completely uninterested in meeting new people at, say, dinner parties. Being pleasant, obviously, but not even going through the pretence of swapping numbers/emails.

f) Being too old for weddings. Thinking, 'I'd better go but, oof, it's *a very long day*.' Plus, see e).

g) Thinking, horribly, about many – though not all – weddings, 'Yeah, good luck with that.' Like a monster.

h) Forgetting people's names. Wishing I were camp enough to say, 'Darling, meet darling.' Not being as camp as I was.

i) Having two-day hangovers. Sometimes three-day. We're talking darkened room and death-feeling axe through the head and Temazepam, not Neurofen Plus and 'plenty of water'.

j) Wondering how it came to pass that the people in charge should be younger than me. Feeling, strongly, that a dreadful mistake has occurred – a rip in the time–space continuum, a grotesque, extra-anomalous anomaly – and that someone needs to *notice*, and fix it.

k) Realizing that young people talk about the Eighties in the way that I used to talk about the Fifties: i.e. as though speaking quite anthropologically about quaint prehistory. Also, noting that the films being remade are the films of my youth. Ditto the clothes.

l) Developing an interest in the weather. Talking and thinking about it a lot. Responding to the weather as if it were a person – more, a friend: being outraged by the rain's behaviour, and wondering why it's doing it. Worrying about slipping in snow, despite snow being my favourite and despite my soles being snow-cautious and grippy.

m) Also developing a strong interest in nature, despite having been the kind of ultra-urban young woman who genuinely didn't understand what the country-side was *for*. Being pleased when I see mushrooms. Smiling at trees. Examining leaves. Pondering sheep. Photographing cloud formations and learning their names.

n) Only finding babies interesting up to a point, unless I'm related to them. Sometimes finding the babies a bit irritating, rather than (as in the past) permanently adorable. Saying 'Oof' when they leave, and having a nice cup of tea.

o) Oh yes: tea. Pints of the stuff. Pints. Rivers.

p) Developing an unlovely fascination with my own bowel movements. Becoming pleased when I 'go' and disgruntled if I am denied my morning poo. Being so breezy about this particular interest (hobby, almost) that I am not shy about discussing it with girlfriends, even though every man I've ever slept with is led to believe that I don't poo or wee, ever, because I am a princess made of special things.

q) Often feeling that there is too much choice. Wishing that there were twenty pairs of shoes to pick from, not 200. Wishing that coffee were just coffee, with three variants, maximum, and only one kind of milk. Preferring small shops to the department stores that I once considered nirvana. Preferring shop assistants not to be versions of my children; craving the matronly.

r) Sometimes overhearing young people talking and, instead of being excited by the fact that language is a growing, ever-evolving, living thing, thinking, 'Language has just died in your mouth. You have murdered words.' Being tyrannically intolerant of bad spelling; equating it with imbecility. Becoming a grammar pedant. Saying things like, 'How can you *think* if you can't even *write*?'

s) Having bits of poetry I learned by heart at school thirty years ago pop into my head unbidden, after a complete absence of three decades. Not unpleasant. Ditto hymns. Also, wandering into churches and having a sit-down, feeling utterly at peace, even though I am not an especially devout person.

t) Minding about manners. This is not new, but now feeling actual rage at people who don't say please and thank you. Saying it for them, in a horrible, sarcastic, old-biddy tone. Speaking of which: noticing how prefixing anything with 'old' makes it a more effective insult.

u) Knowing that I'm more than halfway through, you know . . . my life . . . and pushing the thought away with all my might.

v) Becoming incandescent about 1) litter and 2) dog turds. Chasing people who don't pick either up.

Saying, 'Excuse me, excuse me,' in a fluting, rising tone, almost singing, until they notice me.

w) Flirting in a completely mild, ordinary way with waiters and sometimes seeing the confusion in their faces, and realizing they are thinking that I could be their mum.

x) Knowing that one day somebody will ask my youngest child, whom I had at thirty-eight, if I am her granny. Not now. Not yet. But one day.

y) Hoicking my bosoms and sniffing to indicate disapprobation.

z) No, not really. Not that last one. But it can only be a matter of time.

I

My friend Olive used to narrate her day to herself in her head as a child. 'Olive is walking down the street, her long brown hair swishing, whee. Today it is plaits and they are a bit tight. Olive looks nice, even though she is named after a gross-tasting thing, like being called Anchovy, which tastes of fish's bottoms. Soon Olive will be at school. Maybe it will be sausages for lunch. Johnny says they look like willies. Olive sees a red bus and two lots of blossom.' She told me years later that, as an only child, she found the running commentary kept her company during the many hours she spent alone, travelling to and fro or waiting for her parents to come home. 'Every cup of tea I made, or every plate of beans on toast, turned into a little bit of presenting, like I was in *Blue Peter*: "Olive is lighting the gas carefully. Olive thinks half a tin is plenty for tea, because there is strawberry Angel Delight afterwards."'

She said thinking about yourself in the third person did wonders for her self-esteem. She rarely thought, 'Olive Wilkins is walking down the street looking horrible. Galumph, galumph, goes Olive Wilkins. Urgh, the fat spotto. Round by name, round by nature.' The story she told herself about herself was cheerful, optimistic, with Olive as its star – a mildly tweaked-for-the-better Olive, but a recognizable one. We'd had a couple of bottles of wine when she told me about doing this a fortnight ago, and she laughingly admitted that she had never entirely stopped. 'Obviously, it stopped being every moment of the day by the time I was about eleven,' she said. 'But if I was feeling a bit anxious or insecure it would pop back again: "Olive really hopes David turns up, because she's been waiting outside the Odeon for ten minutes now and it's about to start raining. But why would David not turn up? Olive is wearing her nicest dress and her hair actually looks OK, and he said he'd been looking forward to tonight all week. Ah, there David is."' Once, she said, quite recently and during a particularly unsuccessful sexual encounter, she made herself snort with laughter by returning to her childhood habit: 'Olive hates Harry's back, because it is hairy. Hairy Harry. Olive wishes she had known about the hair, but she couldn't see it through the shirt he was wearing at dinner. Oh no, Olive notices sadly. Harry really doesn't have much of a sense of rhythm. Poor Olive. Poor Harry.'

I'm trying out Olive's technique while walking down the street. Here Clara comes, looking halfway presentable despite the early hour, because she had a meeting earlier this morning and has made an effort. She notices that the builders have started work at number 33; she sees them from afar, milling about the pavement as a scaffolding lorry is being unloaded. Bother, Clara thinks, I'm going to have to go right past them, and even though the law's changed and building firms are all discrimination-aware and everything, you do get the ogle and still, sometimes, the odd catcall. Awful, really, that in 2012 women should still be objectified in this way – that they can't go about their daily business without some brickie shouting out a vague obscenity. And there are about a dozen of them, plus the scaffolders. Oof. Still, deep breath, Clara. Here we go.

How weird. I mean, I know they have to keep their eyes on their important tools and dangerous builder equipment and everything, but really? *Silence?* Here I am, a woman, not actually ninety-five years old and with my head on the right way round: that's good enough for most blokes, isn't it? And these are blokes. But not a peep.

Not that I want a catcall. Not exactly. But – well, come on. Come *on*. I'm wearing quite a tight dress and a pair of heels; I've got on tinted moisturizer, blusher, eyeliner, mascara and lip gloss. I had a blow-dry two days ago. I am only forty-six years old.

Oh, I know. I spent many decades of my life objecting vigorously to objectification. I could bore for England about the theory. Ew, everyday sexism: the horror. Obviously men shouldn't shout things out at women in the street. It's not nice. But I'll tell you what else I don't find nice either, to be absolutely honest with you: this weird silence. What is wrong with these freaks?

I don't like it. Clara is displeased.

I'm just going to go past again, as an experiment. I can see they're busy discussing plumb lines or cement mixers or something; so busy that they're obviously not able to concentrate on passing women.

I walk more slowly this time. I don't saunter – not exactly – but I sashay slightly. I swing my bottom. I am heading towards the biggest group – there are six of them – and as I approach I decide not to swerve awkwardly but to go right through them instead, like Moses parting the Red Sea. Ha! Try and ignore *that*, men with penises. So this is what I do. And they part, wave-like, and as they part I make sure to make eye contact, and to smile – not what I meanly call the full Desperate Nana when my friend Frances does it, but a little smile, with no teeth showing. (Poor Frances. She's so obsessed with her own invisibility that she's fulfilling her own prophecy. Also, she never used to smile like that – I don't know where it's suddenly appeared from. She does it at any single man who ever talks to her: it's a sort of leer, with top and bottom teeth showing. I don't know what it's supposed to denote: a certain 'roar' carnivorousness, maybe. Appetite. It has literally not worked once. You can see the horror in the men's faces the second it happens; she's a nice-looking woman, until she does Desperate Nana and then it's all, 'Woah, is that the time?')

Anyway, here comes take two. And then: bingo. Nothing from the other ones but the main one, the foreman – not bad-looking, actually, thirty tops – smiles at me. Get in! Still got it – I mean, of course I've still got it, but it's pleasant to have it confirmed. One isn't without one's anxieties. And he's about to say something. Success.

'Oops,' is what he says, moving out of my way. And then he raises his hard hat by a couple of inches, and I stand and stare at him as he lowers it again. 'Morning, madam,' he says.

Why is he raising his stupid hat, like he would to his old school headmistress from when he was six? And 'madam'? I have never pined more for the old 'Cor,' or 'Don't get many of those to the pound.' (My most memorable builder line, in the days when they still talked to me, was, 'Your eyes are like spanners. Every time I see them, my nuts tighten.' That would do. It's vulgar, I grant you, but it's no-nonsense. You know where you stand with a line that vulgar.)

I wonder, wildly and for a brief moment, whether I should

actually thrust my arse in his hand, for pinching. 'Madam *this*, baby,' I could say. But I don't. I give the foreman a tight little nod, and then I get a grip and move on. By the time I arrive home, I am in a very bad mood.

Are my eyes still like spanners? They look all right to me as I peer into the hall mirror. I haven't even put my bag down and my keys are still in my hand. There are lines at their edges, obviously, but that's because I'm forty-six and I smile. Smiling is good. I also laugh. I laugh now, mirthlessly and exaggeratedly, to make the bigger lines come: hahaHA. They're not tiny, the lines, but nor are they huge. I mean, they're not *crevasses*. So that's good. It's because I have fat in my face, which is also good. I always knew it would come in handy one day.

Less good: my eyelids seem lower down than they were. They've slumped slightly. You'd have to be on intimate terms with my eyelids to notice this, but then I *am* on intimate terms: they live in my face. Slippage has occurred, as if a tiny but unusually heavy person had sat on my brows and sort of pushed down with their minuscule little hands. But! I can reverse the effect, I note, by raising my eyebrows in quizzical fashion. Having raised my eyebrows, I lower them as much as I can. That's quite a frown line I've got going, actually. When did it come? But never mind. I don't ever frown like that, except maybe at my children, and when I'm helping Maisy with her maths homework.

You know how in films women of a certain age press their palms against their cheeks and pull up, to view the effect a hypothetical facelift might have, and how this denotes 'Our heroine realizes that she is ageing'? I'm not going to do that. No, I'm not, even though I'd quite like to. Just to see. I realize that I am ageing, what with being conversant with the concept of Time. But it's fine. I'm in pretty good nick, actually, considering. I'm healthy and strong and I do proper exercise and always take the stairs.

And I don't think forty-six is old. Not these days. It used to be ancient, of course: I remember the shock of realizing, some years ago, that the ancient old ladies who taught me at school must have been in, maybe, their late thirties. But you couldn't tell, because they wore horrible A-line skirts and cardigans in sludgy colours, and a visible layer of face powder at all times. They had hankies stuffed up their sleeves and sensible shoes that made their feet look like platypuses, and 'done' hair like helmets. I don't have any of these things. I have a couple of pairs of Louboutins, thanks very much. And some kickass underwear, oh yes. I expect my teachers wore enormous white pants, tucking the top carefully into the bottom of their bras for warmth. These are not my pants. Those teachers were not my people.

I realize with a wave of absolute disgust that I am about to tell myself that I am forty-six years young.

Of course it would be at absolutely this point that Sky should wander down the stairs. Now, I like Sky. I like her a lot. It makes me sad that, what with them both being seventeen, her and Jack's relationship is presumably doomed. I want to believe in the concept of childhood sweethearts who stay together forever – of course I do – but logic and observation tell me this is unlikely. But anyway, Sky's great: smart and funny and very pretty. I just wish she'd put some clothes on sometimes. She's not *naked*, obviously, but she's wearing what she usually wears at this time of the morning, namely a T-shirt and pants. The T-shirt covers her bottom, just about, but it doesn't leave much to the imagination. (There's a youthful phrase, I think to myself even as I utter it in my head. There's a thought that doesn't make me feel grannyish at all for having it: 'Doesn't leave much to the imagination.' Works well if you say it in a Sir John Major voice. I don't expect Sky has any idea who Sir John Major is.)

'Morning, but you're already late for school,' I say. 'Where's Jack?'

'It's OK,' Sky says. 'We've got a free first period. He's just in the shower. I'm grabbing us some toast.'

I put my bag and keys down and follow her into the kitchen. Golden hair, legs up to here – she is very aesthetically pleasing, old Sky, and this makes me happy. I don't understand that weird thing whereby women my age (Sir John Major's voice pops up again, saying, 'My favourite vegetable is the pea') – anyway, 'women my age' are expected to dislike or resent younger, fresher models. It seems deranged to me, that, as an approach, to say nothing of unsisterly in the extreme. I may have dodgy notions about wolf whistles, but I'm sane enough to wish the best for other women, young or old. So I'm glad for Sky. I'm glad she's lovely and pert and gorgeous and brainy and ambitious, and not necessarily in that order. Why would I not be glad? If someone's going to mill about my house in a state of semi-undress, I'm glad it's Sky and not, you know, some nerdy girl with a tache. Not that there's anything wrong with nerdy girls with taches: they're usually clever and interesting. But I could do without one in her pants, moping about all gloomily in – what? – black pants. Emo pants, or skull pants. Death pants, gloom pants, the Doleful Pants of Melancholia. I'd rather Sky's red and white stripes, which are jaunty.

And anyway – as I tell myself whenever her lack of familiarity with dressing gowns or pyjama bottoms gets on my nerves – it's good that she feels comfortable enough to wander about in her pants. She has quite a complicated home life – the mother died when Sky was little and the dad has had a succession of girlfriends, not all of whom have been wholeheartedly liked by Sky. She spends a lot of time at ours. Her dad's some beardy weirdo who writes fantasy fiction, if you please. Big on trolls and elves, is Sky's dad. And now rich as Croesus, because apparently there's quite a market for that sort of thing. His trolls and elves have 'gone global', according to Sky, particularly since the recent smash-hit TV series.

I don't suppose she'd walk about in her pants if there were an older man about. Or maybe she would?

'Sky? Would you get dressed if I had a husband?'

'Another one?' Sky says. 'Oh no, did we run out of Nutella?'

'Well, not necessarily a *husband*,' I concede. She's right – I've got two former ones of those already. 'But, you know, a boyfriend. Who lived here. A man my sort of age. Would you cover up? And there's another jar in the drawer.'

'Cool. Why?' says Sky. 'Are you going to move someone in? Who is it? Yeah, I guess so. I wouldn't feel comfortable walking about like this. Not if I was going to be objectified.' She wields the word breezily, familiarly, fluently.

'Who else is moving in? I know about Gaby,' says Jack, appearing in the doorway. 'You might have said. That's just such a weird thing to spring on us.'

'Nobody,' I say. 'Just Gaby. It was a hypothetical question about Sky and her pants.'

'Oh,' says Jack. 'I like her pants. Come on, Sky, we're going to be late. Got to get dressed.'

As they amble back upstairs, I wonder: would I ever move a man in? I used to do it with such breeziness in my youth – come and live with me, or I'll come and live with you, look, here I am with my bag and my wheely suitcase, here you are with your borrowed van and your LPs, it's done – but the fact is, I'm set in my ways. Living alone – well, living alone with biggish, relatively self-reliant children – has quite a lot to recommend it. You can do exactly as you please. You can grab your eight-year-old and lie about watching Disney movies in bed all day without feeling guilty about your spouse's need for adult conversation. You can have exactly who you like to dinner: no more 'Yes, I know he's a wanker, but I've known him since university.' You don't have to pretend to be interested in golf or rugby. There are additional benefits: you can be quite unphotogenic and gross and there's no one to see it. I know some couples have no issue with being unphotogenic and gross in front of each other, but I don't like it. Never have. It's really unsexy to have someone fart next to you, and there's nothing anybody can say – 'friendly', 'relaxed', 'companionable' – that will ever change my mind. Go and fart in your own house, I say, Parp-o-tron. Not in bed with me.

Speaking of which – bed, not parps – my sap is rising and I'm not sure what to do about it. I'm incredibly frisky at the moment, even now, as I screw the lid back on to the Nutella and open the dishwasher to unload last night's plates. What's that about? Rhetorical question, actually. I know exactly what it's about. I swore off what my former mother-in-law calls 'bedroom unpleasantness' when my last relationship – with a man I met in a hotel bar – eventually went south. The problem was that sex with him was amazing. It was *remarkable*. I do not say this lightly, or from the position of an ingénue. It was sort of cosmic, that sex – filmic, magnificent, filthy; like nothing else. All we did was fuck and then lie there swooning. This was fantastic, obviously, but also quite debilitating, because the Man From The Connaught and I were permanently knackered, half-broken with exhaustion because of all the fucking. And then we'd get a tiny bit of energy back and – well, you know. When we weren't fucking, we'd be eating and drinking and talking and laughing until the early hours. It was beautiful, and mad, and at some point I suppose might have become less frenetic – but we shall never know, because, alas, the Man From The Connaught is no more. I mean, he's alive, as far as I know. He has not perished or met with grievous injury. But our relationship has, because he had to go and live in Australia for work and, well, you know – it's all very well emailing and talking on the phone, but eventually we agreed that it doesn't quite cut the mustard.

I didn't think I'd mind that much – you tend not to, with the more sex-based stuff. But I do mind. I mind increasingly, because it turns out it wasn't just the sex. It turns out I was in love with him, which was not a thing I pointed out, or was even necessarily fully aware of, at the time. And so now there he is, being a jackaroo and galloping across the outback, herding sheep, I expect, and wrestling them to the ground while wearing chaps. Maybe. Or maybe not: he works in finance. Anyway, he's there and I'm here and it sucks, especially when I imagine him with a hypothetical new girlfriend called Sheila, all tinnies and sun damage and begging for a 'rooting'.

I'm still, a year later, trying to be brave about it and pretend I don't miss him, or the actual sex. But I do. All the time. I cope with this by pretending that he is the last thing on my mind, and sometimes it works. For example, I will try not to mention the Man From The Connaught again.

Anyway, having been shagged half to death, I thought I'd take a little break and try and have the occasional full night's sleep. Devote myself to the domestic pursuits. Help more with school projects; go back to my language classes; knit. And that was all fine, except at night I'd get this terrible overwhelming feeling of sadness – of brokenness, really. And you can't be having that. Not at my age: life is short and you must carpe the diem, not lie about on sofas howling into space while the yarn on your lap unravels like a metaphor. And then I thought, 'Well – it's perfectly possible to do all of these familial, domestic things and not be a nun.' So I swore back on: I made myself, to help the grieving process. (Also, not having sex is really fattening. You think, 'I'm not planning on having sex,' so you sit there picking absent-mindedly at snacks, the children's as well as your own, in a way that you wouldn't if sex was on the agenda. I mean, nobody prepares for a night of passion by scarfing down a tub of taramasalata and two pitta breads, do they? No one thinks, 'Fwoar, I'm massively in the mood, I'll just eat this really disgusting and inexplicably overpriced stuffed-crust pizza,' or 'I know what would make this underwear look really spectacular: carb-loading.' Sex is exercise, especially if you're being flung about: whatever you eat during the period of frenetic sexual activity comes straight off again. No sex equals 'Hiya, fatso.' Sex is part of one's general physical maintenance, really, at my age, like a decent serum or expensive opaques.)

However, sexing, as my daughter Maisy calls it, with people you're not really massively into is not as emotionally undemanding as you might think: on a bad day, it just serves to remind you of what you lost. I'm pleased that I am emotionally intelligent enough to have fathomed that out, obviously, but now I've got this awful Code Red level of the horn, and nowhere to put it: it's like some awful genie has been unleashed and won't go back in its bottle. I need to act, before I become the sort of woman who leers at people in the street and turns to her friend saying, 'Would.' On top of everything else, the horn feels dreadfully age-inappropriate. I should not be revved up like poor old teenage Meatloaf on a Saturday night.

Plus, you know: logistics. As the Loaf notes, it's a bummer being a) all revved up with b) no place to go, not even Sydney. I can't really have people back here if they're going to be one-offs – I don't think it would be nice for the children: 'Freudian nightmare' pretty much covers it – 'Welcome! Kids, meet the random. Random, fyi, we all shag on different floors. Try and keep the noise down.' I could, and have, gone to people's houses, but I don't really like that either because it's so immediately domestically intimate. And while intimacy is fine – evidently: you're about to shag – I don't like the domestic bit. I'm not interested. I didn't have the domestic bit with the Man From, because we never lived together, but I did with my two husbands, obviously, and with countless boyfriends in my youth. I'm not looking to play house the randoms for a good old while. I don't even want to see their furniture, which is a useless thing to say because there aren't that many men out there who live with their worldly goods covered in dustsheets, more's the pity.

It never bothered me before, to know what the inside of somebody's fridge looked like, but when the men you're talking about – the shaggees, I mean – are in their late forties or early fifties and inevitably divorced or separated, with pictures of their kids pinned to said fridge, it makes me feel a bit gloomy, or rather gloomier. It kills the horn. Their half-pint bottles of milk-for-one make me feel sad. Their childless man-homes, ditto. Their lonely toothbrushes. Their dying orchid, all crispy and brown. Hair-thickening lotion, once, poignantly, at the house of Richard, who was very handsome and very slightly thinning on top. I think it has something to do with the fact that there was obviously once a time when these men thought, 'Freedom! No more ball-and-chain! My very own shag-pad!', envisioning all the hot laydeez passing through and enacting their fantasies – 'Hey, do you want to ask your mates round? I could really do with a bukkake party, it's been two long weeks.' And then, after a period of time, this: hair thickener and, somewhere tucked away, a picture of the ex-family in happier times. It's the death of hope. As a vibe, it doesn't really make you want to wave your knickers in the air, joyfully crying, 'Over here, tiger.'

Also, whereas years ago I'd have forgotten the specifics of various interiors by the time I'd walked to the Tube, these days they're irritatingly lodged in my head: 'I liked the way he'd knocked through in the basement. And putting the utility room to the side like that – it's a really excellent, ingenious use of space.' This is, let's face it, also an age thing, born of decades of overfamiliarity with houses in general and interiors magazines in particular. I don't think you should necessarily walk to the Tube after a night of passion (though it isn't passion, alas and alack) with total recall of someone's white goods/carpeting data.

I wouldn't want you to get the wrong idea: it's not like there have been dozens of these lone-toothbrushed men. There have been a mere few. Three. Maybe four (I say maybe because I do not wish to remember Four, who had a thing about feet, which was perfectly fine *up to a point* and then just tiresome, as well as quite comical in a not-good way). None of whom I had any intention of seeing in anything approaching a regular way.

But that too is awkward, because we're all so easily findable nowadays: you can't escape. You can't say, 'Thanks for the fun evening,' and disappear: there's email, and texts, and Facebook and Twitter and so on and on and on, so that you can never wholly shake someone off. Plus they send distressing, only very slightly coded tweets about feet, in the case of Four. So then you have to go through this rigmarole of doing it again and upping the date ante, even though at least one of you knows the thing has no legs (only feet, ho) and isn't going anywhere. It's wearying. It's like being twenty and doing pity-shags, or politeness-shags, which really ought to be a thing one outgrows.

You'd think men would die of joy if someone sent them a text saying, 'That was fun, let's do it again at some point, maybe.' No strings. Turns out a lot of people like a little string. At our age. Which is damned peculiar: I spent literally decades thinking all men wanted was stringlessness. I wonder when the interest in string kicks off. At around forty-five, I'm guessing, after at least one failed marriage, maybe two; after the initial excitement of thinking 'I could shag any woman in the world!' wears off and Angelina Jolie has bafflingly failed to come knocking, naked under her trench coat and writhing with longing, and more realistic expectations set in. Everyone is so lonely, really. It's piteous.

And another thing: people find the idea that a person – me, for example – should rather fancy the idea of stringlessness . . . not shocking, exactly, but mildly distasteful. Well, I say 'a person' – what I really mean is 'a single woman with teenage children'. I have observed that you're allowed to have those thoughts if you're freshly separated and your children are small, because then the assumption is that you're looking to hook up again, to form another nuclear unit, to provide your children with a stepfather and to start playing happy families all over again. This is acceptable. Whack on ten or fifteen years, though, and it becomes suspect, especially if you point out that said children have perfectly good dads and that nothing could be further from your mind than providing them with an unnecessary replacement. I mean, maybe if the dads were dead, but Sam and Robert are alive, I'm pleased to say. They're not even ill.

But live dads and no stepfather requirements basically mean 'I like sex' and incredibly this perfectly reasonable statement – not that it's a *statement*: I don't march about shouting it out – is still considered suspect. You see some people's thought bubbles and they're saying, 'Slaaaaag.' You kind of get the feeling they would prefer it if you said, 'Sex? Urgh,' and ran out of the room holding your mouth, which had filled with volumes of sick. And then ran back in, purged, to quietly get on with your macramé.

Anyway, it's all very well standing around with ants in your pants, wondering about these annoying mute builders and eyelid droop and laughter lines and pushing back the memory of the glorious Sex of Yore and shoving it in a box and putting a padlock on that box and throwing it in the sea and pretending there is no such thing as Australia, but I need to get on. There will be other occasions on which to test the builders, seeing as they work halfway down the road, and the eyelid situation is just going to have to wait. There's not much I can do about it, frankly, other than take a knife to them, and everybody knows that that way madness lies, plus horrible feline eyes at a strange slant, as though you'd taken a cat and cruelly pulled back all its face-fur and tied it up with an elastic band, like a psycho and as a break from pulling the wings off flies. Bad look on a cat, worse on a human. And the sex: well, you know. It's not going to kill me to go without for a bit. I don't think.

Also, today is a red-letter day – the day my old schoolfriend Gaby becomes my lodger and moves in to the top floor of my house. She's been living in California for the past ten years, becoming, either improbably or crashingly obviously (I can't quite work out which), a sort of yoga mogul. You'd think there would be an embarrassment of yoga moguls – yoguls? – in California, and that they hardly needed a Brit to come along and show them how it was done, but there we are. She started off with one studio and now has a mini-empire, which she's planning to expand over here. Her explanation, when I asked her about it all on the phone, was, 'I took the wankery out of it,' which does seem appealing. Maybe she offers bourbon shots and toasted cheese sandwiches after class. It's a strange concept, Gaby as yoga person – I mean, people change, obviously (Gaby changed so much that she used to be called Laura), but ten years ago she was all about the evenings in with telly and a takeaway, plus she was quite fat. Not like 'Come and winch me out of this sofa, for I am beached,' but fatter than me, and I was a size 16 at the time.

The top floor is empty because my eldest son is now away at university. We moved things around when he left and freed up a space that was used as a general lair. There's a little bathroom up there too – it's like a self-contained flat. I was delighted when Gaby announced she was coming home after all this time – and less delighted when she confirmed what I'd surmised, namely that she and her American husband, Ham, were getting a divorce (yes, that's his actual name: short for Hamble, which if you're British and of the age to remember *Playschool* is arguably even worse). They don't have any children, which simplifies things at one level at least, though I suspect it may have complicated them at another. She always seemed keen on the idea of children, Gaby, and now she won't have any. That must be weird, to know categorically that it's too late for it to happen and that it never will. Not necessarily bad-weird, but odd and disconcerting.

Surprisingly, given her newfound success, Gaby leapt at my offer of the top floor; after an absence of over a decade, she said she wanted to sit back for a bit before hurling herself into the London property market. 'Plus, it'll be cosy,' she said. 'I'm not quite ready to rattle about some Soho apartment on my own. And we've got so much catching up to do.'

Which is true. I love Gaby. She's Team Cheese. You know how some women are Team Chocolate? I'm not one of them, and neither is she. These are the things Team Chocolate do: always pick the sweet thing over the savoury one, and then make a grotesque coy face and say the sweet thing is 'sinful' or 'wicked', as though a cake were a highwayman. They pine for the Nineties, when they could order a spritzer; now they put ice cubes in their white wine instead, and you want to say, 'Hey, why not just bring your sippy cup along?' They also favour fruit-based alcoholic drinks, and 'fizz', and they call their vagina their 'bits'. They use the word 'pampering' without throwing up. They love cupcakes. Cupcakes are everything that's wrong with domesticity (and I'm big on domesticity). When you have a baby, Team Chocolate are the women in perfect blow-dries who organize passive-aggressive, competitive, show-off coffee mornings that would put the Stepford Wives to shame. I've got a theory about that too, having sat through the rigmarole three times, which is that new motherhood is many women's option to reinvent their school days, to rearrange the order of things, the hierarchy. Not one of the cool girls? Ate lunch on your own? Here, finally, is your chance for redress, through the medium of Bugaboos and immaculate homes and a pretend version of How Things Should Be. I didn't have that problem at school, so I've never had any yearning to engage with it – in fact, all of that 'my baby eats more puréed broccoli than your baby' thing makes me want to laugh, flick V-signs and talk about wanking while smoking a fag. Nothing changes. But it's funny how school days still have so much to do with everything, even decades later. I can certainly tell a lot about a person by their child-rearing methods and their perfect child-parties, which when the boys were small sometimes induced hilarity.

So yeah, Team Cheese. Team Tampax, not – the horror – Team Towels. Team A Friend's Ex Is Off-limits Forever, And That's The Law. Team I Eat My Dinner, not Team I'm Pushing Salad About My Plate. Team Make It A Double; Team Why Not; Team I'll Give It A Go; Team Madonna. Still.

And now here we are, and by the time I've done my various yawny chores – because my children still have only the haziest grasp of the function of dishwashers and so on, which I do think constitutes the most appalling parental failure on my part – Gaby will be imminent. I'm excited. She's not only Cheese but one of my oldest girlfriends – the kind you can not see for a decade and still communicate with in shorthand the moment you clap eyes on each other again. And it'll be nice living with a friend, like in those American sitcoms where they have roommates. I'd nip out and buy some flowers for her bedside table, but I don't fancy going past the builders again.

2

Well, blimey. Gaby is still Gaby – lovely Gaby, whom I adore – obviously. She's also very obviously Not Gaby. The first thing I notice, after I've thought how almost tearfully happy I am to see her, is that any Moomin-type physical tendencies she may once have had have so gone away that it is as though I had imagined them. In fact, when her cab pulled up and I was standing on the doorstep hopping up and down with excitement, and she stepped out of the taxi, I very briefly thought, for a nanosecond, 'Eh? Who's this?'

And then I recognized her, of course – you couldn't not, with that shock of red hair and that megawatt smile, plus when you've been friends with someone since you were teenagers and they were called Laura, you'd recognize them anywhere, even if they'd grown a beard and changed gender. But as I helped with her bags and she dragged her enormous suitcases into the hallway, I couldn't help but observe that Gaby is a) half her old width and b) ten years younger – at least – than she was the last time I saw her. She looks amazing. She looks like an idealized version of herself. I can't really get my head around it. Weight loss, fine – she's a yoga freak for starters, plus you just go on a diet, plus she's come from California. It's more her face, which is the beaming, youthful face of a thirty-five-year-old. Thirty-six, tops. In reality, she is three years older than me, and, as I recall, about three months away from her fiftieth birthday.

'Frown, Gaby,' I say as I make her a cup of tea.

'Please, please give me PG Tips,' Gaby says. 'I could cry with joy. I get visitors to bring the tea bags to LA and I'm always so excited, but the milk's all wrong – you can't make a decent cuppa. Awful American milk. Two sugars, please.'

'Coming up,' I say. 'But go on – frown.'

Gaby frowns. Tiny wrinkles appear on her forehead and brow, and round her eyes. She can frown. Kind of.

'Oh man, I can't tell you how happy I am to be here. It's so great to see you, Clara. I love your kitchen.'

'It's bliss seeing you,' I reply truthfully. 'Have you had Botox?'

'Not for ages.'

'It's just – you look fantastic. What have you done? Have you had *work*? I mean, you actually look completely different. I barely recognized you.'

'You look fantastic too,' Gaby laughs. 'Have you?'

'Work? No,' I say. 'But funny you should ask, because I was thinking about my eyes this morning. Look. My lids. What's that about?' I make the face I made in the mirror earlier. 'See? There. And that big frown line. I don't like it.'

'Plenty of time for that conversation,' says Gaby airily. 'Meanwhile, fill me in. How are the children? How are you? How's work? What's up? After the tea, can we go to the pub?'

'It's eleven a.m.,' I say.

'I know,' says Gaby. 'Oh God, this tea – it's ambrosial. All I drink in LA is coconut water.'

'It tastes like come,' I say. 'Don't you think? Watered-down come, at three quid a shot.'

'Totally. But it's fantastically hydrating and full of minerals.'

'Hm,' I say. 'I'm too stupid to understand how anything can be more hydrating than water. I just can't really get past the taste of come.'

'You haven't changed,' Gaby notes.

'Just saying. Time and a place for that particular flavour.'

'Anyway,' says Gaby, 'it's because I haven't been in the pub for ten years. I've been so homesick recently. I started dreaming about rain and dirt and pigeons. And the Tube! Imaging dreaming about the Tube – and then you wake up and it's boiling hot and the sky is bright blue and you go for a swim before breakfast.' She shakes her head. 'Ham thought I was mad. There we were in idyllic splendour, and I was pining for London grot. Tube trains and rain.'

'That's a sex dream,' I say. 'Things pounding through tunnels. Do you want me to explain it to you?'

'It's because I am sexually desperate,' Gaby says, throwing back her head and laughing. Her teeth! Now that I look at them properly, her film-star teeth seem slightly too big. Where are the snaggly canines of yore? They were nicer; friendlier. 'I don't know why I'm laughing, it's not at all funny. I haven't had sex for seven months and eleven days, and even before that there was a marked deterioration in frequency and quality, obviously, what with divorcey hideousness.'

'I haven't had sex for four months and' – I frown, making the bad wrinkle come, while I count on my fingers – 'six days, I think.'

'You're so shit at maths.'

'I know. Roughly four months, say.'

'We should go out one evening,' Gaby says. 'To a night-club or something. Where's fun?'

'What, go on the pull?' I start laughing at this idea – the

last time Gaby and I went on the pull together, we must have been about nineteen. A memory pops into my head, of a club in Soho at about two a.m. and of Gaby glaring at me balefully from a banquette because I'd pulled and she hadn't; she was in a bad mood anyway because we couldn't find anything to fit her at this shop we used to go to called HyperHyper. She was always my plainer friend. Looking at her now, it seems hard to believe.

'Yes,' she says, laughing too. 'Why not?'

'I honestly have no idea where we'd go. I could find out, I suppose. But I'm amazed by your sex drought,' I say. 'You look amazing, you're in LA – how hard can it be?'

'Harder than you'd think,' she says. 'Everybody in LA looks pretty much like this: I'm the basic model. I'm entry-level. And everybody knows everybody. And I'm not in the husband-nicking business, so . . .'

'Well, no. But still. Aren't there hot yogis on tap, in your line of work? Tantric sex for days, that kind of thing? Like Sting.'

Gaby gives me a look and starts sniggering so contagiously that I'm also sniggering before she's even started talking. 'Yeah. I'm going to tell you about that,' she says. 'The tantric stuff. Later. In detail. They really want a drink to go with them, those stories. Anyway, how's Robert? I'm dying to see him. And to meet Sam. I can't believe I never met him. Ships in the night. Anyone else I should know about?'

'They're both great. And not at the moment, no, although when we go to the pub I'll tell you a funny story too. It's about feet.'

'A guy with a foot thing?' Gaby says, looking repulsed. 'I hate that. Of all the body parts.'

'Yep. And also feet are just feet. It's not like they're particularly dexterous or bendy or anything.'

'Feet don't have sex skills,' says Gaby. 'And I'm OK with that.'

We both start laughing again.

'We're like a couple of sex-crazed old biddies,' I say. 'We disgust me.'

'Oi!' says Gaby. 'Less of the old.'

'Well, we're not spring chickens, are we? And –'

'Speak for yourself,' Gaby interrupts.

'I do. You're more, I don't know – a young hen. Come on, I'll show you your coop,' I say, and we make our way upstairs.

Coconut water aside, any concerns I might have had about a wearying Californian lifestyle – egg-white omelettes, wheatgrass shots – having been adopted by Gaby are quickly dispersed, thank God. She looks like someone else, but she's very much herself. Aside from her face and body, nothing's changed – we could still be at school, which was where we first met.

I love my girlfriends. I've always loved them, but I love them even more now that I'm older. I love the way Gaby and I clung to each other, almost weeing with laughter, when I told her the specifics of Four, the foot guy.

As she goes off to the bar, I think about how I love the way I can ask her about Botox before filling her in on what my children have been up to, without feeling guilty about the order of priority, and the way everything is immediately made funnier, sharper and more cheerful by her presence. Not being married or in a relationship for the first time since I was twenty-four has brought many advantages, but the girlfriend thing absolutely tops the list. They've always been around, of course, but I didn't necessarily have time to hang out with them as much as I'd have liked, partly because of having children (which I did earlier than most of my friends, which made me out of sync: they were still going to raves while I was knee-deep in bottles and bottom-wipes) and partly because I do that full-immersion thing with men – here we two are, and everybody else can just butt out and wait. That's been remedied now. I feel so sorry for people without girlfriends.

3

dinner, without pleasure. Actually, I loved the physical sen-
sation. Now to have pure physical pleasure was first rate.
Though on a full appetite, true, it did become almost sickly
to the touch. With the experience of joy came worldliness,
though and disillusion. One way or another I was a sensualist
too,' I say clearly.

'So this is what you do,' Gaby explains a few days later, as the
two of us share a late breakfast. I've asked her, yet again,
how she comes to look like she does. I've been observing her
and as far as I can make out, she doesn't do anything out of
the ordinary. It's beginning to obsess me and so far her
replies have been . . . not evasive, exactly, but I don't think
she's quite giving me the full story either.

'Go on,' I say, already entranced, clearing the newspapers
away to make room for my elbows.

'OK. So. You don't eat. At all. Well, you eat a tiny bit,
otherwise you'd die – whole grains and greens, in my case,
and that's it, in microscopic portions. Maybe steamed fish
occasionally, like in restaurants. No alcohol. No dairy. No
wheat, obviously. No sugar, not even fruit. No nothing, to be
absolutely frank with you. You walk around starving.'

'What, so you acquire some sort of eating disorder?' I ask,
aghast. 'Just like that, all breezily, for no particularly good
reason?'

'No.' Gaby shrugs. 'You just don't eat. I mean, I suppose if
you had emotional issues around this stuff then yes, the
approach could easily turn into an eating disorder. But I'm
just really disciplined.'

'So far, so no use to me whatsoever,' I sigh. 'Also, when
I go to restaurants I like pommes allumettes.'

'It's not for everyone,' Gaby concedes. 'It's a massive

denial of pleasure. Actually, I think that's why I'm so into sex. You have to have physical pleasure somewhere – and food, sex, it's all appetite, isn't it? And then of course you go to the gym. Well, to the yoga studio, in my case, to which I have free and permanent access. You work out for three or four hours a day.'

'Right,' I say. 'Doesn't that make you want to kill yourself?'

'Only for about the first three months,' says Gaby. 'After that it becomes quite addictive.'

'Right,' I repeat, eyeing up my bacon and eggs and trying to recall when last I had a gym membership.

'It's basically a full-time job,' Gaby says. 'I was lucky in that it *was* my job. But yes, it pretty much took up the whole day. I don't have kids and I'm not a born housewife – and anyway, we had staff to do that sort of thing. I'm rich now, you know. So I went to my job, and that's what my job involved. You can't run yoga studios and be a size 18. But you're, what, a 14?'

I nod.

'You're fine.'

'Oh, I know. I mean, I know I'm not a complete disaster. Also, "fine"? What's that – exquisite understatement?' Gaby laughs. 'You do look at least ten years younger than me, is the point.'

'I wouldn't go that far,' says Gaby, shovelling in a mouthful. 'But you know, Clara, if this stuff bothers you, there are things you can do.'

'Also, why are you eating breakfast? And you've had tons of wine over the past few days.'

'I've given myself a fortnight off,' says Gaby. 'While I

acclimatize. After that I'm going to be no fun to eat with at all.'

'I know about the stuff you can have done,' I say. 'I don't think I fancy having things in my face. Toxins and fillers and God knows what. Anyway, doesn't all that sit quite oddly with your devotion to health?'

Gaby shrugs again. 'I guess, but I don't care. I'm vain. We're all vain. We don't know we're vain, some of us. We only realize quite how vain we are when things start heading south, is the thing. And at that point you only have quite a narrow window to act in if you're going to do it properly.'

'But do what, exactly?' I ask again. 'What have you actually had done? And how do you mean, "properly"?'

We're interrupted, annoyingly, by the arrival of my sister Flo, who's come to collect a box of picture books that Maisy, now eight, has outgrown.

'Fucking hell, Gaby,' is the first thing Flo says, or rather shrieks. 'You look . . . *incredible*. Like a really hot cartoon.'

'Thanks,' says Gaby, with the easy confidence of someone used to compliments. 'So do you.' She starts gathering her things; she has an appointment with an estate agent, to see about the possible location of her first yoga studio. 'How are you, apart from all grown up? You have kids now, right?'

'Two,' says Flo. 'They're three and five. I am broken with exhaustion, as you can see.' She points to the faint shadows under her eyes. 'But it's lovely having them, obviously.'

'Mm,' says Gaby, with a smile that strikes me as quite sad, but that I may be imagining: I mustn't go forcing my half-baked, stereotyped ideas about the Agony of Childlessness on to my oldest friend. Oddly enough, while we've talked about literally everything under the sun in the past few days, we haven't mentioned how she feels about this. She's been unbelievably nice to my children; she and Maisy have had a nightie-party twice and yesterday I found Gaby making her those fat American pancakes for breakfast. But so what, really? Liking my children – and they *are* nice children – doesn't exactly mean she cries herself to sleep every night over Her Barren Womb.

'I'm off,' Gaby says. 'Back later, teatime or so, and I'll pick up something for dinner. Or shall we just have a takeaway? I haven't had any Indian food yet and I don't know that I can hold out much longer.'

'Let's do that,' I say. 'I'll order. See you later.'

'See you,' says Gaby, blowing Flo and me a kiss. 'By the way, those builders down the road. Nightmare, right? I have to put my headphones on so I don't have to hear them.'

'She eats *takeaway*?' Flo says, with utmost incredulity, the moment the door's slammed. 'I don't think so.'

'She's having a fortnight off,' I say.

'What, a fortnight off eating air?'

'Something like that, yes. She was just explaining it all to me. Do you want some tea?'

'Yes please. She looks great, mind you. Not creepy-thin, just really fit-thin. But her face, Clara! She must have had everything done. I mean, done really, really well, because you can't tell. Well, you can, but you know what I mean. That is *fine* work. Plus she's lost a lot of weight without ending up looking like a monkey, which I call a feat at that age. You can go quite bonobo after about forty. She's unrecognizable.'

'I was asking her about it when you came in,' I say. 'She's

obviously not that keen about broadcasting the details, because she stopped talking.'

'That's the trade-off, isn't it, with not having children,' Flo says pensively as she sits down. 'You get to keep your body. I mean, I could live in the gym and I still wouldn't have a body like that.'

'You could,' I say. 'You're only thirty-four. I couldn't. My stomach is beyond fixing – three C-sections will do that to you.'

'Hm, tits and stomachs,' Flo says mournfully. 'No kids and you get to keep pert tits and a flat stomach. But,' she says, brightening, 'I'd rather be me or you. With children and the scars to show for it.'

'Would you really, though, Flo? You know – what if you could have the kids and the body, and the new face that was like your old face except better?'

'Oh, Clara, no,' Flo says, looking appalled. 'You know how I feel about that. We've discussed it millions of times. It's awful. There's nothing wrong with getting older. I mean, it's going to happen to every single person in the world. I think lines are *beautiful*. They tell a story.'

'God, you're so young,' I say. 'That's my position: I think I taught you it when you were in your teens.'

'It's *the* position,' Flo says sternly. 'It's sanity. Age with dignity. Don't go dicking about thinking you can be anything other than what you really are. It's delusional, aside from anything else.'

'I know,' I say. 'I know.' But I'm not sure I do know, any more. Would it really be so awful to get rid of my frown line? Why? Who would it hurt? I'd be me, with one line fewer – the one, lone line that remotely bothers me. The only problem that I can foresee is that I'm always reading how Botox is the thin end of the wedge, how this stuff becomes addictive, how you can't stop and then one morning you wake up and you've overdone it and you look like a freak. But I'm not stupid, or blind, and I don't have the money to go mad. And to be honest I wouldn't be that devastated if I woke up looking like Gaby.

'I might get my frown done,' I tell Flo. 'Or rather, I might go and chat to someone about my frown, just to see what they say.'

'I forbid it,' says Flo. 'And anyway, what frown? Everyone has a frown. That's because everyone has facial expressions. Because people are not *eggs*. Get a grip, Clara. No. Please don't.'

'I might,' I say firmly. 'I don't see the harm.'

'I will cull you if you do,' says Flo, looking genuinely distressed. 'Please, Clara. Not your face. Not anything, but especially not your face. I can't go through the rest of my life having a sister who's ruined her face and made herself look weird.'

But the more Flo is appalled, the more determined I become. The thing is, I know exactly what she's saying: she's saying what I myself have been saying for decades. It is a position, and a justifiable position, and it is also a position stuffed to the gills with the arrogance and blitheness of youth: 'Ooh, I can't wait to be old, it'll be so lovely. I'll be all apple-cheeked and well padded and bake cakes all day.' It is massively patronizing, is it not? What's wrong with 'I'm not especially looking forward to being old and I don't like baking. I'm going to have some jabs in my face and wear nice clothes and look as good as I can for as long as possible'?

37

Is that not another reasonable option? Do these things have to be either/or? And why should the rotund, baking old lady be somehow 'better' and more 'dignified' than the old lady sitting in the bar of the Connaught, without jowls, wearing lipstick, crossing her thin legs and toying with a cocktail?

'I'm coming with you if you make an appointment,' says Flo. 'Which I sincerely hope you won't because before you know it you'll look like a freaky egg-cat and your face will be all sinister and your eyes will be too high up.'

But I think I will. It's stupid to dismiss stuff out of hand without really knowing anything about it.

'Did you notice?' says Flo. 'Gaby has liver spots on the backs of her hands. Sun damage, I expect, but still. And her neck's all crêpey when she turns her head. There's no treatment for that. You can't hold back time, Clara. Stop being mad.'

'Talk to me again when you're nearly fifty,' I say.

'You're four years away from fifty. And Kate's not going to like it,' Flo says, heaving an enormously melodramatic sigh. 'Not one bit. The only thing Kate's ever used on her skin is almond oil.'

4

It's just after four p.m. and the house, which has been a haven of calm all day, explodes into its usual afternoon chaos. Maisy's back from school; she and her friend Lulu are playing upstairs – something involving several costume changes and the decimation of her dressing-up box, as ever (and this despite the presence of Meccano. I try, just like I tried with dollies with the boys. No dice).

Jack and Sky are mooching around the kitchen behaving like people who haven't eaten for days, even though they've just said they grabbed a Subway on the way home, literally fifteen minutes ago. Jack's in the fridge and Sky's by the toaster; Jack informs me that 'a couple of people' are coming round shortly. I push away my laptop and the article I'm working on – I write for magazines for a living – wondering if the day will ever come when I am able to work beyond teatime. I mean, obviously it will – these children aren't going to live here forever, but by that time I'll hopefully be retired.

'Stop eating,' I say as Jack pulls out a packet of Cheerios. 'And what's with the bloody cereal all the time? Eat a banana, if you're that hungry. Which you can't be.'

'I am. When's dinner?'

'About seven-ish, I expect.'

'I've got news, Clara,' says Sky, chomping on toast and putting crumbs everywhere. 'You know my dad?'

'Yes. Well, no, but yes.'

'He's going away,' Sky says.

'How do you mean? Where?'

'Oh, only for three months,' Sky says. 'To finish his book. His publishers have banished him.'

'I don't understand,' I say. 'Banished him where? Banished him, why?'

'You know his books, right? The Men of Granite Chronicles. They're, like, this huge long epic saga with dragons and stuff, set in an imaginary land called Lapidosa . . .'

'A harsh land,' says Jack, 'where strong men are unmanned. A land of rocks. A brutal land of pillage and siege.'

'Thanks for that,' I say, giving him a thumbs up. He's doing it on purpose: he knows that fantasy fiction is my least favourite genre in the world. I'll read anything, but there are limits.

'Horlan,' Jack says. 'That's "you're welcome" in Lapidosan.'

I roll my eyes at him.

'Anyway, and there have been six volumes,' Sky continues.

'Bernard's cool,' Jack says.

I think cool is pretty much the one thing Bernard categorically isn't, but I don't say so. 'Yes,' I say instead. 'Can't say I've read them, but yes.'

'Read them *yet*,' says Jack.

'Well,' Sky continues, 'everyone's waiting for volume seven, because they're really gripping and we are all dying to know what happens next . . .'

'Except *Bernard* doesn't know,' says Jack.

'Right,' says Sky. 'He's blocked. He says he can't finish it, and so he told his publishers, and they said he *had* to do it by the end of the year and that the problem was London because it was distracting. So they've rented him a place in Scotland.'

'Scotland?' I ask, perplexed. 'Why Scotland? What can he do in Edinburgh that he can't do in London?'

Sky stares at me blankly. 'Well, he doesn't know anyone, for a start. And it's not Edinburgh, it's those islands, you know, miles away from anywhere.'

'What, the Hebrides? They're sending him to the Hebrides?'

'Yeah. That's them. Totes remote. And, you know, no women.'

'There are women in the Hebrides, Sky,' I say. 'Also midges, as everyone knows. But why is that relevant?'

'Big shagger,' says Jack helpfully. 'Loads of girlfriends. Bernard,' he adds as I stare at him agog for the third time in three minutes.

Wow. I've seen Bernard's books – you can't miss them: they sell by the truckload – which means I've also seen his author picture more times than I care to recall. He's sitting behind a desk, looking like a little angry troll, all gnarly and covered in hair.

'Ah, OK,' I say, not wanting to hurt Sky's feelings by spluttering with derision. 'Sort of like Harold Robbins, whose publishers locked him in hotel rooms until he pushed enough sheets of paper out to them under the door.'

'No idea who that is, but yeah,' says Sky. 'Anyway, the thing is –'

'Could Sky stay here?' interrupts Jack.

'Yeah,' says Sky. 'Could I live here for, like, three months, while he's away? Please.'

'Please, Mum,' says Jack, making big eyes. 'Sharok. It's "please" in –'

'In Bernard book language, yes, thanks, Jack,' I say, giving him a hard stare.

'Pleeeease,' says Sky, chewing her fingers, as she does when she's anxious.

'She's half an orphan,' Jack says with a piteous expression. This is factually accurate but not strictly necessary.

'Erm,' I say, quickly thinking about it. Sky spends over half her time here anyway, so that doesn't make an enormous amount of difference. It's just, she's only seventeen: in loco parentis and all that. It's not without responsibility. 'I guess so, probably. Yes. OK.' Jack and Sky whoop. 'But,' I add, 'I really need to talk to your dad. He could have asked me himself, actually.'

'He's going to. He's calling tonight. I just couldn't wait to tell you,' Sky says. 'I'm so happy you said yes. Thank you so much. You'll hardly know I'm here.'

Jack and she are beaming, lit up with happiness – it's really rather sweet to see. And Maisy adores Sky and will be so pleased.

Still, blimey, I think to myself as they go upstairs to tell her the news, which she greets with shrieks I can hear two floors down. Imagine being in a position where you can just bugger off and up sticks for three months, leaving your child behind: helps to be a man, eh? What would Sky have done if I'd said no? Stayed with someone else, I suppose. At least she's comfortable here, and we all like her. It's fine; it's her second home anyway, I suppose. I do think it's slightly breezy of old hobbity Bernard to assume this arrangement would be such a dead cert by me. I'm curious to speak to him.

I don't have long to wait. The phone goes just as I'm

making the sauce for the children's spaghetti. It is indeed Bernard, who, amusingly, has just the kind of deep voice I expected. I always associate deep baritones with beards, to the point of being disconcerted when someone with a beard is insufficiently gravelly. Sam and I used to know a bearded man who had a high-pitched squeak: it was all wrong and we used to catch each other's eye and smile.

Bernard sounds perfectly pleasant, as well he might, given the enormous favour I am about to do him and his beloved half-orphaned only child.

'You're absolutely sure?' he's saying. 'Because we wouldn't want to impose in any way. Thank you, by the way, for having her over so often. I should really have thanked you before – remiss of me. I've been, er, rather caught up.'

This is an allusion to his shagging, I suppose. I wrinkle my nose at the handset and say nothing.

'Remuneration,' he continues. 'Obviously you aren't a guest house and, er, I'd like to ensure your coffers are replenished. Would you email me your bank details? Or keep accounts? I don't know – what would be easier?'

'She's very welcome to our food,' I say, feeling mildly insulted. 'It's incidentals, I suppose, like clothes and travel and stuff she might need for school. But I can jot down what it costs and let you know at some point, and then you can refund me.'

'Marvellous,' he says, sounding pleased. 'Or I could let you have some cash upfront, if that helped? Some doubloons? Perhaps we should meet – share a cup of the bean before I go? I'm leaving on Thursday.'

'I can't,' I say, aware of sounding faintly rude. But really,

I don't see the need, plus I don't have any burning desire to have coffee with the author of the Men of Granite Chronicles. That dungeons and dragons malarkey: really not my thing. 'Maybe give Sky some cash and we'll take it from there,' I say.

'Perfect,' says Bernard. 'Now, the idea of the exercise is total isolation. For my sins. Unfortunately that means no phone, no email, no nothing.'

'Is that really possible, in this day and age?' I ask. 'I went to Barra a few years ago and everywhere had broadband. Not to be a downer or anything, but I had better mobile reception than I do at home.'

'Mine's a smaller island, population thirty-eight,' Bernard says. 'There is some sort of dial-up Internet arrangement – I know, so old-fashioned – but my publishers have asked for the line to be disconnected. They mean business, I'm afraid. I'm not even going to take my mobile. Odd way of doing things, but total isolation works for me. I did a version of the same thing with my fourth volume, *Brotherhood of Stones: Initiation*, though the words flowed considerably faster then.'

'Ah,' I say, turning my laugh into a little cough. 'But – so, what, there's no way of getting in touch with you at all? What about emergencies? And surely your publishers will want updates?'

'There's a neighbour on the other side of the island who has every facility, apparently, though I'm told these things can sometimes be dependent on the weather. I'll send you the details. And for non-emergencies, there's always the post,' he laughs. 'I'm going to put all of this in an email to you now.'

I give him the address and wish him bon voyage. He thanks me again, profusely.

'One last thing,' he says. 'I know that Sky and Jack share a room, with, erm, everything that implies.'

'Oh!' I say, finding myself blushing (why?). 'I haven't actually asked them, have you? But I . . . I assume so. I mean, I think so. I mean, I think they do it, yes.'

'I haven't either, but I assume likewise,' Bernard says. 'They seem reasonably sensible, for young people. And of course it's a relationship they'll remember all their lives. First love: you never forget.' He sighs; I wonder if he's thinking of Sky's dead mother. 'However,' he continues, 'I'd appreciate you keeping an eye on . . . that side of things.'

'Well, I'm not going to *watch* them,' I say. 'I'm not going to try and listen.'

'No, no, of course not,' Bernard says with a laugh. 'But I'd appreciate any guidance you might be able to offer Sky on . . . on this subject. She is motherless, and the two of you seem close.'

'I'm not going to give her sex tips either,' I laugh. 'But I know what you mean. Of course I'll keep an eye on her. On them. And I'll report back.'

'I don't mean you should sit down and ban them from living their lives,' says Bernard. 'I meant, if she comes to you with any questions, or regarding any . . . feminine matters . . . You see, she's an only child, and there are so few women in our family – I have no sisters, and . . .'

'I'll do my best,' I say, thinking, 'Thanks, Bernie.' So now I'm Marie Stopes, or the period doctor, or whatever it is he means. Still, I suppose it must be awkward at times, being the widowed father of a teenage girl, and I feel myself thaw

45

towards him. It can't be easy for Bernard, or Sky for that matter.

'I'm grateful, I really am,' Bernard says again, and I swear I can hear a little sigh of relief. 'And that email is on the way.'

'Goodbye,' I say. 'And best of luck. I hope you unblock.'

'Like a lavatory,' says Bernard. 'God, so do I.'

5

'Florence told me. It is absolutely out of the question,' Kate says, adjusting a lock of glossy hair. 'I simply won't have it.'

'You don't have to have it, Kate. It's *my* face.'

'Not really,' says my mother. 'Technically, it's half mine.'

I sigh. 'Don't be loony.'

'We spent so much money on your education,' Kate says sadly, pouring out the tea from a china tea set. We are in her immaculate sitting room. Kate has the sorts of sofas that look like nobody's ever sat on them. 'And yet the simplest biological facts elude you. You know when the mummy and the daddy have a special "cuddle", and a baby comes?'

'I understand the biological facts, Kate. Age is also a biological fact, as it happens.'

'Oh, age!' says Kate, waving her hand airily. '"A) it's a question of being sincere and b) if you're supple you've nothing to fear," as Noël Coward so rightly pointed out. Go and get the hand mirror from my dressing table, would you?'

'But it's upstairs, and there's one right there on the wall,' I say, marvelling – as ever – at my mother's unshakeable belief that there isn't a pin to put between adult children and indentured servants.

'Well, *legs*, Clara,' says Kate. 'Wonderful exercise. This wall mirror is hopeless for faces. It is deeply unflattering. *Deeply*. Go on! There's no point sitting there glaring mutinously. Of course I'd get it myself – there's nothing I like more than running up and down the stairs; I do it, like everything else, with delight – but it so happens that the mirror is heavy and that I've hurt my wrists.'

I look at Kate's wrists, which are bejewelled and poking elegantly out of superfine navy-blue cashmere jersey. They seem fine to me: not hanging brokenly, as her tragic facial expression would suggest.

'I sprained them,' she says, 'carrying a bag.'

'What, cement or something?' The idea of Kate carrying a bag of cement starts making me laugh out loud.

'Tsk, so discourteous,' says Kate with a little moue of annoyance. 'Of course not cement. Pears. From Fortnum's. Beautiful, but unexpectedly heavy, for fruits.'

'Right,' I sigh. 'I'll just go and get the mirror.' There's no point in asking Kate how she sprained her wrists carrying pears: my laughter will become uncontrollable and she'll become cross.

Among her many odder convictions, my mother believes my sisters and I to have the strength of packhorses and herself to have the muscle power of a consumptive fairy. This prejudice – which is what it is – is height-based: I'm the tallest, at five foot nine, and therefore supposedly almost mannish in my strength. Flo is five foot eight, which gives her the strength of a pit pony. Our sister Evie is a mere five foot six and therefore only called on to carry the lighter luggage – in the absence of a porter, obviously. This is entirely regardless of any wrist-injury situation: Kate just doesn't like carrying stuff and feels her daughters are more than equipped for the task.

Kate, at five foot four, is appallingly heightist and attributes unattractive, ludicrously masculine qualities to those of us who are taller than her. 'Gosh, you're strong,' she'll say disgustedly, as one of us passes round a plate of vegetables, as though it would be infinitely more preferable – or perhaps just more pleasingly feminine – to stare at the bowl helplessly, eyes big with hunger, too weak to lift it. 'The strength of an army!' she once exclaimed, watching my sister Evie and I shift a chest of drawers for her, regardless of the fact that both of us were sweating, swearing and puce in the face. 'You are warriors!' she shouted when we eventually wedged the thing into place. 'Vikings! Boudiccas!' Being Kate, these 'compliments' were tempered by a facial expression denoting extreme revulsion, as though she were thinking, 'My God, I've given birth to *beasts* of indeterminate gender.'

In fact, none of us are remotely Herculean, except in Kate's head. Her own extreme weakness (perceived) stands her in excellent stead when she tires of babies, whom she likes but not for too long. 'Darling, *arms*,' she'll say, handing back the infant after a pleasant two minutes or so. 'Agony.' Of course, when I was a child, which is to say before she married my stepfather, Max, she lugged a dozen bags of supermarket shopping without a blink and carried all her own cases. Juggled anvils in her youth, probably. Plus she's been doing Pilates for thirty years, and I suspect that if any one of us is inhumanly strong, it's Kate.

Anyway, I schlep up the stairs as requested and into Kate's bedroom in search of the wretched hand mirror. It's on her dressing table, nestled among Chanel lipsticks and discarded jewellery. I pause to admire the dressing table. Everything is gorgeous, lacquered, shiny. Except for that ugly tube at the back. What's that doing there? Very unlike Kate to have ugly stuff out: ugly stuff goes in the bathroom cupboard, hidden from view as though it were shaming. I pick up the tube – an anodyne, atypically functional white plastic number, with writing in German. I don't speak German, but I want to know what's inside, so I untwist the cap and squeeze out a dollop of cream. I rub it into the back of my hand. Impossible to tell what it's for: it's just a cream. White, thickish and now a bit stingy. Smells of nothing. Hm. I go back downstairs.

'Now,' Kate says, taking the hand mirror off me. 'My face. Look: no lines. Well, hardly any.'

'Did you send me running up the stairs so you could tell me a thing that is perfectly obvious to me?' I ask, annoyed. 'I know you've got no lines. I can see. With my eyes. And anyway, stop preening.'

'I am not preening, Clara,' says Kate, beaming at herself delightedly. 'I am the living proof of the efficacy of almond oil, because that's what it's all about. Almond oil.'

'What's that tube on your dressing table, with writing in German?'

'Don't snoop around,' Kate snaps. 'My God. I can't believe you *snoop around* my things.'

'I wasn't snooping.' She's quite put out, I can tell. 'It was sitting there. What's it for?'

'It's just sunblock, for God's sake,' Kate says. Could it be that she's looking shifty? Yes, it could.

'From equatorial Germany?'

'I didn't notice which country it was from,' Kate says loftily. 'I don't scrutinize labels for precise geographical locations. Unlike you,' she sniffs.

'Right. Well. What was it you wanted to tell me? To show me?'

'Ah yes,' says Kate, perking up. 'I wanted to share a secret.

My facial massage technique. Come and sit over here, so you can really see.'

I roll my eyes. 'I know about your facial massage technique. It's nice – I do it sometimes myself. But the point is, you are fantastically genetically fortunate. I too am genetically fortunate, but not as fortunate as you or I wouldn't have this sodding line. Look.' I frown exaggeratedly.

'But you never make that face,' Kate laughs. 'When do you ever frown like that? I've literally never seen you do it.'

'It exists, is the point,' I say. 'And I don't like it.'

'Hm,' says Kate. 'No, I don't suppose one would. It's probably to do with sunbathing, you know. You're obsessed with it. Awful business, broiling yourself like that. I've never done it, and look at me.'

'I'm not obsessed with it. I like sitting on the beach for precisely two weeks once a year. With sunblock on. In *Devon*.'

'Does terrible damage,' Kate says. 'Really dreadful. Do you remember my friend Elsa? Spent her life on beaches. Her cleavage looks like it's made of cheap leather. Cheap *ruched* leather, actually. Reminds me of a bag I had in the Eighties. Awful.' She gives a small shudder. 'Anyway, shall I show you how to massage your face?'

'No,' I say. 'I already know. And if this confirms anything, this whole conversation, it's that I'm going to go and have a chat with the Botox doctor. It's all very well for Flo to be appalled, but she's younger. And you're some sort of genetic marvel, and good for you, but really. I still don't see why I shouldn't do something about my line.'

Kate sighs deeply. 'Thin end of the wedge, you know,' she says.

'So I gather. But there's nothing else actually wrong with me. Just the line. So I get rid of the line and that's the end of that.'

'I've seen it go wrong so many times,' Kate says. 'I mean, half my friends look like this.' She stretches her whole face back brutally, holding it with both hands, which makes me laugh. 'Wind-tunnel sort of effect. One hates to be disloyal, but really.'

'I'm not planning on becoming a monster,' I say. 'But having inherited this, er, fine genetic material' – I gesture in her direction and Kate smiles approvingly – 'it seems a shame to let it go to seed.'

'I suppose,' says Kate thoughtfully. 'Perhaps. As long as you swear that'll be the end of it.'

'It will,' I say.

'You know, with my technique and the almond oil – you only need the merest drop –'

'No,' I say, cutting her off. 'The situation is beyond almond oil. It's a great big crevasse, not a patch of dry skin. And now I have to go and collect Maisy from school, but I'll keep you posted.'

'Chemicals!' Kate mutters as I kiss her goodbye. 'In the face! It doesn't bear thinking about.'

6

'Anything I should know?' I ask Gaby. 'I feel weirdly nervous. And you *still* haven't told me exactly what work you've had done. You're a mistress of evasiveness.'

'I wish I was someone's mistress,' Gaby sighs.

It's been three weeks since she moved in and I have so far resisted her pleas for a 'fun' night out, but I'm not going to be able to put it off much longer. These days my idea of a fun night generally involves a box set, a glass of wine and my sofa, and if it has to be a fun night out, it's dinner with a friend. But she pooh-poohed all of that when I told her.

Maybe I'm just prematurely aged. I don't think so, though: I suspect that I could still drink Gaby under the table and smoke her off the face of the planet, and I don't have difficulty with the idea of talking to strange men. It's more that I can't entirely be bothered: I did that for years, and I was glad when it was over – and it was over twenty years ago, when Robert and I first got together. Obviously you sometimes meet people and occasionally go to bed with them, but I haven't met anyone in a club since before I had children. Friends' houses, dinners, parties, yes. The Connaught hotel, once, very memorably. Standing at some noisy, slightly naff bar looking hopeful, though – urgh. I really don't fancy it.

But Gaby is a mind-reader, because she says, 'Let's fix a date and put it in our diaries. High time. How's Friday?'

'What, this Friday? I can't. There's a car boot sale at school on Saturday morning and I need to get our stuff together.'

'A car boot sale?' Gaby's facial expression is somewhere between 'amused' and 'quite cross'. 'What are you doing going to car boot sales, Granny?'

'I like them,' I say, trying not to sound defensive. 'They're fun. In the same way that I like junk shops and flea markets. Plus it's school – it's raising funds. Much-needed. Plus I get to get rid of our junk.'

'Whatever,' says Gaby. 'Saturday night? In town?'

I'm trying to remember when I last went out on a Saturday night in the West End. 'Things have changed since you've been away, Gaby. It's not nice. It's people from out of town and puddles of sick, plus everybody will be twenty-five years younger than us.'

'Well, let's not go to central London, then,' says Gaby. 'Let's go . . . hey, kids, where shall we go?'

Jack and Sky are, as ever, hovering in the vicinity of the fridge.

'What for?' asks Jack.

'Gaby!' I say. 'He's seventeen. I don't want to go to a place full of seventeen-year-olds. I can do that at home.'

'I'm nineteen, actually,' says Jack, referring to his fake ID.

'Yeah, well, I'm forty-six.'

'No, but where do you go?' Gaby persists. 'Where's fun? Where has cool people?'

'Cool people?' I say. 'Cool people? Are you in the Upper Fifth?'

'Ignore your mother,' says Gaby.

'Gabs,' I say, 'I'm not completely past it. We can do the members' club thing if you like. Or a bit of east London.

Or both. Find some *cool people.*' I start sniggering. 'Find some HOT GUYS.'

'Mum, do you mind?' says Jack, looking repulsed. 'I'm here.'

'Darling,' I say. 'It was just a joke.'

'Kind of a joke,' Gaby says unhelpfully.

'I can ask my sisters,' I say. 'At least they're in their thirties. And I do have a vague idea myself, Gaby, what with occasionally leaving the house and all. But honestly – wouldn't you rather go somewhere that had proper cocktails and squashy sofas? Couldn't we at least *start* somewhere not-edgy? Plus, you get the West End as well, that way. Not that it's any great shakes, as you will discover.'

'Oh, I suppose so,' says Gaby grudgingly. 'If we must. Like where?'

'Like, I don't know. Like . . . Like the Connaught. Claridge's. That sort of thing. A smart hotel.'

'God, how stuffy,' says Gaby. 'But,' she adds, perking up, 'not at all like LA. Old-school English, which actually might be quite nice. Refreshing. So, yeah. I'm going to break my no-drinking rule for the night. The Connaught it is. For starters.'

'Actually,' I say, 'not the Connaught.' I feel pierced with sadness just thinking about it: there is actually an ache. Am I going to have to avoid bits of London forever, because they remind me?

'Oh?'

'They're, er, I think they're having building work. Claridge's. And then I'll take you somewhere grimier,' I say. 'I promise.'

I don't know that I particularly want to be somewhere

grimy aged forty-six and with a girlfriend, I think, and then I immediately think that I am displeased by my own thought. I like hanging out in louche bars well enough, provided it's with a man. What is this? It's crap. I spent my whole teens and early twenties hanging out in louche bars with women, and that was the way I liked it. Hanging out with women is my raison d'être, practically. I hang out with women all the time. But not to pull, and those sorts of places are very pully. I realize that I only like going to pully places if I've pulled already. When did that happen? Do men have this? Why have I apparently become the kind of woman who'll only go to a particular sort of place with a man on her arm? The answer comes quickly: because then I feel safe. This is yet another function of age: the idea of 'feeling safe' with a man has crept up while I wasn't looking. They're coming thick and fast, the functions of age, and I don't think much of any of them.

I'm having a very odd three weeks. I am filled with weird thoughts. I wonder if there's actually a moment when you first feel OLD. If there is, I think I'm having it. I'm in it.

'Anyway,' I say to Gaby. 'Anything I should know before my appointment? Any top tips? You've got five minutes to finally spill the beans.'

'You're only going for a consultation,' says Gaby. 'Calm down.'

'But why are you being so evasive? It's not like I want to copy your face, Gaby. I just want to know what to expect. And anyway, I don't think it's just a friendly chat. I mean, I think there's time built in for Dr Halliday to do stuff; it's an hour-long appointment, after all. I'd quite like to know what the stuff feels like, that's all. What I should ask for. I mean, you'd know.'

'You'll be fine,' says Gaby. 'He's very good. He'll explain everything.'

'I don't think you should have stuff put in your face, Clara,' says Sky.

'Come back to me when you're in your mid-forties,' I snap. 'I'm fed up with people telling me what I should and shouldn't do to my own face.

Sky looks at me sadly and I feel a bit mean. 'Sorry, Sky. I didn't mean it. I'm just nervous,' I say. 'Right – well, since no one's going to enlighten me, I'm off. Wish me luck.'

'It's not luck,' says Gaby. 'It's expertise and skill. You'll love it.'

The first surprise is that Dr Halliday's waiting room contains a well-known actress. This in itself isn't surprising as such, but what is is that said actress is famous – feted, even – for her absolute repudiation of any kind of cosmetic work. She has chosen to age gracefully, and the British public love her for it. She's the pin-up for the 'no to Botox' brigade, the living, breathing proof that women can be in their sixties, as she must be, and look amazing naturally. I should know – I've interviewed her. I remember the quotes, or some of them: 'What people do with their face is up to them, but I'd never do anything to mine. I think happiness comes from within, and if you're happy it shows in your face. It's the best medicine! Other than that, it's down to Pond's Cold Cream, a good night's sleep and plenty of water.' There was a run on cold cream once the interview appeared.

What's she doing here? Dr Halliday is of course also a dermatologist: perhaps she has terrible rosacea or adult acne or something. I peer at her face as I head to the coffee machine. It's the face everyone knows and loves: no spots or red bits. The actress is wearing enormous sunglasses and a wrap that hides her neck, and is reading what looks like a script. She doesn't look up or make eye contact with anyone – well, with me: there's no one else in the room. I wonder if I should say hello, but she'd probably have no recollection of our having met – and anyway, bit awkward, in the circs.

I'm such a ninny, I think to myself. I absolutely believed her about the water and the sleep and the cold cream, on the basis that she looks her age, but a fantastic version of her age. A probable version. She has lines round her eyes, and lines when she smiles. In my idiocy, it never occurred to me that this could be the result of cosmetic surgery. Until a couple of months ago, I thought cosmetic surgery meant a tight face, unblinking eyes and a rigid forehead.

I really feel like saying something. I mean, I feel personally slighted. Affronted. That's quite some lie she's got going there. Because why not say? Why not come clean? Why not give an interview and, when asked about your remarkable state of preservation, say, 'Well, I have a little help,' instead of sending millions of poor sods running to Boots to buy products that have absolutely nothing to do with it?

I'm ruminating on all this when a nurse shows another woman back into the waiting room. With the inevitability of Greek tragedy, this woman is a television personality of roughly my age. Exactly the same vibe going as with the actress: lines around the eyes, mobile forehead, nothing untoward-seeming at all – and many, many public pronouncements about how she in fact likes to eat like a horse but not a pound goes on, because of 'running after the children'. Nobody questions the fact that 'the children' that she makes sound like hyperactive toddlers are in fact by now slothful teenagers.

It slowly dawns on me that maybe everyone's at it. Well, everyone who can afford it and whose face is public property. Maybe there's a vast conspiracy and nobody's telling anyone anything. Not that you'd have an obligation to fess up, I don't suppose: people's faces are their own business.

I'm still standing by the coffee machine, staring absentmindedly at my plastic cup. 'Ms Hutt?' the nurse says, with a beaming smile that shows perfect, quasi-fluorescent teeth. God, people's teeth. I am surrounded by teeth. 'We're ready for you.'

'Fantastic teeth,' I say by way of small talk as we head down a brightly lit corridor. If it weren't brightly lit, her teeth would make a passable torch.

'Veneers,' she says. 'My own teeth were awful. Although,' she adds with a tiny frown, 'I'm thinking of having them redone. It's all about the London Smile these days.'

'How do you mean?'

'More natural. A bit crooked. These veneers are very 2005,' she says. 'You know – that whole Big White American Teeth thing. My friend works at a cosmetic dentist's and now everyone's coming in wanting the London Smile. I blame Kate Moss,' she says. 'Still.' She rolls her eyes. 'The stupid thing is, my teeth were kind of like that in the first place. They had that gap at the front – that's very big at the moment. And not this white. You know, more natural-looking. Couple of shades darker.'

'Well,' I say. 'That's OK, then. You can just have the veneers removed.'

The nurse gives me a look. 'Do you know anything about veneers?'

'Not a sausage,' I say cheerfully. 'I don't give my teeth that much thought, to be honest. I mean, I've only got one filling and I brush and floss, obviously. But otherwise . . .'

'Well, it's really not that simple,' she says. 'But here we are. Dr Halliday, this is Ms Hutt.'

'Clara,' I say, shaking his hand.

Dr Halliday is about six foot tall, and handsome in a disconcerting way. He has dark hair that falls forward on to his face, and Clark Kent glasses with a jawline to match. Behind the glasses are sparkling blue eyes. But as I look closer, I realize that he has a baby's skin – fresh-looking, brand spanking new, as though he'd stolen a newborn and nicked its casing.

'What can I help you with?' he asks, staring quite hard at my face, just as I am staring quite hard at his. We are having a face stare-off.

'Ah yes. This,' I say, frowning as hard as I can. 'You see that vertical line there? I'd like it to be gone, please.'

'Of course, of course,' he says. 'And what else?'

'Oh!' I say. 'I . . . Well, nothing else, really. Just the line. I just came in for the line.'

Dr Halliday smiles. He also has the Big White American Teeth, I note. The smile isn't particularly reassuring. He is still staring intently at me, and for some reason I can feel myself blushing. It's unnerving. I am unnerved.

'What I normally do,' he says, 'is take some photographs. Can we do that?'

'Erm. Yes, of course,' I say, although I don't really see the need. I just want him to jab something in my annoying line and then I want to go home and take tonight's chicken out of its marinade before it becomes too garlicky.

'If you'd stand over there, by the window, in the natural light,' Dr Halliday says, picking up a professional-looking camera from his desk. 'Perfect. Now, look at me.'

'I hate being photographed,' I say pointlessly as he starts snapping away. 'And I'm not wearing any make-up, because I thought it would be better.'

'No smiling, please,' says Dr Halliday. 'I need you impassive, face in repose. Nearly there. I'm just going to do a few closer ones.'

He steps closer, and closer still, until his camera is practically touching my face. I am reminded of horse inspections, when people force their mouths open to pronounce on the quality of their teeth and pick their hooves up to examine their feet, or of tribespeople thinking that the camera is stealing their soul.

'All done,' he eventually says. 'Now, let's upload them and take a good look. Ah, here we are. Well, you can immediately see the obvious asymmetry,' he says as the images come up. 'Most people's faces are asymmetrical, of course . . .'

The pictures are brutal. With no make-up, and with his zoomy lens, my skin – which, if I say so myself, is normally pretty good – looks like some sort of crater-ridden lunar landscape. My eyes look small and frightened, my eyelashes stumpy. The lines between my nose and mouth are like excavations. My pores are gigantic; my forehead leathery and criss-crossed with tiny furrows. The whole effect is terrifying and really, really hideous.

'Quite upsetting, actually,' I tell Dr Halliday. 'It's, er, it's not really how I see myself, to be honest.'

And I do feel quite shaken. Anyone would, of course. But he's still staring at me, evaluating my poor chronically asymmetrical face, and it's unsettling. I rather liked my face, until about three minutes ago.

'So,' I say, partly to cut through the oppressive silence. 'What do you think? What would you suggest?'

'Oh my goodness,' Dr Halliday laughs merrily. 'Where to start?'

I can't believe what he's just said. I stare at him. Eventually I say, 'What do you mean? There's nothing wrong with my face!' I feel indignant and, somewhere underneath, borderline tearful.

'Dear Clara, no. Of course there isn't. But it is a very *improvable* face. A few tiny tweaks . . .'

'Spit it out, then,' I say rudely. 'I need the specifics.'

'In no particular order,' Dr Halliday says, 'I'd recommend the following. The skin needs to be retextured for optimal smoothness. That's a course of peels at some point. Botox, but not just in your frown line, which would look obvious and awful. All over the face. Here, for example' – he points to the corners of my mouth – 'and, well, as I say, all over, in tiny amounts. Filler in the smaller wrinkles and in the prominent marionette lines. Here, do you see, these deep grooves between your mouth and your nose. I can burn off these unsightly freckles, here on the left side, with laser. Actually, a course of laser therapy mightn't be a bad idea either. Pulses of light, basically – terrifically youthening, tightening effect. I suppose you go away in the summer, on holiday?'

'Yes,' I say, my voice sounding small.

'It would be essential to stay out of the sun,' he says. 'Heavy sunblock too, forever.'

'Right. The sun is kind of the point of my holiday, and I –'

'I haven't finished,' says Dr Halliday. 'Now, if it were my face –'

'Which it isn't,' I point out, interrupting because Dr Halliday is getting on my tits. Oh my God, tits. Imagine what he'd have to say if I showed him mine: he would make me hate them forever. I pull my cardigan tighter across my chest.

'Quite so, quite so. If it were my face, I'd have a couple of permanent filler implants around the chin, to give a more defined jawline.'

I raise my hand to my chin to feel, and then grab the hand mirror – horrible and magnifying – that's on the desk. My chin is fine. He's making it sound like I have several and like they're all made out of blancmange, or like my face shelves away to nothing past my lips, but as far as I can see my chin is just . . . my chin. The chin I've always had. It's just a normal chin. Not unusually rounded, not exceptionally pointy. A chin.

'Your lips,' Dr Halliday continues, remorseless in his inventory. 'They were fuller in your youth, I can see, and they are thinning with age, which is perfectly normal. So I'd augment them. Just a tiny bit. You've probably seen photographs of how badly that can turn out in the wrong hands, but' – and here he raises his baby-smooth white hands, with their buffed nails – 'these are very much not the wrong hands. I wouldn't provide you with a pout. The difference would only just be perceptible, but believe me, it would make a tremendous difference to the overall youthfulness of the face.'

'Right,' I say. 'I, er, I like my mouth.'

'Of course you do, of course you do,' he smiles. 'It's a nice mouth. But we could make it even nicer. Oh, and – cosmetic dentistry isn't my field, obviously, but I could give you an excellent recommendation.'

'Are you quite done?' I ask.

'For now,' he says, smiling again. 'And apart from the eye lift.'

'The *eye lift*?'

'Mm,' he says. 'Sounds dramatic, doesn't it? But it isn't at all. And it would really make . . .'

'The most tremendous difference to the youthfulness of the face, yes,' I say.

'Precisely,' beams Dr Halliday. 'Of course, by your age many women have already had the mini-facelift.'

I blink at him. 'I don't know a single woman, my age or otherwise, who's had the mini-facelift,' I tell him. 'Literally, not one.'

'You came to me via Gaby Stanton, I believe,' says Dr Halliday, consulting his notes.

'What?' I practically shout. 'Yes, but . . .' Inside, I'm thinking, 'What the actual fuck? A *facelift*?'

'Give her my regards,' Dr Halliday says smoothly.

'Sorry – are you saying you lifted Gaby's face? She's been gone ten years. She'd have been, what, in her late thirties . . . Oh, come on. I don't think so. She's my mate. I'd have known. Really?'

'Patient confidentiality,' says Dr Halliday, laughing. 'It's true I haven't seen her for years – just before she left for California, if I remember rightly. Do send her my very best. I gather she . . . built a relationship with a colleague I recommended in Los Angeles. Phil Gottlieb. An artist, as any cinema screen will attest.'

'Bloody hell,' I say. 'It's a whole new world.'

'Yes,' says Dr Halliday, flashing his dazzling gnashers. 'It is.'

I had the Botox, in the end. And when he'd finished – he did loads of tiny injections, as he'd told me he would – he said, in the manner of a drug dealer, that I could have 'a minute amount' of filler in my 'marionette lines' as a free taster, and that if I liked the effect I could come back for the full filler monty. And I said yes, OK, whack it in. And now I am standing in the street in Chelsea and my face feels a bit sore and I don't know whether to laugh or cry, whether to feel pleased with myself or ashamed. I'm to go home and not lie down for a few hours, whatever I do, and then apparently I just watch the stuff take effect over the coming days and weeks. I'm also to think about his suggestions, eye lift and all. At the moment, though, all I can think about is Gaby's possible facelift. The sides of my mouth feel bruised.

'You might have fucking well told me, Gaby,' I say, slamming my keys down on the kitchen table. 'It was horrible. He made me feel horrible, like there was something horribly the matter with my horrible face.'

Gaby looks up from her laptop and grins at me. 'You had it done, I see. Botox and filler, right?'

'Yes. Whatever. How can you tell? I can't see anything different.'

'Years of practice,' Gaby laughs. 'And you have little needle marks. Come over here, let me see.' She pushes my hair back from my face. 'Good girl!' she says. 'Welcome to the club. This calls for a drink.'

'I don't know that I'm celebrating,' I say. 'I feel strange and actually a bit sad. He made me feel like a freak.'

'Oh, they all do that,' says Gaby, grabbing glasses from the shelf and some Sauvignon from the fridge. 'But I swear on my life – he's the best. You're going to look incredible. Just do what he says.'

'No!' I say. 'Are you crazy? He says eye lifts and lasers and God knows what. Aside from anything else, I can't afford it. But even if I could . . . no. It's a bloody odd business, isn't it?'

'Only at first,' Gaby says. 'And then it's the most natural thing in the world.'

'In an unnatural way.'

'Yeah. Thin line, as you'll discover. Anyway, cheers! To us!'

I raise my glass. 'Hey, Gaby. He says you had a facelift. Well, mini.'

'Did he now, indiscreet bastard?' laughs Gaby. 'Well, there you go. Busted.'

'But . . . what . . . What, it's true? Why didn't you tell me?'

'I'm not denying it, am I? More than one, actually. But fewer than three.' She laughs again, as if all this were the most hilarious thing in the world.

'Gaby! Face! Knife! Cut cut cut! It's not *funny*.'

Gaby stops laughing and leans across the table towards me. 'Do you think it was a mistake?' she asks. 'Do you think I look bad?'

'Well, no, obviously. You look great. Amazing. As I keep telling you. But isn't it a bit, you know – drastic? He said it was just before you went to LA. You were what, thirty-seven, thirty-eight?'

'Thirty-nine. It was my present to my new, soon-to-be Californian self. New life, new face.'

'But you had that leaving party. You looked normal.'

'I still look normal! But yes. I lied about my leaving date. I didn't think my uptight English friends could handle the bare facts. Rightly, as it turns out – you're flipping out a whole decade later. How's this? That was only a mini-facelift. I had a proper one four years ago.'

'Bloody hell, Gaby. You might have said. It's not like I haven't been asking. All that bullshit about diet and exercise . . .'

'Not bullshit! Absolutely true. With some . . . extra bits. I was waiting for you to dip your toe in the water,' Gaby says. 'It's . . . it's a thing, having work. It's being part of a secret society. Like, I don't know – smoking, or swinging or something.'

'It's nothing like swinging,' I say sternly. 'Or smoking.'

'I mean, it's like a little secret club. Once someone's in it, they're in it. But you don't go around broadcasting information to people that aren't.'

'I'm not in the club,' I say. 'I'm happy with whatever minor improvements he carried out today, or at least I hope I will be when I see them take hold. Whenever that is. I just hated that line. The end. Seriously, Gaby. I'm not you.'

'Right,' Gaby says, laughing again in a really annoying way. 'Right. More wine?'

7

By the following Saturday – the day, or rather the night, on which I have agreed to go out with Gaby – the effects of my little foray are becoming visible. Every day first thing in the morning, I've got up and frowned into a mirror, as hard as I could. And every day the frown has become smaller, weaker, harder to make in the first place even though I put all my strength into it. I have to admit, I'm impressed and pleased, more pleased than I thought I would be. My forehead is still mobile and my face still moves: you'd never be able to tell I'd had anything done. Even I can only tell because I know for a fact that I spent that odd afternoon in Chelsea, but really – Dr Halliday's work is indeed very fine, as promised. And as it should be: the invoice he has sent is astronomical.

The lines – the sinisterly named 'marionette lines', with their suggestion of ventriloquists' puppets – around my mouth are fainter too. This has come at the cost of a degree of increased plumpness – it's as though someone popped their finger into my mouth and pushed the lines out from the inside – but I'm not complaining. (That was the one cheering – in that it confirmed my own belief – thing Dr Halliday said: 'The best thing you can do for your face at your age is keep the fat in it.') I'm still a bit bruised, but it's nothing that make-up can't take care of. I feel pretty good, actually. I feel great. Neither Jack nor Sky seems to have noticed anything different, which is what you want, really. Maisy told me

I was pretty when we shared a bath last night, but then Maisy, bless her, thinks I'm pretty with greasy hair and wearing a onesie.

So yes, I'm pleased. I feel like someone has carried out some magic on me. I'm so pleased, in fact, that I'm quite looking forward to Gaby's and my night out. I'm not champing at the bit, unlike her – I'd still rather we stayed in with a box set – but I'm not as filled with horror at the idea as I was. I'm anthropologically interested in taking my face for a spin.

Tonight I am putting a lot of effort into my make-up. Normally I just whack on what's to hand, in the way I've been whacking it on for years. I have good products, and I put a bit of research into what I buy, but I've never gone a bundle on the half-hour full make-up job with forensically careful application. Tonight, all that changes. I exfoliate and moisturize and use a brush to apply my foundation, in tiny, careful strokes, for a whole ten minutes. I conceal and primp and shade and shadow; I do the whole blending thing with my eye make-up; I spackle on some finishing product that promises to make me look 'air-brushed' and which only half lied. I apply fake tan to my arms and legs, dimly aware that I should really put it on all over, except I can't reach. Were I to pull, I'd have a pale abdomen and brown limbs: it would not look lovely. But I am not planning to pull, so that's fine.

I have a fitted navy-blue dress laid out on the bed: demure and – yes – age-appropriate, but short enough not to look like it's made out of nun's habit. I have heels: the precious Louboutins that I hardly ever wear because they're so hard to walk in. I had my hair done earlier today and for once it's behaving; I had a manicure at the same time. All this effort, for a night out: I should at least be getting married or something. But even I have to accept, as I peer into the mirror, that the effort is worthwhile: I look as good as I'm capable of looking. I go downstairs carefully, clutching the banister in a geriatric manner, as though it were a Zimmer frame, and waiting until both feet are on the same step before proceeding, in order not to fall off my youthful heels.

Gaby is waiting for me in the kitchen, chatting to Sky. And suddenly my cocky, pleased-with-myself feeling fades a little bit. My bulb dims: if I look pretty good, Gaby looks like a model. She doesn't appear to be wearing any make-up at all, though I know that she is because I was with her when she raided Selfridges' beauty hall in preparation for tonight – not that she needed to: I've never met anyone who owns more make-up. Her hair is up in an artless chignon that looks not like she spent an hour in John Frieda, but like she's just gathered it up and twisted it herself. She is wearing a plain green shift, one of those garments that looks like nothing until it's on the right body – and this is the right body. She's all hair and mouth and eyes and limbs, long, defined, golden limbs and eyes that sparkle with both anticipation and the best eyelash extensions money can buy.

'Bloody hell, Gaby,' I say. 'You look even more gorgeous than usual.'

'So do you,' Gaby says kindly, in exactly the tone I used to adopt with her when she was the Plainer Friend. 'You look great. The cab's outside. Do we really have to go to Claridge's? Can't we go straight to the fun place?'

'Absolutely not,' I say. 'I can't stand for very long in these shoes – I'd like to have somewhere comfy to sit for at least part of the evening.'

'Oh, all right. God, it's like going out with my granny. But let's not stay too long.'

Once we're ensconced and halfway through the first Martini, Gaby asks me if I'd like to go to the loo with her.

'I don't need to,' I say. 'I mean, I love loo chats and everything, but not now. We've only just sat down.'

'I think you do,' says Gaby.

'That's what I'm saying. I do like them, but the best loo chats are later on at night. And also, we aren't children. You can go on your own.'

'No, I mean – I think you do,' says Gaby, staring at me in a significant way. 'Want to go.'

'Gaby! I really don't,' I repeat.

Why's she obsessing about my weeing? And then Gaby winks at me, and the penny drops.

'You haven't!'

'Oh, but I have!' says Gaby. 'It's my first night out in London in a couple of decades – you bet I have.'

'Good grief. But . . . I mean, where did you even get it from, aside from anything else?'

'I have my contacts,' says Gaby. 'I'm not dead yet. Come on, hurry up.'

'I'm not sure,' I say, suddenly flustered. 'It's been a while.'

'Come *on*,' Gaby says, pulling me up. 'Stop being such an old woman.'

And that is how, three minutes later, we come to be hoovering up lines of cocaine in the lavatories. We're in individual cubicles, having surmised that the Madame Pipi (as Kate, who used to live in Paris, calls loo attendants) wouldn't take especially kindly to two women with a combined age of over ninety scuttling into the one loo and then making snorting sounds.

'I still don't know,' I say as I meet Gaby by the sinks, my nose stinging despite the smallness of the line I took, and a sour taste making its way down my throat. 'Do you think we're maybe – well, a bit old, darling, to be doing this sort of thing? It's not untragic, is it?'

'Nonsense,' says Gaby. 'And don't be so critical. I'm not suggesting we make a habit of it. But for old times' sake. And anyway, you're as old as you feel, and I feel about twenty.'

She lets out a whoop, startling Madame Pipi and startling me too: it's an annoying enough noise when my children make it. But then I take a deep breath, and suddenly the situation just seems funny, not tragic, and I remember she's in the middle of a divorce, and far from home, and I take her arm and we head back to the bar.

The table next to ours has become occupied in the time we've been gone, by a group of middle-aged men in suits. They look nice – interesting, by which I mean they don't look like a group of accountants discussing audits: they're more *Mad Men* – well, up to a point – than Office Night Out. They eye Gaby and me as we sit back down; a couple of them smile. I can hear an American accent or two. They're all drinking cocktails and laughing.

'Stop looking over there,' Gaby hisses.

'Why? I'm not ogling them, Gaby. I was just seeing.'

'They're ancient,' Gaby says dismissively, which forces me to quickly look again. 'They're geriatrics.'

'That's completely untrue,' I report back. 'Three of them are roughly our age and two are in their thirties.'

'Where, in their thirties?' says Gaby. 'I can't look without turning my head.'

'At your three o'clock,' I say. 'Not that it's relevant to anything. I was just being polite because they smiled at us. Another drink?'

'Yes please,' says Gaby. 'Same again.'

I can't see a waiter, so I head for the bar, and while I'm standing there, I turn around and notice that Gaby has had a change of heart: she is now chatting animatedly to the two younger men in the party next to ours, and then throwing her head back and laughing loudly. It must be the coke, I think to myself. She surely can't be hitting on them.

But she is, it becomes apparent within seconds of my returning to the table.

'Yoga! So I suppose you're, um, super-flexible?' one of the younger men is saying to her.

Gaby is laughing prettily. 'I try,' she says, much too coyly for an adult.

'Clara, this is Ben,' she says. 'Ben, Clara.' I wave a greeting. 'And this is Andrew.'

Andrew is the other thirty-something. I smile at him too.

'Hey, Bel, come over here and meet these ladies,' Ben calls to an older man whom I hadn't noticed standing at the bar.

'And I'm Bel,' says the older man, walking towards us and holding out his hand. 'How do you do?'

He has a southern American accent and must be nearing sixty, though it's not that easy to tell anyone's age in the dim, flattering light. Silver fox, though: one of those men who is manlily handsome, like he's carved out of rock. Well preserved. Strong jawline. Fine head of hair. Patrician.

'Hello, Bel,' I say, wondering when Gaby is going to stop

73

flirting and move her chair back towards our table. I want an olive and a cheese straw thingy.

'Why don't you join us?' Bel says, waving his hand expansively. 'Plenty of room.'

'Oh, no, thank you – we were just . . .'

'We'd love to,' Gaby says, grabbing her glass and mine and moving them to the men's table.

This eagerness makes me want to volunteer that we are not hookers, but I decide against it, partly because I don't know if people our age still hook in top hotels. Gaby is now completely ignoring me: she has moved her chair right next to Ben's and her attention is focused on him and him alone. I smile tightly at the rest of them, thinking that I'm really not in the mood to make small talk to strangers who neither of us will ever see again. I prod Gaby with my shoe, but she ignores me.

'I'm Vince,' says Vince, and 'I'm Sanjay,' says Sanjay.

'Clara,' I say with forced enthusiasm, very much aware I could be on my sofa at home, without these shoes of pain, watching television or reading my book, happy as a clam.

'I hope we're not interrupting your evening,' says Bel, who has nice manners. 'We've been cooped up with each other all day. It's nice to see a couple of fresh faces.'

American teeth, I note, but I think he was born with them: they're white and square, but without the giveaway (I've been observing Gaby's teeth at close quarters) thickness of veneers.

'Not at all,' I say, though it isn't really true.

It's weirding me out, being in a posh bar with strange men. The last time that happened, there was only one strange man and meeting him hastened the demise of my marriage to Sam three years ago. There's no risk of that happening here, and besides lightning doesn't strike twice. But still, I meant it when I said I didn't want to chat to strangers I'd never see again. Jack and Sky are out tonight too, and if I went home now I'd save about thirty-five quid in babysitting. I wonder if I could reasonably peel away and leave Gaby here with Ben, who has now got his arm round the back of her chair.

'What are your plans?' Bel says, leaning towards me.

'Erm,' I say. 'I'm not quite sure. In what respect? We have to be elsewhere in a little while, and, um . . .'

'We have dinner reservations next door, if you'd care to join us,' Bel says. 'It's raining outside,' he adds with a smile.

I smile non-committally back and shrug in the direction of Gaby, hoping to God she doesn't accept. But I don't think she's heard: she's howling with loud laughter at something Ben has said.

Bel is one of those men who give you their entire attention – the full focus of their beam: I suppose it's what's meant by being made to feel like you're the only woman in the room. It's funny how there are silver foxes and not silver vixens, I reflect. All you're allowed to be if you're female is a cougar, and I would literally rather die than be some sad sack who thinks it's an achievement to sleep with people young enough to be your children. I wonder how old Ben is, and I shudder slightly.

'Are you cold?' says Bel. 'Would you like my jacket?'

'No, thank you,' I smile back. I do so love good manners.

I must make an effort myself, instead of sighing internally. So I engage him, Andrew and Sanjay in small talk. Andrew and Sanjay are British; as is Ben, but not Vince, who's from New York. They all work for the same company – a mining business of some description; today they've been to a conference about fracking. I'm afraid the very mention of 'business' makes my ears snap shut, shamefully: I'd be a better and more informed person if I read the financial pages. But anyway, conference here, then on to Munich, and they're all quite high up in this business, from what I can gather.

'Thank you for not making the fracking joke,' Bel says. 'Because it would not have been original.'

'I don't know,' I say. 'Call me old-fashioned, but I think wordplay based on "fucking" is a bit much in the first ten minutes of meeting new people.'

Old Bel roars with laughter at this. 'And what do you do?' he asks.

'You sound like the Queen,' I say, which makes him laugh again. 'I write stuff. I have children. That's pretty much it.'

'That's too non-specific for me,' says Bel. 'Where do you write? I'd like to read you.'

'I don't think you would,' I say, now laughing too. 'But I appreciate the impeccable manners.'

'Let's have another drink,' Bel says.

'That would be my third Martini,' I say, and then trot out the line that everybody's heard before – except, apparently, Bel. 'You know what they say: Martinis are like breasts – one's too few and three's too many.'

This sets Bel off again. He's easily pleased, clearly – frankly his reactions to my attempts at humour are borderline simpleton – but I like making him laugh, so I make some more jokes. Going by his delighted reaction, you'd think I was Coco the Clown crossed with Woody Allen. It's pleasing, though, like making a toddler laugh, so I continue with the quips.

'British women are so refreshing,' Bel announces after a while. 'I don't spend much time in London normally. You should hear the crap that passes for conversation in Houston.'

'I'm sure Houston women are perfectly amusing,' I say, mildly miffed on their behalf.

'Not the ones I meet,' Bel says grimly. 'My wife was, but she was an exception.'

'Oh, I'm sorry,' I say. 'I'm divorced twice myself.'

'She passed away,' Bel says. 'I'm widowed.'

'Oh, I'm so sorry,' I say again. 'I had no idea, obviously, since we've only just met. Commiserations.'

'Sympathies is the word you're looking for, I think,' Bel says.

'Sorry!' I say for the third time. 'Sorry. That I got the wrong word and that your wife, er . . . well, you know, died. Is dead.'

I want to go now. Sitting here with Bel discussing his late wife is a bit discomfiting and it's nearly half past nine and I'd like to be in bed at a reasonable-ish hour; if Gaby wants me to drag her round Dalston and Shoreditch, we're going to have to get a move on.

'Gaby,' I say, but she doesn't hear me. 'Gaby!' She catches my eye and I point to my watch. 'We should go.'

'We should, I guess. OK if Ben comes, right?'

Ben looks at me all expectantly.

'I, er, sure,' I say. Great: not only would I rather be at home, but now I'm playing gooseberry to boot.

'And Andrew, of course,' Gaby says, patting Andrew's

knee. 'And, er, anyone else who wants to,' she adds, looking at the older men with a discernible lack of enthusiasm.

It is amazing to be that ageist when you're pushing fifty; it's like being a bird who hates wings. I fleetingly wonder whether or not it's a form of self-loathing.

'I think they had dinner reservations . . .' I say.

'Oh, stuff that,' says Gaby, who's clearly been to the loo again without my noticing. 'Stuff that. Stuff it. Let's go. Let's party! Woohoo!' And she lifts up her beautiful arms and claps her hands above her head. 'Woohoo!' she repeats.

A couple of people sitting further away turn around to look. It's not really the kind of place in which to woohoo, old Claridge's.

I stare down at the table, focusing on the spiced nuts, mortified, and only Bel catches my eye. He gives me the most complicit smile, and suddenly I am filled with liking for Bel; the liking tamps down my embarrassment at having helpfully told him that his wife is dead.

'I'm sticking to my booking,' he says. 'Join me?'

'Clara!' Gaby says. 'Come on, babe. Come with us. It's our girls' night!'

'I, er, I don't know,' I say. 'I sort of should go home.'

'I'd be honoured if you dined with me,' Bel says in a courtly manner, with his nice twangy accent. He's like someone from an old engraving about cowboys.

'Paaart-ay!' says Gaby. 'P to the A to the R to the –'

'I'd love to,' I tell Bel.

8

I've been awake for hours by the time Gaby's taxi pulls up the following day. I've read the Sunday papers; Maisy and I have made potato gratin and studded a leg of lamb with anchovy and garlic; we've made salad dressing and tidied the kitchen and gone for a stroll in the park, stopping on the way back for coffee (me) and ice cream (her). It's after two p.m. when Gaby comes back. She is followed, ten minutes later, by Jack and Sky, who've also clearly had some sort of all-nighter.

There's a marked contrast, though. The children look as fresh as daisies as they gather up the ingredients for a massive fry-up (brushing aside my protestations about lunch being on the way: 'It's cool, we're starving'). Their hair and eyes are shiny: they beam out health and vitality like it's a force field, even though they say they've barely slept and I don't suppose their evening consisted of drinking smoothies and doing star jumps. Gaby, though. Gaby looks absolutely *insanely* rough, to the point where I say, 'Woah, Gaby. Are you OK? Cup of tea?'

'Please,' she croaks, sitting down dodderily, like an old lady.

I briefly wonder whether she has brittle bones. I don't even know where brittle bones come from, or how you get them, but Gaby doesn't really eat: something's got to give at some level, surely, at some point.

'Did you have a nice time?'

'Great,' she says, smiling weakly. 'Great.'

She makes a rolling motion with her right fist and starts saying 'Partayyy!' but peters out halfway through. She's got panda eyes and her skin is pigeon-grey; her mouth is oddly slack; her hands are shaking. But it's what's happened to her face that's so odd: it's as though someone had replaced smooth, doll-like plastic with crumpled parchment paper. She looks appalling. She looks ill.

'What did you do?'

'Oh,' she says, waving her hand, 'we went to some bars. Lots of them. Ended up in Dalston somewhere. Dalston! Christ, London's changed. It's unrecognizable. Can't remember all that clearly, to be honest.' She lowers her voice and mouths something at me, but I can't make out what she's saying.

'D'you want some bacon, Gaby?' asks Jack. 'We made loads. I could put it in a bun. Mum, do we have any buns?'

Gaby looks like she's about to puke. 'No, darling, but thank you,' she says. 'Excuse me. I'll just go to the bathroom.'

I take this opportunity to shoo Jack and Sky upstairs with their plates of fry-ups, and when Gaby re-emerges – looking less grey and more sheet-white – I ask her what she was mouthing at me.

'Ketamine,' she says.

'You took ketamine?'

'Yes.'

'As well as the coke?'

'Yep.'

'I think I would literally die of a heart attack. It's a horse tranquillizer, for God's sake. What happened?'

'I honestly can't remember that well. Could I have a glass of water? Thank you. We left Claridge's and we were going to go and eat but then we didn't. Went to that members' club you were telling me about. And to a bar near it. Went to some other places. I fell over, look. And my jaw hurts. And my head.'

'Christ, Gaby. I hope it was worth it. Not to sound like your mum or anything, but, you know . . .'

'Oh yeah,' Gaby says. 'It was worth it. Ben's great. I went back with him. He's twenty-nine. What happened with you?'

'I had a delicious supper and took a cab home,' I say. 'I was in bed by half past twelve.'

'With that old bloke?' Gaby says.

'No, on my own. Oh, you mean supper – yes. He's not that old. He's fifty-nine. He's nice. I liked him. He has amazing manners and made beautiful small talk and laughed at all my jokes and was utterly captivated when I ordered a massive plate of cheese for pudding. Not the American lady way, apparently.'

'You can say that again,' says Gaby. 'Also, there's no real cheese in America. But fifty-nine! Jeez, Clara.'

'Gaby! He's thirteen years older than me and we had dinner. Ben is twenty years younger than you, which means you could easily be his mum. So, you know, less of the "Jeez".'

We stare at each other quite crossly for a bit.

'His friends were nice too. Ben's. Or were they Andrew's? Anyway. We hooked up with them at one point. We were doing shots.'

'When you say you spent the night with Ben – how? I mean, you must have been *completely* wasted. Incapacitated. You were heading that way in Claridge's, and that was when it was still early.'

'I don't remember going to bed. But I remember this morning,' she says, perking up. 'Oh yes.' I put another cup of tea in front of her. 'He thinks I'm thirty-four,' Gaby says. 'Which may be pushing it. Normally I say thirty-six, but it was dark and I was wasted and the blinds were still down this morning. The sex was great. Afterwards he said, "I like the sweet freckles on the backs of your hands, I've never seen that before."'

I say nothing, but I make an upside-down face.

'Gaby, do you think it's a good idea to –'

'I must call Dr Halliday tomorrow,' she interrupts. 'Get him to take a look.'

'You can't do anything about liver spots,' I say. 'Or crêpey skin. Even I know that.'

'You can, actually. Newish procedures. You can do everything about everything, if you try hard enough. Anyway, I'm going to have a bath. And maybe a snooze. Do we have any painkillers?'

'Bathroom cupboard.'

'Thanks.' She raises herself out of the chair again, painfully, and wanders shakily off.

Surely, I think to myself, surely it's not worth it. What is the point? I mean, fine, go and get absolutely bladdered every now and then: we've all been there. Go and get bladdered with people you've only just met who are considerably younger than you. Shag them, if you like. But my God – we all pedal hard enough under the surface as it is, just to keep afloat. Imagine how much harder it must be if the thing you're trying to keep afloat is a lie, a construct. Thirty-four! For the first time since she re-entered my life, I feel properly sorry for Gaby, beautiful, gorgeous Gaby, pretendy Gaby, who has made herself a captive of her looks, who can never stop, who is never going to say, 'Sod it, I'm nearly fifty, I think

I'll skip the daily punishment and the starvation regime and just do what I like. And if my arms sag a bit, then so what? I've had a good innings and it isn't the end of the world.' Instead here she is, snaffling down the Class As and trying to keep up with people she could realistically have given birth to. Kate would say it was undignified, and at this very moment I'm inclined to agree. Nights like that should be joyous. Gaby's seems sad to me.

Maybe I'm jealous. Am I jealous, I wonder as I stick the kettle back on? I'm jealous of her looks, certainly: I'd also like to look thirty-six. Wouldn't I? Well, yes, up to a point – but I'm not sure about that point involving a knife, and the deranged-seeming amount of maintenance that being Gaby clearly involves. And anyway, how much can you do, really? Bodies are bodies: you can nip and tuck all you like, but you're still your real age underneath; you are still getting older. Things – invisible, important things – are still slowing down or falling apart. My greatest fear, when it comes to ageing, is dementia, but now I have a new one: dementia when you're seventy but look fifty. It must happen to some people. I bet you see it in LA, or Miami: frisky-looking hottie MILFs who are completely gaga.

I open my powder compact and stare at my face again. Good job, Dr Halliday. But that's probably enough of that.

9

It's not a complete U-turn, though, because having decided that I've gone as far as I'm prepared to go with invasive procedures, I start to think about the non-invasive stuff. If I can temporarily look better without anyone sticking anything into me, is there any harm in that? I discover that you can get a facial that involves microdermabrasion and something called 'high frequency'; that there are spectacular eyelash extensions, which take two hours and apparently obviate the need for any further eye make-up; that there is a Shellac manicure that will apparently last for weeks; that you can get a fake tan from a person rather than a tube (this, I read, involves wearing paper pants and standing in a pop-up tent being hosed with liquid brown stuff, as though one had a peculiar and unsavoury fetish). Also – and, OK, this isn't entirely non-invasive – I have made an appointment with a Mr Kimball to discuss veneers. It's just a chat.

I've lost a bit of weight by accident (and there's a sentence I never thought I'd write). It's to do with the fact that I now eat with Gaby, more often than not, and with her asking if I want whatever she's having. Usually I say yes, especially if the older children are out. I am rewarded with kale and brown rice, or variants thereon, in microscopic portions. Not that I'm complaining: we're hardly in a longing-for-seconds situation. We sit there opposite each other, chewing away: apparently we need to chew each mouthful at least twenty-five times, though Gaby says it's good to aim for fifty. The scallops and chorizo, the chicken tajines, the pulled pork and rare steaks and salads and dark chocolate mousses that I used to make for the Man From The Connaught are all a receding memory, like the tide going out and never coming in again while you stand on the shore in disbelief. The food Gaby and I eat together is frugal, nun-like, entirely shorn of pleasure, and I think how odd it should be that you have to eat like hungry poor people in order to look expensive. Although actually I'm not 100 per cent certain that hungry poor people devour kale in the way that we do.

There is no love in the food we consume, which – as a devoted eater – surprises me too. I don't think I've ever eaten loveless food in a home. I make my children's food with love, even when it's boring and I'm fed up and they're being so annoying that actual love is thin on the ground. I've always associated food with love, which is why I like cooking, and why I've never been skinny. Robert and I ate the food I'd cooked with relish, even though back then my repertoire was initially limited to roast chicken and pasta. Sam and I loved lingering over kitchen suppers with a bottle of wine, the children safely tucked up upstairs. With the Man who I said I'd stop mentioning – and I will, I will – I used to send everyone off to school in the mornings and then sit for ages with open cookbooks, feeling complete joy at the idea of making something delicious for us to eat together.

But now we have this new way of eating. Gaby can barely cook, though she insists on doing it – 'Least I can do, darling' – and there is nothing sensual or enjoyable about eating the results. It strikes me as a sad way to eat and a sad way to live. Except I've lost a stone. And there you have it: the eternal tussle between pleasure and vanity.

Today, though, there will be no kale: kale can do one. Today it's jelly and ice cream and sausage rolls and cake and Rocky Road and brownies, and a massive dish of macaroni cheese as a nod to proper food ('My God, the carbs!' said Gaby when I told her what the menu was). It is Maisy's ninth birthday, which means a gathering of the clan.

I'm obsessed with celebrating birthdays – with any large celebration, actually: see also Christmas. All my family are, because they remind us of when we were little and innocent and happy, when nothing was complicated. Things are no longer uncomplicated, but we muddle through, even though the family gatherings can be as stressful as they are deeply comforting.

Today Sam, Maisy's dad, is coming over early so he can help me with the bunting and then pick her up from school. The hallway is decorated with home-made posters that Jack, Sky and I painted last night; I am especially pleased with the one that says, 'How fine, how very fine, to wake up and be NINE'. There are flowers, and cards propped up the whole length of the kitchen table, and multicoloured streamers dangling from the chandelier.

Sam, whom I haven't seen since a couple of days after Gaby moved in, races in for a parking permit, sticks it on his car and then comes back in carrying a pile of presents. We kiss hello. He pulls back and says, 'Clara? What's going on here?'

'Oh dear, is it happening already? So tragic. So young. It's Maisy's ninth birthday and you've come to tea,' I say. I raise my voice. I don't know why mildly irritating Sam amuses me so much. 'YOU'VE COME TO TEA,' I repeat, taking his arm. 'Come on, love. I'll show you to A COMFY SEAT. DO YOU NEED TO GO WEE-WEES?'

'Tsk,' Sam says, taking his arm away but laughing despite himself. 'I've never known anyone more annoying. You have a mental age of six. It was just, in the light there, you looked different for a second. Have you changed your hair? But never mind. Where shall I put the presents?'

'Do I look well?' I ask.

'What?' He glances at me. 'Yeah. Why? You always look well.'

'But do I look *especially* well?'

'What do you want me to do with this bunting? Yes, you look very well. I told you. Who else is coming to tea?'

'The usual suspects, plus Gaby – you know, my friend from LA who I was at school with and who's living here.'

'Oh yes, that's right. How's that working out?'

'All fine. I thought across the ceiling in zigzags, for the bunting, and then maybe over the doorway and across the window. The ladder's upstairs.'

I continue decorating Maisy's cake as he wanders off to get the ladder. Sam reappears three minutes later, accompanied by Gaby, who despite it being the middle of the afternoon is dressed like she's going clubbing.

'Ah, good, you've met,' I say, not able to take my eyes off Gaby. She is wearing fishnet tights, DMs, a very short skirt, a T-shirt that says 'The Vaccines' and a battered denim jacket. Her left wrist, which usually features a smart, thin gold bangle, is today loaded with friendship bands and silver beaded bracelets that reach midway up her arm. Her nails are fluorescent yellow. She's had her extensions redone and her shiny red waves are now a veritable mane.

'Have you borrowed Sky's clothes?' I say, but in a friendly way.

'You might have told me how gorgeous Sam was,' she says, batting her inch-long falsies at him. 'Matter of fact, I have. Well, the jacket and the T-shirt.'

'I like the Vaccines,' says Sam, looking slightly flustered.

'No idea who they are,' Gaby says cheerfully. 'I like the Stones and Madonna from the Eighties. God, look at all this food. Can I help?'

'Thanks, but it's all under control. So, er, are you and your new look going somewhere?'

'I've asked Ben to tea,' says Gaby. 'He had the day off. I hope that's OK.'

Actually, it's mildly annoying: a complete stranger inserted into the family birthday tea.

'No problem,' I say.

'What?' says Gaby.

'Nothing,' I say.

'It's my clothes, right?'

'I'm trying to work out what I think,' I say, laughing. 'I'm sort-of admiring.'

'Are you thinking mutton?' says Gaby, laughing too, and I know her well enough to detect a small degree of uncertainty.

'Oh, darling, not really. Well, yes. A bit. A tiny bit. But I'm trying to decide whether it's actually mutton when you can pull it off so well. I mean, you've got a better figure than lots of twenty-year-olds.'

'That's what I think,' says Gaby. 'I did wonder, for a nano-second, but then I thought, "Nah, it's fine."'

'I'm uncomfortable,' says Sam from halfway up his ladder, 'with the fact that I am overhearing this conversation. It's very woman-y.'

'Well, what do you think?' asks Gaby. 'I mean, you're a man. An attractive man. How do I look?'

'Um,' says Sam.

'Well?' says Gaby.

'You look great,' Sam says. 'Everyone looks great.'

'I need to be thirty-four,' Gaby tells him, quite disarmingly. 'Do I look thirty-four?'

'You look,' Sam says, 'like an . . . urban . . . ah . . . thirty-four-year-old . . . that . . . mmm . . . likes partying.'

'Perfect,' Gaby says with a pleased smile. 'Thanks, Sam.'

It's so hard to know, with mutton. Part of the reason is that all of these questions only arise when you emerge from the wreckage of having small children, and what you thought you knew isn't necessarily how things actually are, or rather how things have remained. I wear fishnets all the time, for example: they are my tight of choice, on the basis that they are the least claustrophobic. And I own more than one shrunken denim jacket, and I have T-shirts, obviously, though not so much indie-band ones, on the basis that I don't want to dress like my children. (This is also why I don't own any trousers that actually show my arse.) There's nothing wrong with DMs, plus they're practical. The skirt is insanely short, but then she very much has the legs for it. I mean, *technically* she looks great. She certainly doesn't look tarty, which up until now has always been my most reliable measure of mutton: you want a hint of possibility, I think, but at a certain age 'yoohoo' turns into 'sexually desperate', which is really a look a person wants to avoid at all costs.

But there are so many potential pitfalls: the V-neck that's suddenly too deep; the heels that mutate from playfully sexy into 'aged swinger' in the space of five birthdays; the leopard-skin coat that transforms from 'goes with everything, almost a neutral' into 'I charge extra for anal.' Denim shorts, frayed or otherwise; 'amusing' patterned tights; anything that looks like underwear; charms on handbags; leather (rawr); being painfully on-trend – a couple of years ago, this involved being dressed like a Goth, with your Camden Market In The Eighties crucifix and your purple lipstick: I mean, who in their right mind, aged over forty? And then of course there's the full horror of the Little Girl look: bunches, plaits, broderie anglaise, espadrilles with ribbons that criss-cross up the leg, satin ballet shoes; even the harmless sundress is sometimes not exempt. Any clothes that make you look like you skip rather than walk, basically. Any clothes that say, 'Hewwo Daddy, pleathe may I have an ithe cweam?'

But it depends, doesn't it? It so confusingly depends. I bet Gaby would look great in a little-girly broderie anglaise peasant blouse, tanned shoulder peering out. And my own clothes aren't all age-appropriate either: I like a tight frock and I like a tea-dress, where I should probably like rectangular grey shifts and trouser suits and bags that hint at the boardroom. I hate clothes that unsex you, though I have the feeling they're the clothes women my age are supposed to head for: plain, safely androgynous, not putting any ideas in anybody's head, because *God forbid*. Joyless clothes for the perimenopausal. I mean, urgh. It's brutal. It's 'Women, know your place,' and the place in question is 'out to pasture with the old donkeys'. No thanks. Not quite yet, eh?

But it's so hard to know with the stuff I *do* like. I realize

I've been relying on some internal radar, some warning twitch of the antennae. What are the actual rules? I think Gaby looks amazing, but on the wrong side of them – whatever they may be. I don't want anyone to laugh at her. *Would* they laugh, though? Is someone looking great regardless of their age really that hilarious, or is the laughter tinged with envy, as in 'I wish I could wear that, but I can't, so I'm going to snigger at the woman who can'?

If you're one of the sniggerers, you may have embraced the notion of women of a certain age adopting a 'signature look'. This is not so good, because it can go very wrong. It's how you end up with women from Notting Hill in leather trousers, aged sixty-three (which can work, actually, as a look. Sometimes. If you're a former supermodel). And it's how you also end up with retired women who know the little Eighties business suits aren't quite right any more, but have forgotten how to shop and so head for those weird 'boutiques' for the middle-aged, where they sell you enormous, deliberately outsized garments that are supposed to indicate 'relaxed yet stylish' but just make you look like a sack-shaped hippo. Also, fatally, it's how you end up with women who are a size 14 or over wearing smocks and enormous wooden jewellery, with 'interesting' scarves, the tails hanging over the stomach as though to conceal the most improbable, the most grotesque of pregnancies.

There is a sub-genre, which my sisters and I call Hampstead Lady, due to overexposure to the species as children. Hampstead Lady – she is also to be found in other bourgeois-bohemian neighbourhoods – does the smock and the huge jewellery, but with an ethnic spin, as though she were in fact a painter of Rajasthani or Aboriginal landscapes. It's not

ugly, or even visually displeasing, but let's put it this way –
Hampstead Lady isn't batting the boys away with a stick.

I'm interested in being attractive.

And in any case, why should a middle-aged woman who
is fit and healthy not wear a backless dress, or a mini, or a
garment that shows her body? Maybe it's time we took the
mutton and wrestled it to the ground. It's not like the alter-
natives are that terrific.

So many questions – and so many rings of the doorbell,
for here come the loved ones. You see, Kate's got it right.
She's in her early sixties – she had me very young – and she
looks in her early sixties, but in a great and enviable way. It
helps that when anyone is rude enough to ask her age, she
whacks ten years on, and then smiles pleasantly when people
express their amazement at her vitality and superhuman
state of preservation. Neither Kate, nor my sisters, nor
I have ever understood why people would lie the other way
if the object is to impress people, but then all of us are strangers to the knife, which is to say none of us are Gaby. On cue:

'Gaby!' Kate says, whooshing in in a cloud of Shalimar.
'Clara, take these parcels, please. They are too heavy for
me. Good grief, Gaby. You look *extraordinary.*'

'Hello, Kate,' says Gaby, going over to give her a hug.
'Long time no see.'

'You look like an infant,' Kate cries. 'And I can almost see
your nappy.'

'Steady on,' Gaby laughs, tugging at her skirt.

'No, you look like an embryo. A zygote, Gaby. *An actual
zygote.* Hello, everyone. Clara, don't put the parcels like that,
in an ugly pile, all clumped. It's disrespectful to my beautiful
wrapping. Where's Maisy?'

'Changing her dress for the third time.'

Kate's eyes haven't left Gaby. 'Can I see behind your ears, Gaby?' she now asks.

'Kate!' I say.

'Kate!' Gaby squeals, and actually blushes.

'What?' Kate says. 'As Gaby was just pointing out, we've known each other a long time.'

'My ears are private,' Gaby says with dignity. 'And also, Kate – I have this new boyfriend and he's going to turn up any minute, and he thinks I'm thirty-four. So could you, like, not reminisce about me and Clara watching *Bagpuss*, or go on about looking behind my ears?'

'Darling, please,' Kate says. 'Why would I come some-where and talk to a stranger about *Bagpuss*?'

'I know,' says Gaby. 'It's just, it would really suck if you *inadvertently* . . .'

'Let the cat out the bag,' I guffaw.

'The wit,' says Kate. 'My conversational skills are highly evolved. *Bagpuss!* For heaven's sake. Your little secret is safe with me. Now, Gaby, come and sit here and let me look behind your ears.'

'No,' Gaby shrieks. 'Leave my ears alone.'

'I *will* get to look, you know, whether you like it or not,' Kate says, laughing. She can be quite monomaniacal, Kate. 'But maybe later. Impressive work, though.'

'Thanks,' Gaby says uncertainly.

'Mm,' says Kate. 'Of course there's that terrible problem – what's it called: 1664, 1056, 1789? Something like that. Seventeen from the back, eighty-nine from the front. Not that you look eighty-nine, obviously, darling. But still. The turning-around issue.'

'Tea, Mother?' I interrupt.

'On the other hand, I don't suppose you scuttle into rooms backwards, Gaby, and then flip yourself round so that everyone gasps with shock. So it's fine, I expect. Usually.'

'Biscuit with your tea? Cheese straw? Iced gem?'

'I try not to go into rooms backwards, no,' says Gaby. 'Ah, Christ – here's Ben. Please, Kate. Please stop going on about it, just for now.'

'The infant boyfriend! I look forward to meeting him,' Kate says. 'My unaugmented lips are sealed.' She mimes zipping them shut and then laughs to herself as Gaby throws her a dark look.

Jack and Sky have ambled in; Jack's brother, Charlie, understands the momentousness of family birthdays and is on his way home from university, and will be here any minute; my sister Flo and her brood honk to indicate they've pulled up outside. Robert appears at the same time as Ben, having left work early, bearing a huge bunch of flowers. Maisy, resplendent in white sequins and two tiaras, runs around chatting, sitting on everyone's laps, and slowly begins to open her presents while we start drinking tea and digging in to the industrial quantities of food. Ben is sitting by Gaby, who is still throwing Kate anxious looks.

Talking of large presents, a huge FedExed parcel arrived for Maisy this morning. I haven't opened it – obviously: it's addressed to her – and in the general getting-ready chaos of the day, I haven't paid it much attention: I just stuck it on the table with the other parcels that have been trickling in over the past few days, from her Granny Pat (who signs herself 'Granny', in quote marks, as though she were lying to be kind – 'Love you, Maisy, from "Your gran"'), from her various

94

uncles and from my sister Evie, who is away for work for another fortnight. But now it's the FedEx parcel's turn to be opened, and once Sam has sawn through the crazy amount of tape with a knife, I watch as Maisy starts the actual unwrapping.

'Who's it from? Is there a card, darling?'

'I don't think so,' says Maisy, not looking very hard and tearing through two layers of scarlet tissue paper.

The doorbell goes again: Charlie, taller than ever and looking very grown up, dragging a duffel bag. The room erupts into whoops as he walks in. Maisy hops down from her present-opening, kisses him, clings to him like a limpet and then hops back up, returning to the task in hand. I'm in the oven, examining the level of crispiness of the macaroni cheese and thinking that it probably needs another five minutes, when a thought strikes me.

'Mummy, look! I LOVE it!' Maisy is saying.

I turn around to see her embracing a huge, fluffy toy koala. It's gorgeous: not so realistic that it's actively creepy, as is often the case with the more expensive teddies, I've noticed, especially those ones with studs in their ears – I prefer it when my soft toy doesn't look taxidermized. But nor is it so cartoon-like that it seems insultingly for-toddlers. It's beautiful.

'He's called Kevin,' Maisy announces. 'I'm going to sleep *on* him.'

'Who's it from?' asks Jack. 'There's got to be a card or something, Maise.'

'Nah,' says Maisy, rummaging through the box. 'I've looked.' She props Kevin on the ground and moves on to the next present, pausing only to bite into a sausage roll.

I shout at everyone to clear a space on the ridiculously crowded table and put the macaroni cheese down on to a mat. As people help themselves, I gather up the wrapping paper and general debris, including the FedEx box. I have a feeling I know who it's from, and I'm not wrong: buried deep under those pillowy white bits of bean-shaped foam, there's a handwritten note. '*Happy birthday, Maisy. I hope you like your new friend,*' it says. It isn't signed, but then it doesn't need to be.

I crumple up the note, feeling dazed, and make a giant effort to pull myself together, though not before glaring at Kevin surreptitiously and with some fury. Kevin just stares back in a big-nosed koala way. I'll think about it later: for now there's jelly and ice cream and then of course cake, and more presents to get through, and conversation to be made. But even as I push all non-relevant thoughts down to the very bottom of my head, they rise to the top like helium-filled balloons. 'I hope you like your new friend.' Does he like his? Root-longing Sheila, assuming she exists. And why's he chucked an outsize koala into my tea party, like a furry tufty-eared bomb? Argh. Also, because of some level of dementedness I don't entirely seem to be able to control, the stupid koala – Kevin – makes me feel a sharp stab of desire. Well, no: actual *Kevin* doesn't cause me to desire him. (God, though, imagine a life where one found stuffed toys a turn-on. There must be people: if you think of a fetish, it exists, no matter how outlandish. I would really hate teddies to give me the horn. One must count one's blessings.) Where was I? Yes, not Kevin. Kevin leaves me cold Down Under, as it were. Here I pause to laugh at my own joke, all alone by the kettle, like a lunatic; suddenly my nerves seem very close to the surface of my skin. Kevin's sender, though – that's a whole other thing. That's the series of small, sharp stabs in my stomach. Which I must put out of my head. I can't sit at my own child's birthday party thinking about . . . But of course I'm thinking it already, and within ten seconds the inside of my head is so unseemly that I can feel myself blush.

'Clara!' Robert says. Robert is exceptionally beady-eyed at all times. 'What are you doing, laughing all by yourself and going red?'

'I was just thinking of a funny thing,' I say. 'I was thinking about, er, Australia and . . .'

'Good grief!' Robert exclaims. 'Never mind that. I've just noticed something. Come over here, would you?'

He's said this just as there's a gap in the otherwise Babel-like torrent of conversation, so everyone hears him.

'Why?' I say defensively.

'So I can admire whatever you've had done to your face,' he says smoothly.

'Robert!'

'What? You look great. But I can tell you've done some-thing. Come on, hurry up. Over here, under the light.'

So now there's pin-drop silence and everyone is staring at me with intense interest, and apart from it being embarrass-ing, I can't help thinking it's also unjust. I'm not Miss Full Facelift sitting over there. But Gaby is staring too, a little smile on her lips, giving every pretence of being astonished. And then they all start speaking at the same time.

'What, like Botox?' asks Ben, all agog. 'Like poison in the face? That's, woah. That's full-on.'

'I don't want you to have poison in your face, Mummy,' Maisy says, looking aghast.

'Neither do I. Well, I do, but it's not poison. Well, it is, but it doesn't hurt people.'

'It only hurts wrinkles, Maisy,' Robert explains. 'Mummy's fine. Mummy looks great. God, I'd have everything done if I was a woman. Good on you, Clara. Who did you go to?'

'Oh my God,' says Flo. 'You did it. Oh my actual God. That's so weird.'

'Clara! I can't believe you actually went ahead with it,' says Kate, in her best Lady Bracknell. She's been so busy staring at Gaby and trying to get to her ears that she's barely glanced at me, an oversight she is now remedying with some vigour. If she had a lorgnette she'd be raising it. 'Chemicals in your *face*?'

'I thought there was something,' muses Sam. 'I couldn't put my finger on it.'

'I thought it was make-up,' says Sky.

'I think it looks all right,' says Charlie.

'I can't even see the difference,' says Jack.

'Yeah,' says Ben. 'But, you know – stuff in your *face* . . .'

'Anyone else have an opinion?' I ask. 'About, like, my face, which belongs to me?'

'A little goes a long way, with that sort of thing,' says Gaby, between whose artificially plumped lips butter wouldn't melt. 'Don't go crazy, Clara.'

She says this last sentence with a concerned look, Ben nodding in assent. For fuck's actual sake. Is he *blind*? Has he checked out her neck at all? Those adorable liver spots on the backs of her hands?

'Oh, stop going on,' Robert says gallantly. 'So many people have stuff done. It's practically the norm. She looks great on

it. Leave her alone. We'd have it done too – blokes, I mean –
if we thought we could get away with it.'

'I wouldn't,' says Sam.

'I bet you would,' says Robert. 'If you had massive wrinkles
or huge eye bags or facial warts.' He tuts. 'I can't bear that Pres-
byterian ethic that none of us ever apply to anything else – that
all of this is awful vanity. It's not vanity. Your body is yours, and
you matter. You know? You might as well turn down a hip
replacement on the basis that at your age nobody needs to
walk and you've had a good innings. It's false sanctimony.'

'Facial warts?' says Sam, nonplussed.

'It may be the norm in the weird fashion world that you
work in,' Flo says, 'but I don't know a single person who's
had anything done. Apart from my sister, obviously, now.'

Flo is shocked, I can tell. I'm not surprised: I'd be shocked
too, at her age. The mid-thirties is still the period when you
think wrinkles are 'lovely' and 'characterful'. Until you wake
up with a face full of them.

'I'm going to have it done when I'm grown up,' says Maisy.
'And I will look beautiful, like Mummy.'

'No!' I say, slightly louder than I meant to. 'Mummy just
did a tiny thing, once, and it was probably a stupid idea, and
I'm not going to do it again, ever.'

Jesus. What kind of weird ideas am I giving my little
daughter? All the things I'm so conscious of never doing
in front of her – discussing weight, moaning about diets,
overly praising or dissing other women's looks, all of that
stuff – undone in one fell swoop. Robert, who is incredibly
unwise, does strike me as having said a wise thing, though.
It's true: if you're fortunate enough to have been blessed
with a body, or indeed a face, that works and that isn't broken

and that looks OK, why would it be sinful vanity to try and keep it that way? Isn't it just called self-esteem?

'Oh, calm down, everyone,' Kate says, somewhat unexpectedly. 'I was against it, as you know, but you do absolutely look better, Clara, and not everyone is as lucky as I am. Almond oil, you know. A miraculous substance. Regardless of which: do stop overreacting, all of you.'

'Kate's right,' says Flo magnanimously. 'You do actually look pretty good. But no more, right? That's it? Because it's still freaky.'

'Yeah.' Hurrah: now Sam's chipping in. 'You look well but I'd leave it at that.'

'Although,' Kate says, 'I think possibly . . . come over here, Clara, would you?'

I suddenly feel like a little girl again, and like Kate's about to find out that I've done something naughty.

'What?' I say. 'I don't want to. It's nearly cake time. And there's nothing behind my ears.'

Everyone is staring at me again.

'Just come over here,' says Kate, narrowing her eyes and staring intently. 'I think there's something up with your eyebrows.'

'My eyebrows?' I yelp, my hands going up to my face. 'What about them?'

'She's right, Clara. They're rising,' says Flo. 'They're higher up than they used to be. Not by much,' she adds kindly.

'What?' I grab my bag and scrabble around for a mirror. The evidence is incontrovertible: the eyebrows are indeed higher up than they were.

'Oh my God,' I say. 'What are they doing? Gaby, what are they doing?'

'I don't know,' says shameless Gaby, who will pay for her ingénue act later. I'm going to deep-fry her bloody kale and boil her fish in cream and butter.

'I'm sure they'll settle down, maybe, eventually,' says Flo. 'Makes sense, if you think about it. We all have really arched eyebrows in the first place, in this family, and if you have Botox in your forehead then the whole area is sort of yanked up, isn't it? Including the poor eyebrows.'

This seems to me to be indubitably true: the upward trajectory of the eyebrows is undeniable. And as Flo points out, our eyebrows are circumflexes in the first place. Why didn't I think of this? Why didn't Dr Halliday? I wonder how long it takes to grow a fringe, and then I remember that I have a small forehead and that fringes make me look like a monk without a tonsure.

After the cake and the last of the presents, we repair to the sitting room. Sam asks Robert if he meant it about men having 'everything' done if they thought they could get away with it.

'God, yes,' says Robert. 'If we didn't have to let our faces slide downwards, but it was done so delicately that nobody could quite tell? You bet. Look,' he says, smiling exaggeratedly, much as I smiled at myself in the hall mirror all those weeks ago. The sides of his eyes are criss-crossed with deep lines.

'I like your eye lines,' I say. 'They're from smiling. You're pushing fifty. They're in keeping.'

'In keeping with what, though?' says Robert. 'I go to the gym three times a week. I run. Awful thing to say about yourself, but I'm in good nick. You know my line of work and I know it makes you laugh when I say this, but it's part of my job to wear this season's clothes. Hence this,' he says, pointing down at his skinny trousers and his pointy shoes.

'But you look nice,' says Flo.

'But I don't know that these' – Robert gestures at his eye lines – 'are necessarily in keeping with these.' He gestures at his shoes. 'I mean, I don't want to look like a teenager, but I wouldn't mind a tiny bit less of the craggy. What's wrong with that?'

'I went out with a singer once,' Kate says. 'A rock star, I suppose you'd call him. He had a very particular look. Not especially imaginative – tight trousers, lots of hair, rings, you know – silver rings with skulls on them and so on. Very bad karma, to wander about with skulls on you, as I think I pointed out at the time. I made him throw the worst ring in the canal in Maida Vale, I think it was. Anyway, cowboy boots, leather things, you know.'

'A rock star?' I say. 'What? Who? When? Maida Vale?'

'Oh, we needn't go into that,' Kate says airily. 'It was very brief and literally decades ago. My point is –'

'Was it the man with the lips out of Aerosmith?' Flo interrupts.

'No. My point is –'

'Was it Ozzy Osborne?' I ask with an interested face.

'The chubby little one who dressed as a schoolboy out of AC/DC?' Flo tries to say, except she starts choking with laughter halfway through.

'Was it the man out of Def Leppard?' I say, catching Flo's eye as well as her now full-blown hysteria.

'When you say "lots of hair", do you mean, like, lionish?' Flo says, howling with laughter and miming a rocking out motion with her head. 'They hadn't invented conditioner in those days. The hair was massive.'

'Other people's mothers say, "I used to date a dentist,"' Sam observes.

'A dentist! With his hands inside people's mouths all day!' says Kate. 'Rootling about! Revolting. Anyway, as I was saying before my intolerable children started abusing me, this man dressed in a particular way.'

'Levver,' says Flo. 'Levver pants, man. Oh my God – was it Keith Richards?'

'No,' says Kate, 'and if nobody is going to let me finish then I shall go downstairs and make myself some mint tea and check on the children, whose conversation will be more sophisticated than their mothers'.'

'No, no,' says Robert. 'Carry on. I'm interested.'

'So. He was, I don't know, twenty-five at the most at the time. As I say, it was a brief affair.'

'I love how you say "a brief affair",' says Gaby. 'It's so much more elegant.'

Kate shoots her a look like an arrow, poison-tipped. 'Don't be irritating, Gaby,' she says. 'Were you there? No. A brief affair is what it was. A liaison. Anyway, then it ended, which was no great hardship. But of course I saw him occasionally, not in the flesh but on television, or in magazines. And he was thirty and then forty. And then fifty . . .'

'All the decades,' I say.

'And now he must be a bit older than me. Approaching seventy, maybe. And he still dresses in the same way.'

'I wish you'd say who it was,' says Flo.

'There is no need,' Kate says. 'The fact remains, it can be quite hard for men too, the ageing process. He still looks good, if you like that sort of thing. But women can change their appearance any time they like. I mean, look at what's her name, the Italian one that Clara so used to love. Madonna.'

'I still love her,' I say.

'We will always love her,' says Flo. 'She is queen of our hearts.'

'She can wear a sensible frock when required,' Kate says. 'She can wear a suit, or a dress, or thigh-high rubber boots . . .'

'Because she has a stylist,' says Flo. 'And a wardrobe as big as Buckingham Palace. Most women don't. They tend not to be squillionaires either.'

'Leather,' I say. 'Leather boots, not rubber. They're not waders. Waders aren't sexy.'

'Unless you're a fisherman's wife,' says Flo. 'In which case they might be super-hot. "Keep your waders on, Ian."'

'I don't love the way they'd frame Ian's penis,' I reply. 'Still, horses for courses.'

'Yes,' says Flo. 'Who are we to judge?'

'May I finish?' Kate says in her chilliest voice. 'Madonna. She could wear Prada or a corset, or whatever she pleases. Whereas the rock star is still stuck in his snake-skin cowboy boots from that shop in Vegas, and more to the point can never cut his hair.'

'Well, he could. He's not Samson,' I say. 'He could have a short back and sides and rock a nice Church's brogue and go to the cooler end of Savile Row, if he wanted.'

'It's true, though,' says Flo. 'Look at Russell Brand. What's he going to do when he's sixty?'

'I'm sure he'll think of something,' I say. 'I don't think it's a problem for men.'

'You're so wrong,' says Robert. 'I mean, those are extreme examples because they're so famous, but it's absolutely a thing. Leather jackets.'

'What about them?' I say.

'I know what he means,' says Sam. 'They're a fork in the road, leather jackets.'

'No, they're not,' I say. 'Any man can wear a leather jacket.' I think about this a bit and then realize it's not true. 'No, OK, maybe they can't. But this is still really niche – rock stars, famous people, leather jackets . . . Women have to rethink the whole thing, all the time. Year by year, practically. Normal women, I mean, not famous ones with stylists.'

'There *is* such a thing as male mutton,' Flo says pensively. 'Ram. Old ram. There are many expressions of it. We think it's just cars shaped like willies, or running off with a twenty-year-old who has plastic bosoms and does massive sex-moans when she sees their beer gut. But actually, the ways are subtle and varied. How awful to be old ram.'

'Well, except men are allowed to be silver foxes,' I say. 'Being a silver fox is easy. We get bloody *cougars*, who are pleased with themselves for shagging boys Charlie's age.'

'Mum!' says Charlie.

'What? It's true. Women my age ogling kids my children's age! That's not an achievement, it's a psychological disorder. It's incest by proxy.'

'Mum!' says Jack.

'It disgusts me,' I say. 'It disgusts me when men do it, and it also disgusts me in the other direction. Also, cougars. For God's sake.' I am warming to my theme. 'They're not sexy felines, they're maladjusted oddbods who so can't interact with normal adults that they have to pick on children.

They're old woman sex pests. They're the twenty-first-century equivalent of flashers. Urgh.'

'But do we actually know any cougars?' says Flo. 'Aren't they a made-up thing? How many women do you know who are shagging men young enough to be their sons? They don't exist, or not much. They were invented by the *Daily Mail*. There are probably four of them in the entire country.'

I am considering my response to this when the conversation is interrupted by Ben getting up quite suddenly and offering everyone a cup of tea.

'It's funny what you're saying about silver foxes,' he says, now by the kettle and clearly not wanting to talk about cougars any more. 'The silver fox thing. It's reminding me of my dad.'

'How old's your dad?' I ask. 'Is he old ram or fox?'

'Not fox or ram,' says Ben sadly. 'I kind of wish he were. He's much older than my mum. He's seventy-two. He's very sort of *correct*. Old school. And – my stepmother – she . . . she doesn't think any of this stuff matters. His eyes aren't brilliant, you know? And so he has these, these sorts of whiskers on his cheekbones, just from where he hasn't shaved properly. And hair on his ears. And his nose. And – ha, I don't even know why I'm telling you this. I don't even know any of you, but . . .'

'Carry on,' I say. 'It's all fine.'

'It's only a small thing,' Ben continues, 'but it mentalizes me. He used to be a handsome guy. But she lets him have this old-man hair, because she doesn't care. Like, mad old-man hair. Professor hair.'

'Of the face,' says Flo thoughtfully.

'I'm sure she does care,' I say soothingly. 'She probably loves him so much she doesn't even notice.'

'Yeah,' says Ben. 'Maybe. She's all right. She's not horrible or anything. But he took pride in his appearance. He was – what's the word? – dapper. He'd be appalled if he knew what he looked like. I just want to take a razor to him.'

'You should,' says Kate. 'You should make a joke of it, or say, "Let's go and get wet shaves." There's an excellent place in St James's Street.'

'Do you think?' asks Ben. 'Maybe I should. I don't know what my problem is. But we haven't lived together since I was fifteen, so it's not really that . . . easy a relationship. And it shouldn't really matter, should it? A bit of ear hair. So what, right? But it just makes me feel sad every time I see him,' he says, petering out. 'It makes me feel sad for him and in a weird way for myself.'

'I wouldn't worry quite yet on that front,' says Robert. 'You're, what, thirty?'

'Twenty-nine,' says Ben. 'No, you're right. We're spring chickens,' he says, stroking Gaby's thigh and putting on a bright smile. 'Aren't we, babe? Plenty of time for that later.'

'Mm,' says Gaby, snuggling in youthfully. 'Too right.'

It is at this precise moment – just as Kate catches my eye, raising both eyebrows in incredulity at Gaby's breathtaking chutzpah (mine are raised all by themselves, as we have seen) – that Flo's two children come stampeding into the room like mini-wildebeest, breathless and squealing. Flo's husband is halfway up the stairs, I notice, having just arrived from work and bearing yet another present.

'Mummy,' says the youngest. 'Maisy is *chasing us* with a monster's tail, and we are scared.'

'And she's going to put it on us,' says her brother. 'And it's a real tail and it's horrible.'

'And we are *scared*,' the little girl repeats.

They are giggling like mad, frenzied from the game and from a sugar-rush.

'Raah,' says Maisy, who has galloped upstairs and is now framed in the doorway. 'THE TAIL WANTS TO SIT ON YOUR HEADS, BABIES.'

'Waaah,' the children scream, racing about the room and clinging to their mother, at that intersection between terror and laughter hysteria.

We're all sitting about smiling and thinking how sweet they are – or at least, I am – when Gaby leaps out of the sofa and says, in an unfriendly voice, 'Give me that, Maisy. Maise. Give it, now.'

'The tail?' says Maisy, looking nonplussed. 'But we're playing!'

'Give it now,' Gaby hisses, holding out her hand.

'THE TAIL! THE TAIL!' scream the children. They pronounce it 'tay-yool'.

'Darling, give Gaby the tail,' I say, nonplussed myself. 'She just wants to have a look at it.'

'Nooooo!' says Maisy.

'You can have it back,' I smile, getting up and going over to the sitting-room door to see what on earth all this is about. There, in Maisy's hand, is a two-foot-long red hair extension, faintly matted at the tip, sinister now it's disembodied. Gaby, whose eyes didn't even flicker throughout our Botox–mutton conversation, is scarlet. Her back is to the rest of the room.

'I'll have it,' I say, keeping my voice breezy and sticking the tail in the pocket of my dress. 'Come on, children.

Let's go downstairs and find a new game, and then it's bathtime.'

'I don't want to turn around,' whispers Gaby. 'What if he saw?'

'It's fine,' I whisper back. 'Men that age zone children out, unless they have some themselves, and besides, everybody's talking. He won't have heard.'

'Jesus,' says Gaby.

I was right: Ben appears to have been oblivious to the whole episode. When Gaby turns around he's on his Black-Berry, head down, tapping away. 'Drink?' he says to her, looking up. 'A bunch of my mates are in a bar in Kensal.'

'Yes please,' says Gaby, and you can hear the relief in her voice. 'Give me two minutes to pretty myself up.'

10

My eyebrows hit their heights ten days later. Every day they've become slightly more quizzical and arched – fine qualities in a person, less so in facial hair – and by day ten they look like I've stolen them from Ming the Merciless. It is an appalling look. Happily it coincides with the beginning of the school holidays and with an intensive period of work, so I try to leave the house as little as I can and pray – literally pray, every night: health for my children, succour for the afflicted, world peace, my eyebrows – that some miraculous intervention will take place to make them go back to normal. I emailed Dr Halliday photographs of the brows, and he replied saying that yes, this sometimes happened, and he'd know for next time. I'm thinking: there won't be a next time.

The enforced period of rest reminds me of how I lived before Gaby came to stay, before Bel the silver fox, who remains present via text and email and via a smart dinner here, a cocktail there. Before I started preoccupying myself with things that I am slightly ashamed of being preoccupied by. Gaby hasn't been around that much – she's often at Ben's overnight, and in the daytime, having finally found a site for her first yoga centre, she's busy racing about getting things organized. But she had something done to her hands three days ago – something called 'fat transfer hand rejuvenation', and so now she's at home, lying at the other end of the sofa from me, reading a magazine. The backs of her hands will remain covered in weird mittens for several more days, so she doesn't want to go out in public.

Sky – also on holiday, obviously – has rather taken to our newly home-bound existence, and appears now bearing two mugs of tea and a bacon sandwich (for me. I've started to rebel. I'm fed up with the kale. I don't think the kale is worth it. So what if I'm a size 14? I mean, really – so what? Also, I went round the supermarket feeling childish excitement at the Christmassy tins of biscuits and the pyramids of Christmas puddings and the jars of Stilton, except that every time I went past something I liked the look of, I thought, 'Not for me.' I found it quite depressing).

'There's some post,' Sky says, handing me a bunch of envelopes. 'And one for me from Dad! He always draws a baby Beakstrel when he writes to me. Look, Clara. It's a bird, from the Chronicles.'

'Ah yes,' I say. 'Very nice. How's he doing?'

'He's still majorly blocked, he says. He's sounding a bit desperate. I was wondering – should I go and see him, do you think? Or would that be, like, really unhelpfully distracting? It's crucial that he delivers this book. The Lapidarians – that's his readers – are pleading with him for volume seven. The blogosphere's gone mad and his website keeps crashing. He's had to close the comments section.'

'I'm sure he'd love to see you,' I say. 'He must be really missing you. But the point of the thing is isolation, so I'm not sure. Why not write back and ask him?'

'Yeah, I will,' Sky says. 'I just wish I could think of something to help. He's trying to link back to this stuff that happened two volumes ago, when the Hornfels laid siege to the Amphiboles, but he just can't get it right. It's an ongoing siege and a very parlous situation for the Amphiboles, but he can't resolve it in a way that makes sense.'

I'm touched by the way Sky speaks like her dad's books sometimes, and I smile at her.

'What?' says Gaby, looking up from her magazine.

'My dad,' says Sky. 'He writes these books.'

'I'd love to help, darling, but I haven't read them,' I say. 'The Hornells mean nothing to me.'

'Hornfels,' says Gaby. 'What – what are you saying, Sky?'

'Huh?' says Sky, puzzled. 'About what?'

'Your dad,' Gaby says, sitting bolt upright. 'Are you saying that your dad, your *dad* is Bernard Frossage?' She gives a wild little laugh. 'You're not, right? I mean, he can't be.'

'Uh,' says Sky. 'Yeah. Yes. He is.'

'Oh my actual fucking God,' says Gaby. 'I love those books.'

'You and about ten zillion people,' I say, laughing. 'There's no need to look like Brad Pitt just goosed you.'

'Clara!' says Gaby. 'God! Don't you remember?'

'Remember what?'

'When I say I love them, I mean I *really* love them. I love them best in the world. I loved them before they became well known.' Her eyes are shining: I haven't seen her so animated in weeks. 'Way before the TV thing. *Way* before he was famous.'

'Cool,' says Sky, smiling. 'I really love them too. They're the best.'

'What year did I change my name?' says Gaby, addressing me.

'Um . . . I don't really remember,' I say. 'Long enough ago for me never to think of you as Laura.'

'Do you remember what I changed it to?'

'Well, er, yeah. To Gaby. To Gaby, Gaby.'

'No!' yells Gaby triumphantly. 'Not Gaby. I changed it to Gabbro. *Gabbro*.'

'You've lost me,' I say. 'Lost me utterly. What kind of name is that? You've always been Gaby.'

'Short for Gabbro!' Gaby practically shouts.

'What the fuck is Gabbro?' I ask, now beyond puzzlement.

'Gabbro!' says Sky. 'Oh my God! That is so cool. High five, dude.'

They slap palms, beaming at each other.

'Anyone want to enlighten me?' I say. 'I'm feeling a bit baffled, to be honest.'

'The Lady Gabbro,' says Sky. 'She's the main female character in Men of Granite. She's The Matriarch. She's in it from the first one. After her husband . . .'

'The Magma of Magma,' says Gaby.

'. . . The Magma of Magma, perishes in battle against the Greywacke, The Lady Gabbro rules over Caldera.'

'The Lady Gabbro?' I can't quite believe my ears, so I say it again. 'Seriously, Gaby – The Lady Gabbro?'

'But her ambitions are greater than the smallness of the land,' says Gaby. 'And soon she invades Pippilin, home to the Pippil peoples.'

'Dad's little joke,' says Sky. 'Get it? The Pippil People.'

'Right,' I say. 'What humour.'

'They are very rich, the Pippil,' says Sky. 'Their coffers are plump with gold.'

'The Pippil's wealth is abundant, their natural resources infinite,' says Gaby. 'And their men are hornèd.'

'Hornèd?'

'Yes, when they reach manhood. But Gabbro, The Matriarch, lays waste to their lands. She subjugates them and harvests their riches. It is only the beginning. There are many checks and reversals of fortune, but the Chronicles chart the course of her ascent to power over all of Lapidosa. There's a hint of irony in the title: *Men* of Granite. Do you see? Oh, Clara, I can't believe you still haven't read them. They're epic.'

'This is so great,' says Sky happily.

'It is very astonishing,' I say. 'Though now I think back – yeah, you were always trying to shove those books at me.' When you were still plain and nerdy, I want to say, as opposed to hot and, clearly, even nerdier. 'But since I never read them, I just didn't make the connection. The Lady Gabbro, eh? By Bernard Frossage, rhymes with sausage.'

'So,' says Gaby, ignoring me. 'What needs to happen with the siege? That's the central question, isn't it?' She has risen from the sofa and is now pacing up and down the sitting room.

'Well, yes,' says Sky. 'You remember when Horno, son of Hornki, finally routs the Amphiboles, after, like, three years of trying, and they retreat to the Citadel?'

'Of course, of course,' says Gaby. 'Horno is invigorated by drinking from the Cup of Thark, and there's the skirmish with the Plumèd Few at the Gates.'

'Exactly. But even during the siege, Bold Olivine remains. Remember? And she is great with child by the end of that volume.'

'Horno's child. They calve early, the Amphiboles,' says Gaby, looking thoughtful and nodding. 'And the needs of the Hornfels are known throughout the land. I mean, woe betide the Amphibole maid who finds herself before a Hornfel's lust.'

'And then there's the Quest going on in the background, and Dad says something about needing to tie the two together, and it's all extra complicated by the fact that Calcite, that *other* son of Horno's, has now reached manhood and . . .'

'I feel like I'm on drugs,' I say. 'Am I on drugs?'

'. . . and he's now narrating the odd chapter,' says Sky. 'Calcite, I mean. And Dad's also stuck with a thing to do with that. He said something about "unreliable narrators". You know? Because it's going to be Calcite telling some of the Bold Olivine story. And you know the state of play between them!'

'Hm,' says Gaby. 'Hm. I do indeed. And then there's the Hippolith, of course. That needs to be resolved too. Oh God' – and here her voice darkens, like a shudder – 'and Strong Gossan. What's he doing with Strong Gossan? I mean, there's only so many places he can go. Now. After the massacre that happened in Gneiss.'

'Dude, you should write to him,' says Sky excitedly. 'I'd say call him up, but there's no phone. You could maybe help him.'

'Oh!' says Gaby, and she actually blushes. 'God, no. Imagine! Ha! God! No! Help Bernard Frossage! Hahaha!'

'He really *is* stuck, though,' says Sky. 'He'd really appreciate it. He's getting desperate.'

'Darling,' says Gaby. 'There are five zillion fansites and forums where all people do all day is discuss the Men of Granite Chronicles. He just needs to dip into one of them and he'll get millions of ideas.'

'Oh, he does that,' says Sky. 'But he says if the fans have already predicted it, he doesn't want to write it. That's part of the problem. They've thought of everything. Dad says they're "forensic". They're kind of ten steps ahead. Five steps wrong, usually, but still. It was bad enough a couple of years ago, but after it was on telly – well, it just went mad. It gets him down badly sometimes. It freezes his creativity.'

'Really?' says Gaby, sounding awed. 'Do you think? I mean, he wouldn't even have to read it – it would be such an honour just to communicate with him. Oh man!' she says. 'Bernard Frossage! Bloody hell, Sky. You might have said.'

'Here,' I say, opening my laptop. 'Here's the address. Jot it down. Or have it tattooed across your face, or something.'

'I've got to go – I'm going to meet Jack in town,' says Sky. 'I wish I could stay a bit longer: this is amazing. Do write to him, Gaby. He'd love to hear from you, I know he would.'

'Haflorka!' Gaby says. 'Haflorka, Sky!' And here, unbelievably, Gaby makes a salutation at Sky: she extends her right arm in front of her, folds it across the lower part of her face and nods her head into the crook of her elbow. She does this slowly, at a stately pace.

'What the actual fuck are you doing, Gabs?' I say.

'Haflorka, Gabbro,' says Sky, returning the greeting. They look like a pair of shy elephants, using their trunks to hide.

'Haf-whatty?' I say, turning to Gaby, who is pink with excitement.

'It's sort of "cheerio", "au revoir",' she says, looking misty-eyed. 'In Lapidosan. And this' – she does the salutation again – 'is either "Thou hast returned" or "Strong voyage".'

'I don't know what to say, really.'

'You know what?' Gaby says, ignoring me. 'I think I'm going to do it. Why not, right? What have I got to lose? God,

I queued for three hours just to get him to sign my book once. I flew to San Francisco. Do we have any writing paper?'

'Anything for The Lady Gabbro,' I say, still utterly incredulous at the bizarre turn of events the morning has taken. 'In the desk drawer. In the, ah, the broogle finnibo, you'll find ample gromble.'

'Not funny,' says Gaby. 'And anyway, the scribes' tablets are called pikera.'

II

The eyebrows don't show any sign of moving downwards, which I suppose was only to be expected. I become used to them, sort of. Which is funny, in a way, because it presumably means I could have got used to my frown. Instead I am now a woman with ridiculous eyebrows – galling, because I used to be a woman with really great eyebrows. I am a woman with ridiculous eyebrows and a smooth face, like an egg you've drawn on in black marker pen.

However. It's not actually that bad a look. I mean, I wouldn't go out of my way to choose it, but it doesn't seem to be diminishing my charms when it comes to Bel (what *is* that short for? Beloved?). He doesn't know my face well enough, unlike my family, to start pointing and laughing at its upper reaches. He's been scooting about Europe – and Africa, quite thrillingly – but every ten days or so returns to London, and to Claridge's, and to a succession of dinners with me. We have a lovely time, and eventually it occurs to me that perhaps you can't base your love life on explosive sex (it occurs to me, but then a voice in my head says, 'Really? Why not?' This voice is unhelpful and quite insistent. I will silence it). There is no sex with Bel, possibly because he is called Bel (Babybel?), though there is perma-flirtation. The dinners couldn't be nicer. He pays charming compliments, he laughs enthusiastically at all my jokes, he says gallant things and listens attentively to my opinions.

He knows his way round a wine list, which is neither here nor there because so do I, but I like it anyway. There are things grown-up men should be able to do: navigate a wine list; navigate a menu without looking thick (not looking thick tout court is itself a winner); speak at least one foreign language passably; change a tyre without appearing toddlerishly puzzled; wear a suit with aplomb; have da sexual skillz; give beautiful, rather than garage, flowers; put up shelves; know the words of the better-known hymns and the subtexts of the better-known pictures; carry your cases or bags without asking; use a drill without making anxious squeaks about self-electrocution; complain about bad service in a charming manner; buy you underwear that a) fits and b) is sexy; make omelettes, so nobody starves; dispose of dead animals, e.g. rodents, without fuss (and catch bird-sized moths and spiders with faces and put them outside); hold a manual driving licence, because an automatic one is unmasculine; play sport with children – not be the mimsy one on the sidelines saying, 'I don't play football, actually'; swim properly, i.e. get in and do the crawl; drink alcohol without becoming giggly or tearful; not go to bed before you, so that you find them all tucked up like a nan; be kind to animals but, if he has a dog, never refer to himself as 'Daddy'. Oh, and go bald gracefully.

A subjective list, obviously, and I do realize it is something of a contrast with the things that some kinds of women want men to be able to do: have sympathy period cramp, express their emotions freely through the medium of interpretative dance, start sentences with 'As a feminist'. Unfortunately, I find most of these things completely unsexy. I mean, they're grotesque. I'm not big on men crying, for instance.

Obviously, fine in the context of illness or bereavement, though even then, less is more. Not so fine during rom-coms or soaps, or about pets of yore, or with self-pity (instant dumping: nothing more unattractive in either gender). I like a man who can cook – see omelettes – but I wouldn't love one who was, say, an obsessive and perfectionist baker who sulked all evening because his crème anglaise was too runny. And I only like them metropolitan up to a point. I'm all for the grooming, but it can reach a stage where you think, 'Oy, why don't you stick on a frock and be done with it?' A man preening in the mirror for more than forty-five seconds – no thanks. Also, grown-up men don't need to preen: they really should have worked out what kind of look works for them by now. And yes, I know I have become sexist and retrograde in my old age. I don't care. I don't fancy men who drink herbal teas either, or who enquire anxiously about the components of certain dishes in restaurants. You're a man: eat a bloody steak.

Bel (Belvidere?) eats steak. Owns cattle too, I shouldn't wonder. Eats steak straight from the haunches of his cows, probably, crouched on all fours, chewin'. I'm embarrassed to ask, because there's already something of the television show *Dallas* about him, and the cattle thing would just start me laughing. I expect he can do all the things on my mental list, with the addition of wrestling bulls and branding them himself (it would be quite funny if Bel lived in a condo with a grand piano and dozens of orchids, but from what he's told me that seems unlikely). So yes, he ticks all the boxes. And it's not that he's unattractive: au contraire. On paper, he's so weirdly great that if you met him online, you'd think, 'This can't be right,' and suspect him of being a murderer *at best*.

And yet . . . I don't think I've ever heard him venture a single opinion on a serious subject himself. It's as if he thinks it would be bad manners to do so. No current affairs, no politics, no religion, no nothing. If I were to think about it properly, I'd find it quite unsettling.

So here we are again, at 'our' usual table, and Bel is talking about his daughter Carlice (pronounced Carleece, obviously, not Car-Lice. If you judged the well-being of a country by its names, America would be some way below the Congo. America would probably call its children Congo, come to think of it. Or Togo. 'Hi, I'm Guinea-Bissau, and this is my sister, Comoros. Our parents named us after, like, poor nations').

Anyway, Carlice. Carlice is twenty-two and gorgeous – as evidenced by the stream of photographs Bel shows me on his phone. Except for her ankles, with which she has 'a problem'. In every single photograph, Carlice is wearing boots, which seems incongruous given that many of said photographs have been taken in forty-two-degree heat. And looking at her, I think of how crap this all is, that women's self-esteem should be so irrevocably tied to their looks. Her ankles! This golden girl, with her golden hair and her golden smile and her Harvard degree, disabled by the fact that her ankles – her ankles! – aren't the slimmest. It actually does my head in.

'It does my head in,' I tell Bel. 'The way people – well, girls and young women – treat a tiny thing like that as though it were a deformity. She's twenty-two! She's perfect! She has no idea of how perfect she is, and by the time she realizes she'll be fifty-five and filled with regret.'

'I know,' Bel (Beluga?) says. 'It upsets me too.'

'It's a confidence trick,' I say. 'The whole shebang. You have two choices: you're either seen to be incredibly vain – I mean, disastrously vain, self-obsessed, and by extension shallow, empty, superficial, incapable of reading a newspaper without your lips moving. That's if you really care about how you look. Not that many girls want to be viewed that way. Or adult women. It's why we're so sniffy about plastic surgery.'

'Well, no. Or?'

'Or you think, "No. I don't want to be the ninny cheerleader; I want to still be seen as an interesting and desirable person if I wear a sack and get fat and don't bleach my moustache." Which sounds admirable, but which is complete bullshit too. It's its own kind of appalling, off-the-scale vanity, for a start: "I'm so special that I need no embellishment; I am not like other women." Plus, ironically, it's unsisterly, because the moustache-women *despise* the ninny-women in ways the ninny-women couldn't even begin to imagine. Do you see?'

'Huh,' says Bel. 'I'd never thought of it that way. But don't the ninny-women hate the moustache-women? I don't think I know any moustache-women.'

'No. If they think about them at all, they think how they'd like to give them a makeover. They don't view them with contempt. But they're both extremes. Those women – well, all women, really – have been sold a pup. There's no acceptable middle way, in the current set-up. You're either a vain, shallow ninny or some sort of fembot in dungarees. And the truth is, most women aren't either.'

'Well, you're a woman,' Bel says. 'What do you do? To yourself, I mean? What do you tell your daughter?'

'Funny you should ask,' I say. 'The first time we met, I'd recently had Botox and fillers.'

'Oh, that. Botox and fillers,' Bel laughs. 'Who doesn't have Botox and fillers?'

'Quite a lot of people,' I say. 'I've started to feel bad about it. Well, good-bad. Bad-good.' I sigh. 'I don't know. It's complicated.'

'I've had 'em,' Bel (Belvyn? Belanie?) says. 'Right here.' He taps his face. 'My wife suggested it years ago, round about the time it was first available.'

'Good grief,' I say, almost yelping. 'Let me see.'

'Sure,' says Bel easily, leaning his face closer to mine and obeying my orders – 'Frown', 'Smile', 'Do angry face', 'Now happy face' – good-naturedly.

'Undetectable,' I say, impressed despite myself.

'Hell, I'm nearly sixty.' Bel shrugs. 'I need all the help I can get.'

'Do you admit to it? When you're hanging around doing oil things with a bunch of macho blokes?'

'I don't sidle up to folk and give them the details of the doctor, no,' Bel laughs. 'But if anyone asked – sure.'

'Have you ever been tempted to do anything else? Oh – and hey, your teeth. Are they actually your teeth?'

'Yes, ma'am,' he says. 'All mine. All-American teeth. And no. Nothing else. I'm not . . .'

'A woman,' I sigh. 'You're not a woman.'

'Your fish is going cold,' Bel says.

'OK, so – cards on the table. Do you think a face full of work is attractive? Because I know some men do. I have a male friend who actively prefers plastic tits, for example.'

'Homosexual, right?'

'Not as far as I know, no,' I say. 'Quite robustly heterosexual, I'd say.'

'Hm,' says Bel. 'That's kind of unusual. In my experience. I mean, they don't move properly. They feel hard.'

'Have you met many plastic tits?'

'More than my fair share, ma'am,' Bel says. 'My recollection is that they aren't especially, uh, responsive. And also, you know . . .'

'This is a weird conversation,' I say. 'Sorry.'

'It's interesting,' Bel says. 'I was going to say, you want a breast to behave like a breast. To, er, *feel* like a breast.'

'You want wobble,' I say. 'I think I'd want wobble too, if I were a man. Otherwise it'd just feel like massive pecs, I imagine. Which have their place. But not necessarily on a woman who isn't a professional bodybuilder.'

'I think so,' Bel says easily. See, that's another nice thing about him: he doesn't say anything saucy after discussing wobble, or segue into some sort of clumsy attempt at sexy-talk. He just takes a mouthful of steak and gestures again to my bream. 'Eat,' he says for the second time. Maybe Bel is a feeder, I think to myself, intent on making women immobilized with obesity, which while not being as bad as being a murderer would not be ideal. I saw a documentary about them – feeders, not murderers – once: one of those times when you realize you're not as broad-minded as you think (see also adult babies).

I wonder what Bel (Belladonna?) wants. Maybe: nothing. Maybe: just company during this extended European sojourn, light, undemanding, borderline vacuous conversation, someone outside his world to amuse and entertain him, like a geisha without the other thing. On the other hand, we must be realistic: Bel is a man in possession of a penis. And unless his penis is broken or absent – if not a murderer or a feeder, perhaps a eunuch? – then the whole question of snogging/ shagging is going to raise its head imminently, like – in fact – a penis. And then what will happen?

It's not like I think Bel (Belmondo?) wants to marry me. But he's so easy to be with – so civil and civilized, so elegant and sane – that I wish I would hurry up and find him sexually attractive. He is a grown-up, and that is good. Good, grown-up Bel. We've moved on from breasts to basketball, about which I know next to nothing, but I'm happy to be enlightened. Well, up to a point. The problem, clearly, lies with me. Here I am, with a technically attractive and attentive adult male, and all I can think is Slight Yawn. Slight Yawn is the bane of my life – as in 'Oh yes, very nice, Slight Yawn'. I think it more often than I'd like, about anything from human beings to people's new kittens to TV programmes to certain forms of political protests to organic vegetables. It's a by-product of age, like Interesting But Very Long and Bored Now, Bye.

The reason I am thinking Slight Yawn about Bel is that I evidently do not value maturity enough. I totally value it in cheese, obviously. In cheese, it's a must, which is why I am about to order it for pudding ('Lord,' says Bel, when my Stilton arrives. 'I can't believe you Brits eat that stuff').

It occurs to me that I could do a lot worse than to start thinking of myself as a cheese, and of ageing as *ripening*. This cheers me immensely. Of course! Cheese is the solution, here as elsewhere in life. Do I want to be a Brie, all seductive and oozing, the cracks on top denoting especial deliciousness, or a Kraft slice, plastic and flavourless? Do I want to be, to extend the metaphor, a piece of spongy, mass-produced white bread, or some delicious hand-made sourdough number? Do I want to be a can of Heinz soup, or the home-made roasted tomato version, with herbs? Oh. Confusion. I want to be the Heinz, because Cream of Tomato is the food of the gods, and sometimes cheap and unmysterious and downright delicious is best.

Why is nothing simple?

I should really try and be more encouraging to Bel. I should not get a taxi home. I should accept his offer of a nightcap, and see where that takes us. Nude Bel. Nood Bel. Bel in the mood. All nood. I start smiling to myself as I imagine the noodness, and inevitably the smile is misinterpreted. Bel (clothed) pats my hand and smiles warmly back at me. Here's my chance: I could wiggle my fingers suggestively, or wrap them around his (I could also grab his balls, obviously), which would encourage Bel, which – as we have seen – would probably have perfectly manageable consequences, possibly even downright pleasant ones. *Good* Bel (Bellatrix?), all nood and matoore, with his pats. (My mother, Kate, one summer long ago, face convulsed with repulsion: 'Clara! Look out! There's a, a . . . a *dog-pat*.' My sisters and I still call things pats: birds-pats – 'Sorry I'm late, a bird patted on my coat'; cat-pats; the horror of cleaning the children's aquariums – 'Urgh, fish-pats'; even, on one traumatic occasion, 'And afterwards he LAID A PAT in my loo.')

But I can't do it, with Bel. I just can't. 'I was thinking about cheese,' I say, slowly withdrawing my hand. If you want a romance-killer, cheese – O useful cheese! O best of foods! – is your friend, especially with Americans, who fear it because

126

many of them believe that proper, non-plastic cheese – cheese
with veins, cheese with mould, full-on cheese – is dirty. The
Man From The Connaught loved cheese, as it happens.
(I wouldn't want you to get the wrong idea. I'd be perfectly
happy with the Man From The Premier Inn, and to be having dinner at the Travelodge. It's just, happily, that for some
reason we've gone all five-star here. It's hardly indicative of
any other aspect of my life.)

(Maybe not the Travelodge. You'd want a sense that the
person had made a tiny effort.)

In the cab home – no nightcap, a kiss on the cheek due to
ingenious, last-minute angling of my face, for Bel, post-hand
clasp, is ramping up – I chastise myself for having invented
this faintly ridiculous Bel, who is cheese-fearing and to me
by extension sexually unadventurous. Plus I've somehow – it
might have been the wine – conflated him with pats in my
head, an unattractive link that I can neither explain nor shake
off. I have broken Bel in my mind, and I'm annoyed about it
because now I can't unbreak him. First of all, this is unkind.
Second of all, Bel is not remotely ridiculous. Bel is what
my grandmother would have called A Catch – mind you,
she was from the generation that called their dogs Nigger, so
let's not get too misty-eyed about ancient wisdoms. But,
having had Nood Bel (Belly pork?) pop into my head –
disporting himself erotically among Claridge's' fine period
furnishings, all bare, all frisky, not in urgent need of a pat –
I can no longer seriously contemplate any Bel-action. Nood
Bel's rood is out of bounds to me. It's actual mental retardation on my part, all of this, or emotional retardation at the

very least. And it's incredibly unfair to heap ridicule on a person when you yourself are a person that is currently practically obsessed with ridicule-through-mutton.

Like I said, it's because I'm immature. At least, I think I am. I'm either chronically immature or incredibly wise, and I can't tell which it is, even though at this late stage you'd think I might have worked it out. For example – well, not for example: this is the crux of the whole thing. So, in full: I think that the more time marches on, the more important it is to seize the day and have a laugh, and not be cross or sad or mean. I believe, quasi-religiously, in a dirty, tears-of-laughter laugh, as often as possible and ideally all the time. A perma-laugh. I don't mean a laugh in the Gaby 'take ketamine and shag children' sense, because that seems like extraordinarily hard work and, I'm starting to realize, not that funny, what with the knives and needles and hair-tails and the frantic pedalling underwater. We all pedal quite hard enough, I feel, without suddenly having to acquire some sort of submerged outboard motor.

But, a laugh. Less stress. More joy. More shagging, more wine, more jokes. More fun. You know? It's so incredibly exhausting having small children, and we all wander about knackered and half broken, and then one day they're big, or biggish, and all of that stuff suddenly starts looking after itself. Well, more or less. And so you're free (well, more or less). No wonder it's called your prime. And it seems to me that this is the point at which you want the laughs, the naughtiness, the excitement and the risk and the second teenagehood – except a million times better because the crap bits have been removed. You're a beacon of confidence compared to your teenage self. You have more (which is to say, some) money. You're better dressed, better educated, cleverer, funnier, more assured. It's better than being a young woman too: you're not getting up three times a night or panicking about the PTA or staying at home for a bit with the babies, wondering a) what happened to your career and b) whether you could get away with doing the school drop-off in your nightie with a mac on top. Either you're still deliriously in love with your husband, or you've addressed the fact that, one day, you're suddenly not. But you've done the things – got married, had children – and you're out the other side. Surely it is time to let your hair down and – well, if not quite party, have a little band following you about in your head, honk honk, toot toot, time for a high kick or two, a little joyful conga?

Isn't that right? I'm fully aware of the alternative. I admire it. You stick to your guns and crack on. You lie in the bed you've made, because you're no spring chicken and better the devil you know. You push aside ridiculous notions about not being dead yet and seizing the day, even as the day dims. You are a good person, a decent person, and you get on with it, because wanting all laughs all the time is selfish and self-indulgent, and here you are, and everything's fine, and you watch like a hawk for signs of perimenopause ('Is this department store insanely overheated, or is it my woolly coat, or is it – daaa daaa daaah – the withering of my womanhood?'). You sigh lovingly at your husband, fondly exasperated, as though he were a comically wind-troubled Labrador; you go to parties and tell funny stories about his ineptitudes as he stands right there next to you. You flirt with your boss, and with anyone flirtable with, safe in the knowledge that Nothing Would Ever Happen, even though you sometimes imagine it's not your husband lying next to you. You're probably very content: I'm not knocking it. But I've never been good at any of that stuff. I'm selfish and I get bored. I get claustrophobic. It sounds melodramatic, but once or twice – in serious relationships, in the past – I sometimes felt like I was suffocating and like there wasn't a paper bag big enough to help me regulate my breathing. And I never want to talk about my partner as though he's a farty Labrador. I can't think of anything I'd want less.

I want to stumble down the street, holding hands and laughing – and then come home and make a pie: I'm not wishing myself into some rock 'n' roll scenario where I have panda eyes and the children go hungry and the house is dirty. I'm neither an aristocrat nor grimly poor – and therefore otherwise preoccupied: I am bourgeois, which means that I like making supper and that dirty houses disgust me.

And at forty-six, I don't see why I shouldn't have both: the stumbling and the chicken and mushroom, the cosy sofa and the non-pretendy shagging. I want the real thing. The Man From The Connaught sent me a text, after he'd left for Australia and we'd not been in touch for months. It was two a.m. his time, and maybe he was drunk, but it said, 'It's you I wank to, Clara.' I quite see that some people wouldn't find this romantic, but I did. It was so dirty and so desolate, and so out of the blue. I was also intrigued by his use of 'to': I'd have said 'about' or 'over'. It took a superhuman effort not to reply, obviously.

I must not think about the Man From The. I'd like the second teenagehood without the moping. Where was I? Ah yes. There comes a point where time starts feeling like looking through the wrong end of a telescope, and suddenly things that seemed far away are dramatically closer, and really – if I'm not going to be blissfully happy romantically speaking, I'd rather be happy domestically and pootle on, hope springing eternal. Basically I just want the lolz, even if wanting the lolz is a form of midlife crisis in itself, which I suspect it might be.

I let myself in. There's a note from Gaby on the kitchen table – 'Gone to Ben's, there's a party, come any time, text me. Or back tomorrow.' I smile and push it aside and make myself a cup of tea to take to my bath, and when I get into the bath I actually groan with pleasure, like a nan. I want everything, is my problem.

12

'What are you doing about your teeth?' Gaby asks a few days later. I am transcribing an interview at the kitchen table.

'Nothing,' I say, turning off the tape recorder. 'Why? My teeth are perfectly OK.'

'Weren't you going to go and see about veneers?'

'I did, yes. Mr Kimball. I think he thought he was being persuasive. He explained that they'd have to rough up my teeth so the veneers could stick to them. Also file them down into little stubby vampire teeth. He added that veneers do fall off, but not to worry because he was always on call. So, er, no. On balance.'

'Hm,' says Gaby. 'You don't see that bit. You only see these.' She smiles widely.

'I can't hack it,' I say. 'Aside from the fact I'd have to take out a bank loan, and that the mere idea of it makes me want to cross my legs, it just seems like a really mental thing to do. Given that there's nothing wrong with my teeth in the first place.'

'A bit of crookedness,' says Gaby pleasantly.

'Normal crookedness,' I reply. 'Which I gather is fashionable. But I did get bleaching trays made, to avoid red-wine teeth.'

'That's something, I guess,' says Gaby.

'And anyway – do the Men of Rocks have immaculate teeth?'

'Men of Granite,' says Gaby. 'Their teeth aren't really discussed in the Chronicles.'

'Another thing to put in your letter to Bernard,' I say. 'Have you written it yet?'

'I'm halfway through,' Gaby says, and actually blushes.

'Well, there you go. Make the case for twenty-first-century dentistry while you're at it.'

'Don't be silly,' snaps Gaby with an irritated tut. 'It's set in Lapidosa. It's a daily struggle to stay alive. People have other things to think about than teeth.'

'I don't think people care that much about teeth in real life either,' I say. 'I mean, provided they're clean and flossed and not crazily crooked. And not, like, walrus tusks, or just empty bare gums.'

'Stay with the project!' Gaby says. 'I can feel you drifting. Concentrate, Clara. You're looking great, but there's so much further to go. Nobody said it was easy.'

'I can't,' I say. 'I can't do it. I'm OK with how I look, broadly speaking. And I'm happy – delighted – with the, er, improvements, eyebrows aside, and that's that.'

'But you could look so much better,' says Gaby, who really doesn't know when to stop talking.

'Yes. But I look fine. I'm grateful for all your advice and input and everything, but enough. And anyway – no offence or anything, Gaby, but it's not so much the stuff itself but the secondary stuff. The stuff that comes with it. The upkeep. The maintenance.'

'Well, yeah.' Gaby shrugs. 'You're making a thirty-, forty-year commitment. Who did you interview?' she asks, pointing at my tape recorder and notes.

'Emerald Cunningham,' I say. 'You know, the model.'

'Emerald Cunningham!' Gaby cries. 'I used to have pictures of her plastered all over my walls. Wow. How old is she now?'

'Late sixties,' I say. 'As in her heyday.'

'Oh wow,' Gaby repeats. 'What does she, you know, what does she look like?'

'She looks great,' I say. 'She runs a bed and breakfast in Wales, with her husband, on an organic farm. She's got all these rescued battery hens and some quite manky-looking sheep. She's terrific. Made a cake.'

'I saw some pictures a few years ago,' says Gaby. 'Paparazzi shots. She didn't look *that* great.'

'She's got good bones and that long, lanky body, and she's nearly seventy,' I say. 'She doesn't wear make-up and she was in jeans and a jumper. I thought she looked lovely.'

'Completely grey, I suppose.'

'Yes,' I say, sighing.

'What?' says Gaby. 'You dye your hair. Everybody dyes their hair.'

'I know,' I say. 'I'm kind of hoping that I might be allowed – allow myself – to stop at some point. Or not. Whatever. It's not a competition. Are you planning on keeping your extensions well into your dotage?'

'As long as I can,' says Gaby, who is being good-humoured despite my souring tone. 'Shorter ones, obviously.'

I picture Gaby with thinning old-lady hair, the extensions bonded stubbornly to the wispy roots.

'Hm,' I say. 'That's kind of what I mean, about maintenance. It makes me exhausted just to think of it.'

I am becoming irritated because Gaby is actually half

right. Emerald Cunningham did look lovely, in her rural idyll with her animals and her pat-stained wellies. But she is very much a recluse, and I can't help thinking – well, assuming: I tried to discuss it with her but she shied away from answering properly – that this is partly to do with the effect that time has had on her once-legendary looks. We think it's hard for us, all of this stuff, but it's harder still for the great beauties, the once-in-a-generation drop-dead stunners. Are there only the two options available? Do an Emerald, let your hair go grey and turn into straw, avoid mirrors and proclaim yourself delighted with your new, beauty-tyranny-free existence. Or go Gaby-max: have everything done, all the time. Have a Caesarean of the face, and full-body surgery. Wear film-star make-up at all times; own wigs. Be the seventy-year-old hottie who men sort of want to jump until they realize she's older than their mums. (Obviously, there are exceptions. But not many. For lots of people, being, as Kate calls it, 'genetically blessed' comes with a use-by date. Not many cheekbones can hold up a face forever.)

The terrible thing is that, while I was interviewing Emerald, I thought – and I wouldn't have thought this a year ago, when I still believed that 'ageing with dignity' was the answer to your face collapsing – I thought: 'If she'd had stuff done really well twenty years ago, she would still be drop-dead gorgeous.' She had really deep marionette lines that looked like fissures, like the wood carvings on a totem pole, and I almost said something, more than once. I almost gave her Dr Halliday's number. Surely there's a path that's somewhere between lunatic levels of intervention and just giving up? She didn't look like she used moisturizer, or conditioner, or any of the things that clutter up most women's bath-rooms. Her skin was wind-lashed, her lips chapped.

I'm annoyed with myself for thinking this was a shame.

Poor Gaby is knocking back the white wine tonight, because Ben's come round and bonded with Charlie, who's on holi-day from university and with whom he apparently shares musical tastes. I literally understand maybe one word in five of what they're saying; Gaby even less so, judging by the fully perplexed expression on her face.

'I need some sort of primer,' she says. 'A little vocab list, to keep in my pocket and consult as needed.' She is looking especially spectacular tonight, in a short sequined shift and a teeny leather jacket, bare-legged despite the fact that it's freezing outside.

'Talk to me instead,' I say. 'For all I know they could be speaking Aramaic.'

'I should participate, though,' says Gaby anxiously. 'They keep saying "boom".'

'Boom's easy,' I say. 'Boom is like, wham, done. Boom's old. Trusay, cuz.'

'I know sick,' says Gaby. 'I know loads of words, but none of these.'

'Nobody says sick any more,' I say unhelpfully. 'But I don't know what they say instead. Well, I know nang and peng and cat,' I add helpfully. 'But I don't really know what they mean either.'

'God, it's baffling,' says Gaby. 'Just baffling. Like the dancing. I think I've got a handle on the dancing, but still. It's not doing the YMCA, put it that way. And I do occasion-ally wonder about putting my back out, you know?' She sighs. 'Not that I think that would happen. Thank God for yoga.'

We sit and chat and drink our wine. Eventually Charlie peels himself away – he's going to a gig, appropriately enough, and asks Ben and Gaby if they'd like to come along. Ben looks desperate to go, but 'We have dinner plans,' says Gaby firmly, and so Ben waves Charlie off dolefully and has a glass of wine with us instead. I wonder how aware Ben is that we're old enough to be his mother and auntie. Is there a little voice in his head saying, 'Hm, for some reason this feels slightly weird'?

'Nice kid, Charlie,' says Ben. 'Well, they're all nice. They're great. I like hanging out with them. And with Sky. Who's gorgeous,' he adds with a carefree laugh.

'Isn't she?' says Gaby tightly. 'Lovely young woman.'

'Poor Sky, she's in bed with food poisoning,' I say. 'Otherwise I could ask her down so you could feast your eyes.' I don't know why I say this: it isn't helpful.

'Hahaha. That won't be necessary,' Ben says. 'And she's nowhere as lovely as you, babe,' squeezing Gaby's waist. There is a perfect beat, like in a sitcom, and then he says, 'Ever thought about kids?'

Pin-drop doesn't even begin to cover it, but Gaby's powers are infinite. After only a tinily too-long pause, she says, 'I can't. I'm . . . you know, women problems.'

'What, never?' says Ben, which seems ungallant.

'Ah . . . Um . . . Not necessarily *never*,' Gaby says. 'But it's not looking, er, enormously likely.'

'Ah well,' says Ben. 'It's not like I'm desperate to breed or anything,' he laughs. 'But at some point . . . Still, early days, eh? I don't know why I'm even bringing it up.'

'Me neither,' Gaby laughs, incredibly convincingly, as if this were the funniest conversation in the world. 'Moving on: shall we go? Our table's going to be ready in ten minutes.'

'I asked the guys if they wanted to join us,' Ben says. 'So they might turn up.'

'Ah. Right,' says Gaby. 'Sure. The guys. Well, that'd be fun. But I've only booked for two, so I should probably let the restaurant know. It gets quite busy . . .'

'Nah, it'll be fine,' Ben says airily. 'They might not turn up. They might get a better offer, haha.'

'Right,' says Gaby again. 'Haha.' I can tell she is broiling with rage about her romantic dinner à deux in the fashionable restaurant that she had to book a fortnight ago because it gets so rammed, but only because I've known her for so long. Honestly, this is world-class acting. She could win Oscars. Something about Los Angeles must have rubbed off on her. The fleeting thought occurs to me that Gaby is very rarely herself in company.

'Are you coming, Clara?' says Ben.

'No,' says Gaby, shooting me a ferocious look, 'she is not.'

'Thanks, Ben, but I've got plans, actually,' I say. 'I've got an old friend coming round for a drink. Her daughter was at primary school with Jack.'

The doorbell goes just as I finish my sentence. I haven't seen Annie for years. She's come round for a drink because she wants to ask me about something she's written, with a view to getting it published. Now, Annie: you know where you stand with Annie. Annie is mutton, pure and simple. Tonight she's wearing a glittery sausage dress with a deep V-neck, all the better to show off the sun damage on her chest (leathery); pointy stilettos of the kind Gaby and I used to buy from Kensington Market in 1980 (scuffed); mucho cleavage (squishy); wild hair, half grey, and the contents of a medium-sized make-up stall, including too-dark lipliner and three shades of eyeshadow, worn in stripes. Annie is not wraith-like; she has one of those bodies that never quite stopped looking pregnant. Funny thing is, she kind of looks great. Like a working girl that's knocking on a bit, obviously, but still great. And sexy. Oddly sexy. I make a mental note: if you really, really *embrace* the mutton, if you grab its woolly little back and hug it tight, as Annie so wholeheartedly has, it can be a look of sorts. Not for everyone, granted. But a look.

'Sorry about my get-up,' Annie laughs, pointing at herself, 'but I'm meeting Tilly later. It's Friday. Girls' night out.' Tilly is her daughter, who was in Jack's class and is therefore seventeen. Annie is older than me and, from memory, must be somewhere in her early to mid-fifties. Also, Annie's always looked like this, night out or school run, egg race or pub quiz, so I don't know what she's apologizing for. 'Am I bright red?' she asks. 'Bloody hot flushes. Never-ending. And night sweats. D'you get night sweats, Clara?'

Gaby looks aghast at this last remark, and turns to get her scarf, which is silver and adorned with tiny pink owls.

'Not yet, thank God. You look great,' I say, kissing her hello. 'Annie, this is my friend Gaby, and this is Ben. They are just going out to dinner.'

'Hello,' says Gaby frostily.

'Hi,' says Ben, holding out his hand. 'Nice to meet you.' He seems mesmerized by Annie and is grinning at her encouragingly.

'Ooh, hello, young man,' says Annie with a giggle. Mr Annie, I dimly remember, is a not massively jolly-seeming Something In The City. 'And . . . young lady. Off anywhere nice?'

'Just round the corner,' says Gaby. 'We should go, Ben.'

'Youth, eh?' Annie says cheerfully. 'Well, have a good time. Have one for me! Have two!'

'That would be a pleasure,' says Ben. 'Maybe you and Clara would like . . .'

'They wouldn't,' says Gaby. 'Come on, Ben. We really have to go.'

'How's Tilly?' I ask once Ben and Gaby have finally left. 'Haven't seen her for years.'

'First year of A-levels,' says Tilly proudly. 'Legs up to here. You should see her. Gorgeous. We're best friends.'

'Are you going out to eat?' I ask politely.

'No. I thought I might have a bite with you,' Annie says. 'If that's OK. Just a bit of cheese or something. Line my stomach. We're going to a bar we like with some of her mates. I'm meeting them all at half nine.'

'Ah, right,' I say.

'You had a little girl, didn't you? After St Michael's?' Tilly asks, already rootling round the fridge. 'She'll become your best friend too,' she says. 'Keep you young. Just you wait.' She emerges from the fridge with a block of Cheddar and a bowl of olives. 'These'll do. Do you mind? I'm starving.'

I don't ever want my daughter to be my best friend. I want my daughter to be my daughter. And I really, *really* don't want to be hanging out with my daughter and her mates when she's at university.

But 'Not at all!' I say. 'Help yourself.' It occurs to me that, children aside, nobody ever rootles inside the fridge saying they're starving any more. Certainly not Gaby, and increasingly not me. It's incredibly refreshing: I feel like Annie has given me a mini-present merely by being here and being hungry.

'Or,' I say impulsively, 'I could cook us something.'

'Got any pasta?' says Annie. 'I saw you had bacon. I fancy carbonara. Mind you, when *don't* I fancy carbonara?'

I could hug Annie and her normal impulses, her fearless embrace of the carbs, her *appetite*. 'Yes!' I say. 'I've got the other ingredients, I think. Coming up!'

'Yum,' says Annie happily, pouring herself a second glass of wine. 'Now look, before we go on and get distracted. Thing is, I've written some porn.'

'Ah. OK.' I like the way she's saying this, much as someone might say, 'I've written some poetry.'

'And I wanted to know – you know about this sort of thing – should I publish it myself, or get a publisher, and if it's "get a publisher", then how?'

'What kind of porn?'

'Oh,' says Annie, laughing and winking at me. 'You know. The usual. *Positions*. Name calling while pulling the old hair. *You dirty slag,*' she growls, in a convincing and unsettling man-voice that takes me aback. 'Bit of bumming. Three-ways. Tits. I love tits, don't you? Nice pair of knockers never hurt anyone. Couple of bigger group scenes. Umm, what else? Can't remember. Pretty vanilla really, though there's some dogging in it. Old school!'

She laughs again. I really like Annie, despite – or maybe because of – the unexpected and faintly startling turn the conversation has taken. She's like a proper person. As soon as I have the thought, I think, 'Why don't I think that about my oldest friend?'

'Ah,' I repeat. 'Right. Do you, I mean have you . . .' I start laughing too. 'Autobiographical, is it?'

'Hahaha,' laughs Annie. 'Wouldn't you like to know?'

'I really would, actually,' I say, slicing up some bacon. 'I'm dying to.'

'Only some of it is. Let's just say Mervyn and I keep ourselves busy,' says Annie, winking again. 'Very tame, aren't they, the young people? Did you read that book?'

'Yes. And yes,' I say. 'I felt like a perv for thinking it was . . . adolescent. But then I, er, I like real porn.' The Man From The Connaught flashes into my head again: lost afternoons. But I'm getting better at pushing him away.

'High fucking five!' says Annie unexpectedly, slapping my hand and spilling some wine. 'Oops, sorry, Clara. Here, give us the kitchen roll. It's just, nobody ever says that. I like real porn too. My porn's proper. It's *dirty*.'

'Good for you, writing it,' I say, meaning it. 'Let me think about the best thing to do. I could certainly give you some names.'

'Thanks,' Annie says. 'I knew you'd know.' She takes a sip of wine. 'Your friend,' she says. 'Gaby, is it?'

'Yep. She's staying with us for a bit, in Charlie's old quarters – poor Charlie's on the sofa, now he's back. She's from LA. Well, she's from here, but a long time ago. We were at school together.'

'What's her age, if you don't mind me asking? Here, chuck me the Parmesan, I'll grate it.'

'That's a funny question,' I say, handing her the cheese

and thinking how nice this companionable approach to cooking is. 'Why do you ask?'

'She's gorgeous,' Annie says. 'Absolutely *gorgeous*. That's some work she's had. Five-star. Don't get me wrong. But she's somewhere between you and me, right? Age-wise.'

'Er,' I say, feeling intensely disloyal. 'Something like that, I think. Maybe. Yes.'

'Hm,' says Annie.

'How on earth could you tell?' I ask. I'm genuinely amazed: if I met Gaby for the first time, I'd say late thirties. I can't believe that Annie – Annie, of all people – has some particular insight, some radar that I, beady-eyed I, don't possess.

'Oh, I can always tell,' says Annie. 'Usually by their reaction to me.'

'How on earth do you mean?' I ask.

'They don't like me. I'm how they might have ended up if they ever thought it was possible to have fun past forty and keep eating their dinners. If they were happy in themselves, you know. I'm not saying it in a big-headed way – I'm just happy, always have been. They're half sorry for me: size 18 on a good day, tits in a push-up bra, control pants up to here, tarty dress, too much slap, do my own roots, when I can be arsed. But it half freaks them out. I don't mind,' she says kindly. 'I get it. They think that at our age there's only one way of being contented and of getting blokes to look at you, and that it involves a ton of cash and a ton of pain. I'm like some horrible reminder that it ain't necessarily so. So they don't like meeting me. I unsettle them.' She shrugs. 'I wouldn't be happy to meet me either, if I had scars behind my ears and only ever ate bleeding egg-white omelettes. Here, more wine?'

'Thanks,' I say, holding out my glass.

'I'll have to go, after this,' Annie says as I dish out enormous – and why not? – portions of pasta. 'I'm not against it, you know. Surgery, I mean. It's stupid to be against it. I had my tits done when I was thirty-five.' She holds her bosoms to illustrate her point. 'They looked amazing for a bit, but then I was trying for Tilly and I had the implants removed, which was just as well, it turned out, what with all those leaky ones.'

'Gaby doesn't have implants,' I say.

'I think you may be mistaken there,' Annie says, laughing. 'But good on her. That whole "ooh, it's unnatural" thing – that's just stupid, isn't it? General anaesthetic is bloody unnatural. Dentistry. Any surgery. Die in childbirth, eh, because otherwise it would be *unnatural*.' She snorts. 'What a load of old bollocks. I don't have a problem with it. Just with some of the people who have it done. Lot of them are mentals,' she says matter-of-factly. 'Hacking away at bits of their bodies like that. You know. It's not nothing, is it?' She puts on a whiny, wheedling voice and says, '"Don't like it, chop it off." Urgh.'

Annie's barely drawn breath and now, having wolfed down her pasta and another half-glass of wine, she's off, like a whirlwind, if a whirlwind had cheap-looking shoes that clacked. I feel weirdly uplifted as I kiss her goodbye. It's not that I'd like to *be* her, but after two months of Gaby, her approach to life seems refreshingly, giddyingly straightforward. It's joyous, is what it is. Gaby's – for all the money and the glorious looks and the hot boyfriend – seems, by comparison, curiously joy-lite.

Gaby, of course, disagrees. When she reappears the

144

following afternoon – looking half dead, as she always does after nights out with Ben – the second thing she says, after 'Hello', is, 'Who was that *ghastly* woman last night? I didn't know where to look.'

'I know her from the boys' primary school, years ago,' I say. 'I like her. She stayed and had some supper.'

'What, from a trough?'

'Gaby! She's nice. She's funny and straightforward. She's just herself. I like her,' I repeat. 'Also, she's written some porn.'

'Ha!' snorts Gaby. 'Yeah, right. Because she'd know all about *that*.'

'Well, why wouldn't she?'

'Ha,' Gaby says again, a withering expression on her face. 'I don't think so.'

'Very sisterly,' I say. 'Why wouldn't she have or like or know about sex? I wouldn't particularly want to look like her, but so what? There are loads of people I wouldn't want particularly to look like. I can still appreciate that they kind of look great, in their own way. Doesn't mean you have to be mean about them.'

'She'd top my list,' says Gaby. 'She doesn't look great – have you gone mad? She looks like a desperate old slapper.'

'She's not a million years older than you,' I say. 'And anyway, why's it making you so cross?'

Gaby shrugs. 'To let yourself go like that,' she says. 'She doesn't have any self-respect.'

'Oh, come on. That's just not true. She's incredibly confident, as it happens. I was just thinking, she'd be a great role model, in a way. And she's the size a lot of women are. And there's a difference between self-respect and self-denial.

She's not self-denying – I'll give you that. But so? It's no skin off your nose, is it? Why does it make her *ghastly*?'

'I just didn't like her,' Gaby says, picking up on my increasingly narked tone and giving me a tired smile.

Because I am not always as kind as I might be, I say, 'Ben seemed to take to her.'

'The fucking twat,' Gaby says instantly. 'Couldn't take his fucking eyes off her. I made a joke on the way to the restaurant. I assumed, like a normal person, that he was staring because she was so ghast . . . so ridiculous, and that he'd take the piss out of her. But no. "Sexy," if you please. "Weirdly hot, MILF." Well, whatever MILF is called when it's menopausal.'

'I knew it,' I say, laughing. 'That's why you're in such a rage. I wouldn't assume it means he wants to shag her. He was just making an observation.'

I pause and drink my tea, weighing up my options. I can't not say what I am itching to say, so I say it.

'Also, I really wonder about what's going on in your head sometimes. Seriously. You'd be happier if your boyfriend "took the piss" out of a woman he'd only just met – a woman who happened to be my guest, in my house – based on what she looked like? Fuck's sake, Gaby.'

Gaby has the good grace to blush. 'Yeah, sorry about that,' she mutters. 'I don't really mean it.' She pauses. 'Well, actually, I sort of do. I don't mean to insult your mates, obviously. But women like that are like a slap in my face.'

'Eh?'

'All this,' she says, pointing down at herself. 'All *this*,' she repeats, now pointing at her face, her teeth, her hair. 'And what – so my boyfriend, who by the way thinks I'm

146

thirty-four, says he fancies some fifty-something slapper who's a size 30?'

'More like 18,' I say. 'Same sort of size you used to be, Gabs.'

'Who's got bingo wings like, like *a fat Batman*, and two chins and more make-up on than a fucking *tranny*?' Gaby continues, voice rising, ignoring me. 'You'd be pissed off too. We have to stop talking now. I'm pissing myself off even more just thinking about it again.' She takes an angry sip of her coffee. 'Urgh. Who'd walk around like that, looking desperate, like she'd be grateful if somebody knocked her to the ground and fucked her?'

'Stop,' I say. 'You really *do* need to stop talking.'

'What?' says Gaby. 'It's true. She'd probably pay them. Ask them if they had any mates.'

'*Stop talking*,' I say. 'You're teenage-levels of jealous. It's pathetic. It's making you sound like a crazy person.'

I want to ask Gaby if she thinks the way she looks has made her more insecure, but it seems like a mad question: the obvious answer is no. How could becoming more beautiful than you ever used to be make you insecure? How could it make you sound so desperate – so absolutely the definition of the thing she accuses Annie of being?

And yet: here's all the evidence I need.

'Go and write your letter to Bernard Frossage,' I say. 'Cheer yourself up.'

'What kind of porn?' asks Gaby.

'Annie? Oh, you know, just stuff. Three-ways, I think she mentioned. Bit of dogging – very Nineties.'

'Married, is she?'

'Yep.'

'What's he like?'

'I can't really remember. City type. Corpulent. Just leave it, eh?'

Gaby heaves an enormous sigh. 'Yeah, I think I will. It's not good for me. I'm probably still wasted from last night,' she adds optimistically. 'Don't mind me. Having a funny turn. It's just I sometimes wonder if I've . . . If I'm on the right track.'

'It's OK,' I say. But actually, I don't think it is, and I have to force a smile as she shuffles upstairs.

13

One more date with Bel: I'm going to try and find him sexy. I'm going to really make an effort before giving up the ghost. Strange, apt expression, that, and of course it isn't Bel that's the ghost.

Jack and Sky have a double free period first thing this morning, so I'm making them a cooked breakfast before heading off to the West End to buy myself a new outfit. I feel like I owe it to Bel to make an effort. One last try, to atone for the unforgivable way I have made him comical in my head. We are not going to 'our' table in Claridge's' grown-up, sepulchral restaurant tonight, but, for the first time, to a trendier, younger place in town. Bel (Belated?) in a more normal context: I always think hotels are like little islands – lovely, luxurious, safe-feeling little islands that bear no relation to the Outside World, and that by extension anything that happens in hotels is somehow not quite real. This will be Bel on land. I'm looking forward to it, in a way. Plus, the restaurant doesn't have an upstairs with a super-king bed and a marble bathroom, which I find less pressurizing.

Sausages, bacon, mushrooms, tomatoes. 'How do you want your eggs?' I ask the children. 'You need to coordinate your answers because despite appearances I'm not a short-order chef.'

'Fried,' says Jack. 'Please.'

'Um . . . could we have them scrambled?' asks Sky. 'Fried eggs are so . . . fried.'

'Are you all right, Sky? You're a bit pale,' I say. She's actually sheet-white, with a thin sheen of sweat overlay. She looks like a doll made of wax.

'I'm fine,' says Sky.

'Hm. You don't look that fine. You need some breakfast,' I say. 'Fry-ups are the solution to most things. Scrambleds coming up. Put the toast on, Jack, would you?'

'Did Gabbro write to Dad yet?' asks Sky. 'I really think she could help him out, big time. I think they should talk.'

'Gabbro, is it?' I laugh, amused.

'Yeah. And she calls me Massicot.' Sky smiles. 'We've been hanging out a bit. Massicot is The Matriarch's friend – her sidekick, really.'

'Right,' I say. 'That's nice. Anyway, she's just upstairs finishing her letter now, I think,' I say. 'It's never taken anyone so long to write anything – she's been at it for days now.'

'She's posted it!' announces Gaby, framed in the kitchen door and waving what appears to be a dissertation at us. She does her weird arm-greeting to Sky, who does it back at her. I ignore this.

'Have you written the book for him?' I ask. 'And what's that you're holding, then?'

'Just jotted down some ideas,' she says. 'I really hope he can make use of them. Oh my God, are you making a fry-up? Can I have some? Is there enough?'

'You can have mine,' says Sky. 'I'm not that hungry.'

'Nonsense,' I say. 'There's masses, enough for everybody. Put some more toast on, Jack.'

'I'm like a slave,' Jack says to himself. 'I'm the Bread Servant.'

'You can be the Kettle Elf as well,' I tell him. 'No, Jack – fill it up properly. Otherwise you're boiling two inches of water, which is no use to man nor beast.'

'Jawohl, mein Führer,' says Jack crossly, as though I'd ordered him to spring-clean the house from top to bottom using his own hair as a mop. Why do teenagers behave like you've violated their human rights when you ask them to help around the house? They really are extraordinary.

'So,' Sky says excitedly. 'What have you said, Gabbro?'

'I'm trying to think of ways in which the ramifications of the siege impact on the Quest. Obviously, there are lots of issues that need to be addressed there,' Gaby says.

'Obviously,' I say.

'Mum loves this chat,' says Jack. 'She's totally into it.'

'And they really need resolving, otherwise – I mean, I totally see what he means: the plot gets stuck,' Gaby continues. 'Dead end. But I think I may have found the answer. Well, I'd imagine Bernard' – she flushes, as if she'd called him something intimate – 'has thought of it too, by now. But I think it was right to tell him, don't you? In case he hasn't?'

'God, yeah, totally,' says Sky.

'And then there's a load of other stuff,' says Gaby. 'I mean – the Plumèd Few, for starters. They are the Amphiboles' warrior elite, and Horno badly needs them on his side. Which means, if you ask me, that a pact with Bold Olivine is inevitable. She leads them, after all.' Here she pauses for dramatic emphasis. 'It must be so,' she adds, in what is clearly meant to be a dramatic fashion.

'Oh my God. A *pact* with Bold Olivine?' Sky asks. 'You're

kidding, right? I mean – *how*? Actually – woah. Tell me in two minutes. Excuse me, just a sec.'

And she rushes out of the room.

'Sky's got a bug,' says Jack. 'One of those puking ones.'

'What? How do you mean?' I ask.

'She's puked *a lot* in the last few days,' Jack says matter-of-factly, just as I put his breakfast down in front of him.

'Well, she's had food poisoning recently, but it doesn't last that long,' I say.

Sky reappears, her cheeks now pink. 'God, that's better,' she says. 'Sorry.'

'I'm going to make you an appointment at the doctor's,' I say. 'Jack's right – you may have some strange bug. That's a long time to be unwell.'

'Anyway, anyway,' Sky says to Gaby. 'How would she ever countenance a pact with Horno, of all men? He was her raper.'

'He is indeed her nemesis,' says Gaby. 'It's kind of hard to get your head around. But there is a way.'

'What is the way, Gabbro?' Sky whispers, agog. The possibility appears to have blown her mind, and she sits down heavily.

'Totally gripping,' I say. 'I'm sorry that Olivine and Horno are on such non-speaks, but you're going to have to excuse me because I have to be in town. Sky, I'm going to text you with a time for the GP appointment, so check your phone. I hope you feel better. Jack, put the stuff in the dishwasher. See you all later.'

The last thing I hear, as I pull the door to, is Sky murmuring, 'Oh my God, Gabbro. That's genius. Genius!'

*

Buying clothes used to be one of my great pleasures. And it still is, of course: who doesn't love buying something that makes you look good and feel better? The problem is that these garments – the magical ones that suddenly make you think, 'Cor, I'd totally do me,' to yourself, and make you feel sorry for all your other clothes – grow increasingly elusive. I mean, they absolutely exist – it's just that tracking them down can take an eternity, at my age. This is partly, as I have said earlier, because department stores offer too much choice. You end up taking whole trolleys' worth of things into the changing room, and who likes changing rooms enough to be bothered to try on twenty different dresses, in the heat and unflattering lighting, especially when sales assistants lie through their teeth and tell you every single one of them looks fantastic? (Plus, underwear. Dingy is bad, sturdy is unattractive to the point of mild humiliation, but sexy is weird, like your thing is hanging around changing rooms in see-through knickers and with your nipples showing.)

It's also because – and I don't think there's a solution to this – the suitable clothes are scattered all over the place. I wish they were just lined up in obedient, broadly age-appropriate pods, but no: sometimes the thing you're after is with the young people's clothes; sometimes it's with the 'occasion dressing' – one great frock nestling among a couple of dozen mother-of-the-bride atrocities (who are these clothes for? Who decided that mothers-of-the-bride had to dress in cocoon-shaped clothes in the more nauseating colours and were only allowed to denote their playfulness through the medium of hats?).

Sometimes the thing you like is cheap, sometimes it's expensive; sometimes it's an 'edgy' brand, sometimes it's with the nan-clothes. And you have no way of knowing where The One – the perfect dress, the pair of sodding jeans – is. (Jeans! That's another thing. You now have to pick from literally hundreds of different brands and cuts. I remember when jeans were by Levi's and cost £30 and everybody looked great in them.)

Increasingly, I approach clothes shopping like I'm Scott of the Antarctic – might make it, might not, might be some time – except without useful huskies to sniff out the good stuff. So I gird my loins as I approach Selfridges, and take myself off for a coffee first, which is probably a mistake: I want to soothe the nerves, not jangle them. (Reactions to coffee: yet another manifestation of one's decrepitude. I remember the days when I necked mug after mug of black coffee without feeling – one mug in – like I'd taken industrial quantities of cocaine and might actually just short-circuit. I remember the days when I stayed up all night writing essays, fuelled by black coffee and 'energy pills' called Pro-Plus, and then climbed into bed and slept like a baby. Today, one coffee makes me feel enervated. Two, and I get the jitters. Three, and I'm so deranged that I could spend the rest of the day raping and pillaging, making loud martial cries.)

To make matters worse, I quite often find that the clothes I like are in fact the ones in the young bits of the shop – well, young-ish: I'm not talking Peter Pan-collared dresses in Hello Kitty prints. This means that they're often shoddily made, plus I'm quite keen on buying clothes that aren't made by children. The young people's clothes actually break – seams unravel, buttons fall off, fabrics bobble, washing machines mangle sizing. If you get them from the rock-bottom-cheap shops, you can sometimes only wear them once, twice tops. And even then, a cheap dress that looks great on a twenty-year-old often looks just cheap on someone her mother's age. Older clothes – clothes for older people – are better made, stouter, more robust, but . . . well, they're clothes for older people, which is very much reflected in their design: the 'pencil skirt' that's as wide as a dining table; the cardigans that fall to the hip and have huge, wing-accommodating sleeves; the trousers that are shaped exactly like elephants' legs; the things that button up too high, a look that can only work if you're thin as a rake and flat as a pancake.

It's not even like you can narrow things down by sizing, because sizing's all over the place: I'm a 12 in one label, a 16 in another, which would make me a 14, except some 14s are huge and some are tiny, so you can't rely on that either. You have to scoop everything up in a variety of sizes, and in the process temporarily empty the racks so that if the next shopper is my size, she'll find nothing there. Vanity sizing, it's called, because people like to believe they're thinner than they are. With American labels, Gaby is a size 0, or sometimes a 2: a completely nonsensical state of affairs given that Gaby is a size 8–10. But we can't say that in case anyone (who? What manner of nutjob?) thinks, 'Ooh, here comes the giant heffalump in her size 10 dress.' It's completely mad. And then of course there's the fact that most women aren't a size 8, which means the 12s and 14s and 16s always sell out first. Do shops replenish their stock in these sizes? They do not. More 8s than you know what to do with, but 'We only got a few 14s and they sold out on the first day.' And you say,

'Maybe order more next time, given that this happens every single time in every single shop in the entire country?' And the reply is always a shrug.

But today I'm in luck: today the God of Clothes is smiling upon me. Practically the first thing I see is a lovely dark green dress in a pencil shape, with a wiggly skirt but a modest neckline, and sleeves: an excellent example of Porn Secretary, a look I favour strongly in the right circumstances. It's demure, but not entirely; correct, except not. Bel (Belch?) isn't necessarily the right circumstances, but there's nothing wrong with him, and lots wrong with me for even thinking that there was, and I'm going to give him my best shot, yes sirree Bob-Bel. I wonder briefly about underwear, but decide against buying yet more expensive lingerie, partly because I have enough at home and partly because the thought of Nood Bel pops into my head and nearly spoils my mood of Zen-like denial.

In the hosiery department, I bump into Alice, an acquaintance of fifteen years' standing, as I am bulk-buying fishnet tights; we have a pleasant catch-up. She points at my stack of tights and says, 'For you?' and when I say, 'Yes, I love fishnets and I'm not super-keen on ordinary tights,' she says wistfully, 'I wish I could wear fishnets.' I stare at her in bafflement for a minute, and then say, 'Er, why can't you?' trying to think of a reason, and wondering if maybe she's very anti-depilation, or has knob-like protuberances on her lower legs, like the Gruffalo.

'Oh,' she laughs, 'I could never get away with them.'

'Get away?' I ask, still none the wiser. 'How do you mean? They're a pair of tights.'

'I just don't think I could wear them,' says Alice.

'Alice!' I say. '*They're a pair of tights*. They're not a, I don't know, a pair of directional leather antlers.'

'Yeah, but,' Alice says. 'All the same.'

'I am buying them for you,' I say. Honestly, I can't believe my ears. 'They're five quid. If you like them, buy more. If you don't, throw them in the bin, or give them away, or keep them in your drawer. They're *tights*, Alice. They're not Satan for the legs.'

'I do so like the look of them,' Alice says uncertainly.

'What *is* this?' I ask. 'You're sounding a bit mad, if you don't mind me saying. Is this an age thing?'

'Yes,' Alice says sombrely. 'It's an age thing.'

'Alice,' I say, galvanized by indignation and coffee. 'Lots of things are age things. For example, I can't really drink much coffee any more. I wouldn't wear hotpants. I don't go out clubbing until three a.m. I'm really weirdly over-interested in my own poos.'

'You too?' says Alice interestedly. 'I'm obsessed.'

'However. We are talking about a pair of tights. Tights are not "an age thing". They are tights. Just tights. If you like them, bloody wear them. God's sake, Alice.'

'I wish it *were* just tights,' Alice says, leaning wearily against a display of Wolford Opaques, above which disembodied, hose-clad mannequin legs wave gaily in the air. 'I don't suppose you have time for a coffee? Or a cup of tea, if that suits you better.'

'Why not?' I say. 'Let me just pay for these. What size are you?'

'Medium,' says Alice. 'You don't have to buy them for me! I can buy them for myself.'

'But you won't. And then you'll always wonder. In the

way that some people wonder about bisexuality. Except about *tights*. Here,' I say, handing her a pair. 'Enjoy. Go wild.'

'Fishnets!' says Alice, with the sort of wonderment most people would reserve for a ride on the back of a woolly mammoth. 'My goodness. It'll be red lipstick next!'

'I'm taking you in hand, Alice, for the next half an hour,' I tell her as we glide up the escalator to the café. 'You seem to have whatever the age version of body dys-morphia is.'

'I just get so *confused*,' Alice says, as we settle down with our tea and buns. 'I know I'm not super-old. I'm forty-three.'

'You're in your prime,' I say. 'But dressed like a granny.'

'But I do find it really muddling, don't you? I mean, what I am and am not supposed to look like. So I err on the side of caution.' She gestures down at herself: black shift dress, baggy cardigan in an unattractive shade of beige, flat shoes, the whole thing richly dolloped with that hard-to-describe, intangible thing: mumsiness. 'It's hardly cutting edge, but at least I'm sure – well, as sure as I can be – that I'm not embar-rassing my children. Or myself. I mean,' she continues, 'Alan – do you remember Alan, my husband?'

'Of course,' I say.

'Alan . . . Alan's started – God, I can't even say it.'

'What?' I say, hoping she doesn't say 'having an affair'. I'm on safe ground with hosiery, but I wouldn't really want to advise anyone on how best to rescue their marriage.

Alice takes a dignified bite of her bun. 'He's started skate-boarding,' she says.

She looks up and catches my eye and holds it for three seconds, at which point we both burst into laughter.

'Sorry,' I say. 'I barely know Alan. I'm not really laughing. Good for him. In, er, in a way.'

'He's forty-six,' she says. 'He wears special skate shorts. You know, those long, baggy shorts. He skates to the shops to get the milk. He's rubbish at it.' She starts laughing again, as do I. Soon we are crying, wheezing with laughter, becoming more hysterical with every detail Alice provides – 'he bought a baseball cap and it cost £47, can you imagine, and he wears it with the brim to the side'; 'he can't really do turns, only go in a straight line, and he can't really stop, so he sort of hops off'; 'he's not good enough to go on the road, so he stays on pavements'.

'And you're worried about tights,' I say when I've recovered my composure, which takes a while. I wipe the mascara smears from under my eyes.

'Tights,' Alice says. 'God, I've laughed so much I've given myself hiccups. Where was I? Oh yes. Tights. Red lipstick, which some part of me still thinks is for women who aren't like me.'

'It's for hussies,' I say.

'I know how absurd I sound, but there's an element of that,' Alice says. 'It's for the sexually confident. Or the more sexually confident than me. Tights, lipstick, very high heels. Black flicky eyeliner. I love black flicky eyeliner, but . . . Make-up generally. I've worn the same make-up for about twenty years. It's Bobbi Brown, mind you. I mean, I'm not *tragic*. But there's tons of other stuff I have difficulty with. I really like handbags, you know, in the way that some women really like shoes. But the handbags I like – love, actually – look stupid with my clothes. Or is it that my clothes look stupid with the handbags? Anyway, they're out of bounds to me, for whatever reason.'

'It's that your clothes look stupid with the handbags,' I say helpfully. 'Sorry.'

'Don't apologize,' Alice says. 'It's helpful to hear, in a depressing way. I thought it was probably that way around. But I have no idea where to start.'

'Because you're scared of mutton,' I state.

'Yes,' says Alice. 'Exactly that. I'm scared of mutton in the way that I was scared of the big bad wolf as a child. I used to imagine his shadow, for some reason, so that he was all distorted and looming, standing on his back legs with his forelegs up, and his claws. I used to have to get away from him, because he was following me.' She pauses. 'A mutton wouldn't make such a scary shadow, I'm thinking. Squatter and woollier. But still.'

'I'm scared of mutton too,' I tell her. 'We all are. I'm beginning to think the best thing might be to ignore the fear.'

'It's terribly inhibiting, isn't it?' says Alice. 'It's made me feel sort of trapped inside my own dullness.'

'Alan's not feeling trapped,' I point out. 'Alan is embracing the ram.'

'I know,' says Alice, smiling fondly. 'He looks so *absolutely* ridiculous. But only when he's skating. The rest of the time – in his everyday life, at work and at home and so on – he looks fine. He looks nice. Age-appropriate. He looks like a middle-aged man in good nick. I mean, he wears suits: nobody looks bad in a suit. Men are so lucky. There's really only a problem when he's alone on pavements. Which I can live with. Whereas my problem is permanent. I permanently have the feeling that something's not quite right, and that I'm impotent because I don't know what to do about it. What do you do about it? Not you, Clara – I mean, one. What is one supposed to do?'

'Do you remember when everyone had their "colours" done, years ago?' I ask. 'That was all part of the same thing. There's a whole industry that taps into that malaise. Middle-aged women not knowing what to wear or what to look like.'

'We were watching *The Graduate* the other night,' Alice says. 'Did you ever see it? With Dustin Hoffman as the young man who's seduced by his girlfriend's mother.'

'Haven't seen it for years,' I say, 'but yes, of course. Anne Bancroft, all old and sexy.'

'Do you know how old Anne Bancroft is in that film?' Alice asks. 'I hadn't seen it for ages either.'

'Mm, mid-fifties?' I hazard. 'She looked amazing.'

'Thirty-six,' says Alice. 'The predatory, shockingly older woman is thirty-six. Dustin Hoffman – the victim – was thirty in real life.'

'Blimey,' I say.

'And I noticed all this other stuff. Everything associated with Mrs Robinson's character is animal. Bestial. Leopard-skin underwear. Zebra stripes. Jungle-like plants. She's got that streak in her hair, remember, like some sort of wild beast? Everything about her is carnivorous and devouring. And, yeah – thirty-six years old.'

'See also "cougar", my least favourite word,' I say. 'Same thing, though: uncontrollable, wild, not to be trusted, flesh-eating, predatory – an animal, not a human being. As opposed to a normal woman who likes shagging and who could be your mum, your sister, you.'

'It's mad, isn't it?' says Alice.

'There's nothing wrong with wanting to be attractive,' I say firmly. 'And – it's subjective, obviously – there's quite a lot wrong with giving up on the whole thing before you've even hit the best years of your prime.'

'I'm going to buy some new clothes,' says Alice. 'Nothing too out there, but no shifts in neutral colours. And I *might* go and have a look at the beauty hall and try not to feel discouraged and overwhelmed.'

'I have to go,' I say. 'But here, take my number. The sales assistant will tell you you look amazing in anything, and it won't be true. Photograph yourself if you're unsure, and text it to me. I will give you a blunt opinion. Easiest way of doing it if you feel confused is to think of a look you like, and try and incorporate it.'

'The look I like best,' says Alice, 'is those girls you used to see a lot, with prom dresses and tattoos all the way up their arms, but really pretty, with great make-up.'

'That would be quite a departure,' I say.

'I know,' Alice says, looking cast-down again. 'It would be startling. I love tattoos.'

'It's never too late,' I say. 'Maybe not the full sleeve, though, to begin with. Good luck. Text me pictures.'

'I will,' says Alice. 'I feel quite inspired, actually. If Alan can wear his special shorts, I don't see why I shouldn't wear a dress I actually like, rather than this weird uniform. Lovely to bump into you, Clara. And now I'm going shopping.'

I have an interview and two appointments in the afternoon – plus a deluge of photographs from Alice's phone to analyse and respond to – and I don't get home until just before six. When I get home there is no sign of Gaby; Maisy is having a sleepover at her friend Grace's and, atypically, Jack and Sky are sitting at the kitchen table, in silence, not eating the entire contents of the fridge. They straighten up as I come into the room, standing to attention like meerkats.

'What are you doing?' I ask, turning on the lights. 'Why are you in the dark? You look like you're at school and I'm the teacher.'

'Muuuuum, fuuuuuck,' says Jack. 'Where have you been?'

'What?' I say. 'Has something happened? Speak to me. You're making me anxious.'

'I'm pregnant,' says Sky.

'She's pregnant,' says Jack.

'What? Fuck,' I say, sitting down. 'Fucking fuck. Oh God. Are you sure?'

'I went to the appointment,' Sky says. 'For my food poisoning. Except it wasn't food poisoning. It was a baby.'

'Jesus,' I say. 'Fuck.'

'Innit,' says Jack.

'Oh fuck,' I say again. 'What do you want to do, Sky? It's probably not a good idea to hang around. How far gone are you?'

'Twelve weeks,' says Sky. 'I'm due my first scan.'

'Right,' I say. 'I'm going to make some tea.'

My brain is whizzing all over the place as I reach for the tea things – not mugs, but a pot: I feel the occasion demands it. Fuck. What are we going to do? Quite aside from the fact that I feel absolutely terrible: I'm in loco parentis for a few weeks and the child in my care gets up the duff. It's not impressive. But then I do the maths and realize she must have been pregnant before she moved in, and feel marginally less guilty. But not much. Pregnant by my son. Who could become a dad. Fuck, is the point. *Fuck.*

'OK,' I say, putting the tea things on the table with a calmness I very much don't feel. 'Well, you know what your options are, presumably.'

'Dr Bellingham explained,' says Sky. 'Not that it's rocket science. We did it in Year 10.'

'Well, obviously I'll help in any way I can. I'll come along with you, whatever you decide, for the, er . . . the thing. Jesus – we need to tell your dad. I really, really need to talk to him. Like, now.'

'He's not going to be pleased,' Sky says, looking like a little girl. 'He's going to be livid.'

'Not necessarily,' says Jack, putting his arm around her protectively. 'You said your mum was your age when they had you.'

'Yeah, but it was different in the olden days,' wails Sky. 'He's going to go mad – or will he just be sad? Or both? I can't stand the thought of it.'

'How did this even happen?' I say, but as nicely as I can. 'Do you not understand how contraception works? Jack?'

'The condom came off a couple of times,' Jack says, blushing scarlet. 'I'm really not comfortable discussing this with my mum.'

'Bit late for that,' I say briskly. 'The condom came off and what – you haven't heard of the morning-after pill?'

'I didn't . . . Oh man, try and fill in the blanks,' Jack says, now puce with embarrassment. 'And because I didn't, not inside, we didn't think . . .'

'I was going to go on the pill,' says Sky, chewing her fingers. 'I was waiting for the start of my next period.'

'And when it didn't come, you thought, "Ah well, never mind"?'

'They're really irregular,' says Sky. 'It's happened loads of times before. I didn't think it was a very big deal.'

'Well,' I say. 'There's no point in discussing that now, I don't suppose. We need a plan.'

'I've got a load of leaflets from Dr Bellingham,' says Sky. 'Mostly I'm worried about my dad.'

'Fucking Hebrides,' I say. 'Is there really no way of getting hold of him?'

'No,' says Sky miserably. 'Only by letter. What's he going to say? What's he going to *do*? He's supposed to have no distractions. Oh God, I so can't face telling him.'

'There's that neighbour on the other side of the island,' I say. 'But I'm going to have to go and see your dad myself. I need to tell him face to face. Not by neighbour, not by letter. In person.'

'I could come with you,' says Sky. 'Should I? Or would it make it worse?' She looks really green.

'We'll think about it,' I say, though even now I'm not convinced that an arduous journey to the outermost edge of the country is the best idea for Sky at this moment. 'We'll sleep on it.'

I go over and give Sky a hug. Poor little thing, half-orphaned and pregnant and seventeen. I need to get to her dad as quickly as is humanly possible: his daughter, my son . . . Oh God. *God*.

'I thought you'd be really angry,' says Jack.

'Well, I'm not doing a dance of joy,' I point out, stroking

his arm. 'You are a pair of complete idiots. But it'll be fine. Don't worry. I'll talk to your dad and we'll work it out.'

'Um, Clara?' says Sky, in a little voice. 'But will we all be able to fit in here? Will that be OK, if we're all here?'

'What? What do you mean, all?'

'All of us,' Sky says. 'Me and Jack and the baby.' She and Jack are clinging to each other like love's young dream. 'I'm going to keep the baby.'

14

'Oh my God. He must have replied on the very same day,' Gaby says, almost swooning, stroking an envelope. The extravagantly curlicued writing looks like it's been done by quill. No need to ask who it's from: next to the stamps is a two-inch-square pen and ink drawing of some sort of crest featuring birds of prey.

'He's good at drawing,' I say. 'I like those eagles.'

'They're not eagles,' says Gaby, rolling her eyes. 'They're Beakstrels. You know, like he sent Massicot. Man, I can't believe he's drawn *me* some Beakstrels!'

'Ah,' I say. 'OK. I'm not even going to ask.'

'Anyway, shush,' says Gaby. 'This is the most important letter I've received in my life.'

'I need to talk to you, though. It's urgent.'

'What, now?' Gaby is reverentially opening the letter, pulling at the flap in tiny gestures, unsticking rather than pulling.

'Why are you opening it in such a weird way?'

'I am opening it with reverence,' Gaby says. 'Because it's from Bernard Frossage.'

'I'd worked that bit out,' I say. 'Speaking of which . . .'

'After my letter,' Gaby says firmly, holding a palm up at me. 'I really need to read this, Clara. Everything else can wait.'

'I suppose it can, for a few minutes,' I say, taking a sip of tea and flipping my laptop open. I have to figure out how to get to the Isle of Muck in the Inner Hebrides. It's two miles long by one mile wide; population thirty-eight. Well, thirty-nine if you include Frossage. It seems I need to get myself to Mallaig, on the west coast of the Highlands, which is doable by train from Fort William, and then cross by ferry.

'Gaby,' I say. 'I don't suppose he mentions coming home in the next couple of days? Or going to Glasgow or Edinburgh for a little light relief? Or to anywhere at all on the mainland?'

'No. Oh my God,' says Gaby. 'This letter is amazing. This letter *blows my mind.*' She puts it down on the table and actually puts her head between her knees, something I've only ever seen in movies. She takes deep breaths and then re-emerges, fanning her face. 'He says I have already helped him "immeasurably" and he is begging me, actually *begging me*, to share any other ideas I might have.' She looks up at me, eyes shining with happiness. 'He's invited me over! Listen: "Your remarkable insights have renewed my faith in my abilities . . . what had started to feel extraordinarily unwieldy and complex now begins to feel manageable . . . The blinding audacity of your resolution concerning the Amphiboles and your suggestions regarding the aftermath of the siege . . . I know that with your help, I am now, finally, able to move forward." And so on. And then he invites me. He actually *invites me*. He says, "I would be honoured, Gabbro, if you would join me here, and spend a couple of days brainstorming the concluding chapters of Volume Seven."'

'You signed it "Gabbro"?'

'Yeah. It's my name.' She looks electrified with happiness. 'Where actually is he?' she asks. 'Hebrides, right? I can't even remember where I sent my letter. I was feeling a bit giddy.'

'He's on Muck,' I say. 'The Isle of. And as it happens, I'm going to have to pay him a visit too.'

'Road trip!' says Gaby. 'But, er, why? You don't even know him.'

'Because, dear Lady Gabbro of Beakstrels . . .'

'Don't even try to do it,' says Gaby disdainfully. 'A) You can't and b) it's not funny.'

'Because Sky's pregnant.'

'Oh my fucking God,' says Gaby, sitting down and blanching. 'Why didn't you tell me? Why didn't *she* tell me?'

'Because you weren't here. This was only last night.'

'Oh, Massicot, my little pal. Oh my God. When? How? How long have you known? Fuck. What are we going to do?'

I'm touched by the 'we'.

'I've told you: nobody knew until yesterday. We're going to go and see Bernard,' I say, 'because my son has impregnated his daughter and it's hardly the kind of news you break by letter.'

'In his books, it's exactly the kind of devastating news that would come by Beakstrel,' Gaby muses.

'Enough with the Beakstrels,' I say. 'And I'm telling Sky she may not in fact be devastated, so stick to that line. Poor thing's got enough on her plate without fearing what you might call the Wrath of Bern.'

'Don't call him Bern, it's disrespectful. How pregnant?'

'Three months.'

'Christ.'

'I know. Explains the puking.'

'I know a very good doctor,' Gaby says.

'Of course you do. But Sky says she's planning to keep it. She's having it, she says.'

'Oh my God,' Gaby says again, her mouth dropping open. 'Oh my God.'

'Well, she's exactly the age her mother was when she had her. She doesn't have a mother. She *is* great with kids: look how lovely she's always been with Maisy. Who knows? And she may well change her mind. She only found out yesterday.'

'I don't think people change their minds,' Gaby says. 'Once they start thinking about it as an actual baby. God, little Sky. Little Massicot. Where is she now?'

'At the library, revising,' I say. 'She's fine, you know. She was chipper at breakfast. I mean, bit spaced-out, bit pukey, but cheerful enough.'

'How's Jack?'

'Jack seems OK too. He just keeps saying he loves her and he'll stick with her whatever she decides. He's saying it like a kind of panicky mantra. He's worried because Sky's worried, though. Her main concern at the moment is Bernard, which is why we need to go.'

'What, today?'

'I'm just looking at trains and planes and ferries. Probably tomorrow – I'm going to ask Sam if he can move in for a couple of days. But imminently. Better start packing.'

What with one thing and another, I'm not really in the mood for dinner with Bel (Belt?), but I had to cancel our date last night for reasons of teenage pregnancy, and he asked if I was free tonight instead. Not unkeen, ole Bel, I sense: matters are coming to a head. Gaby said she'd cook 'a nice dinner' for the children – one involving both carbohydrates and fat – and take the opportunity to have a chat with Sky. So here

I am again, dressed in my new frock, sitting in Dirty, a happening new restaurant on the edge of Bethnal Green. Dirty looks like the grimy version of a dive bar in Fifties America, with prices very much not to match, and serves burgers and cocktails. It occurs to me, too late, that my choice of restaurant is a bit coals-to-Newcastle for Bel, who must have sat in places like this for several decades and probably doesn't find the inclusion of sliders – fashionably minute burgers – on the menu that exciting.

But I do, I reflect as I sip my nearly finished second Martini, even if the penumbral, speakeasy-darkness of the restaurant made it necessary for me to use the torch app on my phone to read the cocktail list, like a potholer. I had to get here early because, maddeningly and like all fashionable restaurants, Dirty doesn't take bookings. I've secured a booth, which is good. The Martinis are going to my head, which is – well, it's also good, actually, because I am finding everything a bit overwhelming, what with pregnant children and so on. Happily my fellow punters are able to distract me, for tonight at least: one of them is wearing a furry hat with enormous panda ears and a tabard, and another appears to be wearing a dress made of bark.

And now my phone pings, and it's a text from Bel (Bellicose?) saying that he's running fifteen minutes late and is very very sorry but the traffic is appalling. 'No problem,' I text back, and order a third cocktail, which is perhaps injudicious, but they are delicious and – well, in for a penny, in for a pound. I didn't sleep last night for thinking about Sky and Jack, and tomorrow I set off for the Hebrides: why shouldn't I have three cocktails? The thought of Bernard Frossage residing on Muck makes me feel that mild hysteria again, until I remember that I have to tell him about our predicament. Well, at least he's no stranger to this particular scenario, given Sky's mother's age when they had their child. Perhaps he can give us some tips.

The phone pings again and interrupts my ruminations. 'Where are you?' reads the text. 'Still here,' I reply. 'Embarking on my third Martini.' It is only as I press Send that I wonder why Bel (Beleaguered?) should suddenly feel confused about my location, which he has in full including postcode: he's not *that* old. I tap back on the handset, to Messages. It wasn't from Bel: it was from the Man From The Connaught, the man who has been silent as the tomb, give or take a koala, for nearly a year. I'm wondering what to do about this, apart from feel my stomach plunge down ten storeys, which is my first response, when another text pings up. 'Lucky you,' it says. 'Would you like some dinner to go with them?' This, of course, is when Bel appears.

'I'm so sorry,' he says, kissing my cheek and easing himself into the booth. 'The traffic was *atrocious*. I should have taken the Underground but I've never been to this part of London before and I thought a taxicab would be easier. Sorry,' he repeats. 'Two more of those,' he tells the waiter, gesturing at my drink.

'And some water, please,' I say. 'Tap is fine.'

'Well, this is different,' says Bel, peering about him. I've only ever seen Bel in a suit, but tonight he is in casual wear, in chinos and a blazer and a crisp, immaculately pressed pink shirt: City mufti, which isn't entirely my bag. It's funny how some people look rich whatever they're wearing: Bel exudes quiet wealth, though his clothes are normal-seeming as well as very square. It's to do with his skin and hair, and teeth, and with his patrician air. The jawline, maybe. He probably looks rich naked. Some people do. With women it usually has something to do with incredibly expensive highlights and a certain fine-poredness.

'You're not in Mayfair any more,' I smile. What am I going to do about my text? What am I going to *do*?

'It's great,' says Bel. 'I'd never come anywhere like this normally. Very hip.'

'I suddenly thought it was a stupid choice,' I say, forcing myself to stay on-topic, 'given that you must have been to dozens of diners like this at home.'

'Not quite like this,' says Bel, looking around. 'Different atmosphere. Different clientele.' Our drinks arrive, and a pair of menus. 'And never with anyone quite like you.'

Here we go. I don't quite know what to say to this, so I smile. Judging by the look on his face – an expression of infinite tenderness – smiling was also a stupid choice. Because I am tiddly and have no self-control, I start laughing: Bel is looking at me with wonderment, like I am a newborn foal and he is my horse-mummy. He is like the baby Simba in *The Lion King*, beholding for the first time the pride lands of Africa. This seems an overreaction, and strikes me as absurd, as does the next item to pop into my head: a picture of Timon, a cartoon meerkat, and Pumbaa, his flatulent warthog friend. I push these away. I am aware that I am grinning manically. I should drink some water.

'I – we – should eat something,' I say. 'Shall we order?' Perhaps Bel will reply that he needs no nourishment other than the food of love. I need to get some sort of grip on myself. My phone pings again but I don't look at it.

'Well, cheers,' says Bel, raising his glass to mine. 'Bottoms up.'

'Hakuna matata,' I say.

'I'm sorry?' says Bel.

'Just a saying,' I shrug. 'A saying of multicultural Britain. It's nice, I think. Now – what do you want to eat?'

Bel looks at me for two seconds too long. Oh dear.

'Er, why don't you order?' I say. 'Here, use my torch app.' The words have only just come out of my mouth – I am in the act of proffering my phone – when I remember the texts. I take the phone back. 'Actually, don't,' I say hastily, practically snatching it back. 'Silly me. There's nothing wrong with your eyes.'

'It *is* very dark,' Bel says. 'But I have my own torch app, as it happens.'

'Oh good. If they come before I get back, could I have my burger rare?' I say. 'And will you excuse me for a second?'

Bel (Belch?) stands up, because his manners are so reliably impeccable and his demeanour so reliably courtly. It's nice – there's nothing I like more than good manners – but I'm never quite sure about the standing up when a woman goes to the bathroom thing. Instead of slinking away peacefully for your wee, you have it announced to the whole room that, yep, it's time for a slash for the woman on table 7. It lacks mystery. It breaks mystique. When you're having dinner with a whole group of men with old-fashioned manners, they all stand up, every single one, and you feel like you should head to the bathroom doing a special little loo dance, just in case anyone's failed to notice that YOU'RE GOING NUMBER ONES because YOUR BLADDER IS FULL.

I sit on the loo and try to think. I'm almost scared to look at my phone. But I do. There are the first two texts, and then a third, which says, 'Apols for the short notice – unexpectedly in London. Expect you're busy. Would love to see you. Understand if not.' He might well apologize: asking someone to dinner at seven-thirty p.m. is uncharming and booty call-ish. I am filled with indignation, actually. So I text back, 'Asking someone to dinner at 7.30 p.m. is uncharming and booty call-ish.' The phone rings almost immediately, but I send it to voicemail. And then another text: 'I know. My flight came in early. So not as bad as looks. Answer the phone.' 'I can't,' I reply. 'I am at dinner with a very attractive and hot man.' This is only half a lie: lots of people would find Bel very attractive and hot. 'OK,' he texts back. 'I'll try you later.' Many replies suggest themselves: 'Actually, matey, *I'll* try you later if *I* feel like it'; 'I might be really busy shagging'; 'I miss you so much I can barely breathe. I feel like climbing out of this loo window and jumping into a taxi.' None of these seem especially wise, so I stare at the phone for a bit and then put it in my handbag, like a mature adult. Then I sit on the loo and regulate my breathing.

Back at the table, I'm aware that I need to normalize the conversation: I need to stop laughing at every thought that passes through my head – because of a combination of Sky, drunkenness, hunger and text-related butterflies – and I need to defuse Bel's expectations, pronto, because if there's one thing that my reactions to the texts have shown me, it's that forcing myself to find Bel attractive is flogging a dead horse. Unfortunately, the brief text exchange with the Man From The Connaught has made me feel mildly hysterical, jangly, rattled, which on top of the cocktails has the unhappy consequence of making me gibber. More unfortunately still, Bel interprets the gibbering as either nerves, excitement or both.

'You suit this environment,' he says. 'It animates you. Not that you're not usually animated,' he adds hastily. 'But you thrive in this informal setting.'

He's making me sound like a retired butler who's moved out of the Big House.

'I guess you'd call it bohemian, huh?' he says uncertainly – and quite endearingly – looking about the room. 'Not Claridge's, put it that way.'

'Hotels are strange places,' I say. 'Not quite real, I always think. Lovely cocoons. Best-behaviour sort of scenario.' This isn't even true: some of my worst behaviour has taken place in hotels. I know I shouldn't, but I take two more big gulps of Martini number four, and find it so refreshing that I follow this by two more. Mmm, Martinis.

'Wine?' says Bel.

'Why not?' I say. 'Why not, Bel?'

'Why not indeed, Clara?' Bel says, his voice deep and resonant. I like his voice and I like his accent. It's not enough.

'You should record audiobooks,' I say.

'Huh?' says Bel.

'Your voice,' I explain. 'It's nice. Warm. Bourbon-y.'

'Ah,' says Bel, looking a bit nonplussed. 'Er, good. But you say it so sadly!'

'Clara! Oh my God, what are you doing here?' squeals someone to my right. I turn my head and see my sister Evie, accompanied by our other sister, Flo, and I remember that it was Flo raving about Dirty which made me book it in the first place. 'Claaaara!' says Evie. 'Shove up. I must embrace you and these heels are very high and my balance is poor. I'm back! Have you missed me?'

'A lot,' I say. Evie's been away for nearly a month on business. 'Hello, Flo.'

'Wotcha,' says Flo, easing herself into our booth. 'Nice dress. And who's this?' she asks, gazing interestedly at Bel.

'Yes, who's this?' says Evie. 'Who is this fox?'

'Silver,' says Flo. 'You have to say "silver fox". Normal foxes are red. Well, orangey. Hello! I'm Flo, and this is Evie. We're Clara's sisters.'

'Hello,' says Bel pleasantly. 'I'm Bel. Very pleased to meet you.'

'Cool name,' says Evie. '*Ding-dong.*'

'We've been drinking,' says Flo.

'Me too,' I say.

'Have you?' says Bel. 'It's not spelled like that, by the way.'

'Yep,' I say. 'I have, Bel.'

'Let's drink more,' says Evie. 'I love to drink when I haven't seen my sisters for ages.'

'So are you on, like, a date?' says Flo, and then laughs, rather wildly, in my direction.

'We're just having something to eat,' I say, just as Bel says, 'Yes.'

'Shall we shove off?' says Evie. 'I sense we may be in the way.'

'Look at Clara's face, Eev,' says Flo. 'She had stuff done.'

'I heard. Let me see!' says Evie. 'I wish it weren't so dark. Can I borrow your torch app?'

'Not to shine in my face right at this moment, no,' I say. 'Not in the middle of what might be a date.'

'You just said it wasn't. Come on,' says Flo, grabbing my phone. 'Evie needs to see. Oh,' she says. 'You have a text, Clara.' She hands me the phone back, giving me a long look.

'It's nothing,' I say, not looking at it.

'I do not concur,' Flo says solemnly.

'So, what are you guys up to?' says Bel, with slight desperation in his tone. This happens, usually, when people meet my relatives. We can be a bit much en masse.

'We're having a drink with you, Bel,' Evie says sweetly. 'And hopefully some hearty snacks. Or do you mean *in life*?'

'Yes. What is your line of work?'

'My line of work is domestic and procreative,' says Flo. 'That is my life.'

'My line of work is clothes,' says Evie. 'They are not my life, but I scoot about buying 'em. For shops, you know. Not for me. Although also for me, otherwise I'd be running about naked. Clara, can I have some of your burger?'

'Maybe we should go back to our table,' says Flo. 'Get our own. Except it would break the serendipity of bumping into you. You told me you were busy.'

'I am busy,' I say. 'Having dinner with Bel.'

'And us!' Evie says joyfully. 'This is so great.'

'Are you going to reply to your text?' says Flo.

'What text?' says Bel.

'So, Bel. Bel, Bel, Bel. Tell me every single thing about you,' says Evie, who has perfect timing. 'Omit no detail, starting with your name.'

Flo leans in to my ear and whispers, 'Do you want to leave? Me and Evie are on it. We will hold the fort.'

'What, go to the loo and climb out the window?'

'Yes!' whispers Flo. 'So romantic.'

'Not romantic,' I tut. 'Mean and childish.' I don't tell her the idea had – very fleetingly – occurred to me earlier. I discounted it, obviously, though to be absolutely honest this was partly to do with the fear of getting stuck halfway through. And then Bel (Bellyache?) would come looking, and he would have to address my bottom, because my face would be in the street. And he would be sad, or cross, or both, and you can't have people going, 'Why, Clara? Why?' at your actual arse.

'Also,' I hiss at Flo, 'I'm not on call. I do not respond to finger-snaps. Especially after, like, months.'

'Yes, I know, but sigh,' says Flo. She actually says 'sigh'. 'Some people are just meant to be together.'

'Hrmph,' I say.

'. . . bottom-founded drilling rigs,' Bel is saying to Evie.

'Gosh, bottom-founded,' Evie repeats, seemingly enraptured and talking louder than is strictly necessary in order to mask Flo's and my exchange.

'And then of course there are combined drilling and production facilities,' Bel continues. 'And deepwater mobile offshore drilling units. MODU.'

'MODU!' says Evie. 'Beautiful modoo.'

'And, er, yeah,' says Bel. 'That's how we drill. Well, some of the ways.'

A terrible geyser of laughter is building up in my depths: an actual explosion. I close my eyes for a second, trying yet again to regain my composure. 'She sounds like she's taking the piss even when she isn't,' I tell Bel. 'Just so you know.'

'It's true,' says Evie. 'It is one of the banes.'

'It's no problem. Right,' says Bel. 'Let's get you gals some food.'

'Gals!' says Flo. 'I am delighted to be called a gal.'

'I am delighted to learn about MODU,' says Evie. 'Is Clara a gal?'

'Clara is a lady,' says Bel, smiling at me.

'Hahahaha,' says Flo.

'Hahahaha,' says Evie.

'No, she is,' says Flo, clearing her throat. 'She totally is. In absolutely 99 per cent of the respects.'

'Well, 95,' says Evie. She notices my face. 'Even 96 or 7.'

'Have you finished?' I say sternly.

'You *are* a lady,' Evie says. 'You're once, twice . . .'

'Evie!' I say.

'What? It was a roundabout way of saying "I love you". I love you, Clara.'

'I love you too, Evie. Now stop it.'

'OK,' says Evie. 'But I was just saying.'

'We mean it in the best *possible* way,' Flo tells Bel. 'Who'd want to be "a lady" all the time?'

'Not me,' says Evie. 'I am content just to be a gal.'

'I'm working towards being a broad,' says Flo. 'When I enter my prime. Or maybe a dame.'

'I agree with you both,' says Bel, laughing appreciatively. 'There is nothing more boring than a lady all the time.'

'Kate's a lady all the time – our mother, you know,' says Flo. 'She's not boring.'

'I don't think Bel meant to impugn Kate,' I say.

'I should hope not,' says Flo. 'Talk about overfamiliarity.'

'It's like being with mad people, isn't it? Sorry,' I say to Bel.

'Not at all, not at all,' says Bel.

'You are a charming man, Bel,' says Evie. 'Like in the

Smiths song, except not a jumped-up pantry boy who never knew his place.'

'I'm sorry,' says Bel. 'You've lost me.'

'Popular beat combo,' I say, meaning to be helpful.

'Now you're talking in code,' says Bel.

'Never mind,' says Flo. 'Tell us about Texas.'

'Texas!' Evie says. 'The romance. Horses and really big hats!' she cries. 'And . . .'

'And oil,' says Bel.

'And so near Mexico, where I went on my honeymoon. Fact,' says Flo.

'Goodness!' says Bel. 'Mexico, huh? Did you like it? It's kind of a dump.'

'We loved it,' says Flo. 'Such wonderful people. And food. And landscapes.'

'Well, the ones who are shooting each other in the face aren't that wonderful,' says Bel. 'Nor are the lazy bastards trying to smuggle themselves out.'

'Er,' I say. 'How do you mean, lazy? Surely they're looking for work? Or trying to get away from people shooting them in the face?'

'Don't get me wrong,' laughs Bel. 'Some of them are perfectly decent folks.'

'I wouldn't say self-smuggling was lazy, exactly,' says Evie.

'Gosh,' says Flo.

'The ones I've got working for me are terrific. Work like burros, like donkeys, all the hours the Lord gives.'

'For the minimum wage, of course,' says Evie. 'And comfortably accommodated.'

'Hahahaha. Not quite,' says Bel. 'Not quite. Or what

would be the point of Mexican labour?' And he roars with laughter.

Ah. So here we have the considerable fly in the Bel ointment. It turns out he's some sort of bigoted Republican who thinks with contempt of the people who work for him. I knew there had to be something, and here it is. Here's why I don't have to feel bad for not wanting to get it on with Bel. Here's why I'm not going to feel like a heel when I don't reply to his next call. There's no point in poking around Bel's other political opinions: I've got the gist. The relief! It occurs to me in a blurry, drunken way that the politics only provide me with a pretext: I've got plenty of friends with political persuasions that differ from mine. It's not like it's a deal-breaker. But I literally exhale with the relief of it: I don't have to try and make myself fancy him any more.

'What?' says Bel, as we sit in silence for a second. 'Are you gals all . . . Ah, what's that great expression I heard the other day?' says Bel. 'So British. Champagne something.'

'Socialists,' I say. 'Yes, we are.'

'That's kind of a funny thing, huh?' says Bel.

'Not particularly hilarious to us,' says Evie. 'Badge of honour, I'd say.'

'You don't seem the type,' Bel (Bellend?) says, still laughing and gesturing vaguely in the direction of our clothes.

'We try and leave our cloth caps at home,' says Flo. 'We prefer to roam without disguise.'

'But Clara,' Bel says to me, sensing – surely – the chilliness that has descended on our booth. 'You like nice things, right? Luxury?'

'I love them,' I say. 'And it, when I meet it.'

'And you work hard for them,' he continues.

'Well, hard-ish. It's not like I'm down the coal mines. It's not like I'm one of your Mexicans,' I say.

'Haha,' says Bel, and then stops laughing.

'As far as I'm concerned, it's very simple,' I say. Bel is getting on my nerves. 'I'm fortunate, and blessed, and privileged, and all those things. I don't need to be a cunt as well.'

'Language, Timothy,' says Flo. 'Also, hear hear.'

'Who's Timothy?' says Bel, looking shocked: funny how the c-word can still have that effect.

'We are very much *against* cunts,' Evie tells Bel in a confidential tone, leaning forward right into his face.

'And we are *for* champagne, where available,' says Flo, 'to toast the welfare state and our beautiful National Health Service.'

'To not being cunts!' says Evie, raising her glass.

'Not cunts,' I say, clinking.

'Not cunts,' says Flo, doing the same.

'It's not that complicated,' I say when I put my glass down. 'No need to look perplexed, Bel.'

'I thought the expression was, uh, pejorative,' says Bel. 'I'm confused.'

'Oh, it's massively pejorative,' says Evie with a shrug. 'But merely descriptive, in our case.'

'Spoiled, but uncuntish,' says Flo, for clarification.

'Well, as uncuntish as possible,' I say. 'I expect a bit of cuntishness sneaks in occasionally.'

'You can't have everything,' says Evie, nodding.

'True,' says Flo. 'We're not the Baby Jesus.'

'No,' I say.

'Who is?' says Flo. 'Apart from Him, obviously.'

'Speaking of all that, in a roundabout way,' says Evie. 'Guess what Bel's name is?'

'I've been asking myself that for weeks,' I say. 'What is it, Bel?'

'Rebel? Decibel? Jezebel?' says Flo.

'It's Belvoir,' says Bel, smiling with his white teeth. 'Bell-vwahr. Old family name. French, I think. Belvoir.'

If I catch either of my sisters' eyes I am going to do myself a laughter injury and it will be fatal: I will actually die laughing. I can already feel myself in the final throes. I stare very very fixedly at the table, praying that neither of them say anything. I am trying so hard not to howl with mirth, not to fall to the floor and bang it with my fist, screaming with laughter, that tears spring to my eyes.

'It's not pronounced like that,' says Flo. 'Well, not in England.'

'How do you mean?' says Bel (Belvoir!).

'There are names that aren't pronounced the way they're spelled,' says Evie, looking straight at me.

'Cholmondeley, for instance,' says Flo, spelling out the name letter by letter. 'It's pronounced Chumley.'

'Crazy,' says Bel, laughing. 'Who knew?'

'And Featherstonehaugh,' says Evie, spelling that out too, 'is pronounced Fanshaw.'

'Heh,' says Bel. 'How about that?'

'Please,' I say weakly. It comes out as a strangulated croak. 'Evie, please.'

'And Belvoir,' says relentless Evie, 'is pronounced Beaver.'

There is a beat, during which Bel stares at all of us in turn.

'You are *kidding* me, right?' he finally says.

'It's true,' I say, not able to meet his eye.

'Beaver?' says Belvoir. '*Beaver?*'

'Yeah,' shrugs Evie. 'So I'd totally stick with Bel.'

In the end, sliding away from Bel was easier than I'd thought. Having put him off with our bad language, and absolutely appalled him with our revelation, all that remained was to peck him decorously on the cheek as I got into my cab and to smile non-committally at whatever it was that he said – I was too drunk and elated by my escape to listen properly. A cheery wave goodbye and – done. But then – and this is why women are so deeply weird – then, of course, comes the feeling of panic. What if, what if, what if? What if Bel appeared in my life because he was a sort of human sign – a sign that it was time to be a grown-up, and have grown-up expectations, and do grown-up things with grown-up Bel? What if, a year down the line, I realize that Bel was, in fact, a terrific idea? What if I'm too old and Bel was my best shot? What if I am insane not to cling on to him while falling to my knees thanking God for the late opportunity and for pro-viding me with a consort named Beaver?

I'm thinking how horrid it would be to have to be with someone you didn't fancy, out of gratitude and desperation. Or is that just a romantic notion? Would it be a great deal more horrid to grow old alone? I can't see that it would be, but it's so subjective. And then I start thinking – who do we want to be attractive to anyway? I mean, all this stuff, all this work and effort and so on – who is it actually for? For Bel, or the possibility of attracting a Bel? Not when push came to shove. The builders who wouldn't whistle at me? Random blokes in the street? Other women, who are better than men at making you feel that keeping yourself youthful is somehow a duty, and that failure to do so lets the whole side down? Is it for the *Daily Mail*? For me and my self-esteem? It used to be, in youth, that I was interested in being attractive to everybody – a reasonable position, I think, when you're twenty-five. But now I know this doesn't apply any more: I don't want to be attractive to young men who are my children's age: it's creepy, and you have to be really a very desperate and unfulfilled kind of woman to take pride or pleasure in being the 'hot mum'. I don't want to be attractive to, say, good-looking waiters, because they could be my sons and it's weird and confusing for everybody (it's also weird and confusing if they don't flirt. It's lose-lose). I don't especially want to be attractive to the very old, though I rather wish I did – presumably ancient old men would find one ravishingly lovely and positively bursting with youth even without the Botox. And then I remember: they have form when it comes to dumping their lovely wives in favour of plastic-chested twenty-three-year-olds. It's come to a pretty pass when even ancient, toothless old men only fancy women half your age: no wonder so many people become a bit deranged.

I think about this all the way home and I still can't come up with a satisfactory answer. Who is it *for*? Is it for men in their thirties, for silver foxes, for the husbands of our friends (to this I can categorically say no), for dads at the playground, for colleagues, for exes, for strangers? The obvious answer would be 'It's for me, for myself,' but that isn't really true. If it were down to me, I'd lie about in my onesie eating cheese, happy as a clam, the notion of Botox not even a notion. It's like that thing that people always say about wearing expensive lingerie – 'Oh, I wear it for myself.' But you don't. You wear it because you want someone to rip it off you with their teeth, regardless of whether you know such a person or just hope to meet one, one day. Sexy knickers are about hope. If you're not interested in ripping, you wear giganto-pants that come up to your waist and sturdy four-hook bras.

The best answer I can come up with is 'people'. I want to be attractive to 'people'. It's unsatisfactory – it suggests that all women who are reasonably vain would actually be child-frighteners if they didn't force themselves to try and look reasonable. But my internal conversation with myself has sharpened my thoughts, particularly when I got to the bit about posh pants and teeth. It sort of *is* for myself, all this stuff, to the extent that it's about being the best version of myself that I can possibly be when it comes to pulling. That's all it is. It's as crude and basic as that. It's biological.

When Bel had gone and Flo, Evie and I had finished cling-ing to each other just saying, 'Beaver, Beaver,' over and over again, crying, and when we were standing in the street look-ing for taxis, Flo said, 'Are you going to text him back?'

But when I get home, I don't. Not now. It's late, and I am confused by his sudden reappearance, and I am going to the Hebrides tomorrow.

'What on earth are you wearing?' I ask Gaby at seven the following evening. I haven't slept much and still have a terrible hangover: I could puke, actually, due to my age-related inability to cope with too much alcohol. I also feel like I'm hallucinating. Three hours ago Gaby was wearing a short striped dress and a leather jacket, accessorized with red lips and heeled boots. No longer.

'Oh, just, um, just . . . country clothes,' says Gaby. 'I got them yesterday. I didn't have anything suitable in my wardrobe.'

'Ah,' I say. 'Right. Where did you buy them from?'

'A shop,' says Gaby.

'What is the shop called? It's quite a look.'

'Pert Damozels,' Gaby mutters. 'I found it online.'

Gaby's hair is twisted into two fat sausages, which are looped droopily on either side of her head, rather like dog ears, flapping furiously back and forth every time she moves her head to speak. The front part of her hair is tightly braided across her forehead, giving a headband effect. Gaby is wearing a dress that I would best describe as medieval: tight bodice, laced up the front, ridiculously full, knee-length skirts (plural) with a bustle effect at the back, and absolutely enormous hanging sleeves that must be at least four feet long; the whole thing made of red – she'd say 'scarlet' – velvet. If you were being charitable, you'd say it was reasonably flattering on the tit front. You'd struggle to say anything else complimentary – the proportions are so odd, for a start – though of course Gaby is so good-looking that things could be a lot worse. Below the wench's frock she wears tall, sturdy socks, of the kind men wear for Scottish dancing except made of rougher wool, pulled right up and held in place by leather ribbons. Her feet are shod in flat pods, with a groove at the front that suggests clovenness. She looks like an escapee from Chaucerian bedlam.

'We're going on the sleeper,' I say. 'I'm doing jogging bottoms, a nightie and a big jumper. How are you going to sleep in all that garb?'

'I'll be fine,' says Gaby. 'It takes ages to put on. I didn't want to change into it in a tiny cabin or in a loo. This way I can just tweak it a bit in the morning.'

'Uh, OK. And are you going to take a coat?' I say. 'It's December, Gaby, and it's going to be absolutely freezing and we have to get on a boat tomorrow. Do you want to borrow one of the boys' parkas?' The more I look at her, the more I'm actually slightly wondering if she's lost her mind.

By way of answer, Gaby slips into the hall and returns wearing a cloak – almost floor length, heavy wool, with bone toggles as fastenings.

'I have this,' she says simply, flipping up the hood.

'You look . . . very unlike yourself,' I say. 'You look unimaginable.'

'That's where you're wrong,' says Gaby. 'I look 100 per cent imaginable by Bernard Frossage. Also, it's because I'm not wearing any make-up,' Gaby says.

'I think it may also have something to do with your get-up,' I say. 'And why no make-up?'

'I am dressed,' Gaby says, 'as The Lady Gabbro. This is what she looks like. The TV series gets it *completely* wrong. The Lady Gabbro needs no wanton's paint. Just cloth of crimson and the sturdy wool of prangs. Prangs are sheep,' she adds helpfully. 'Or – argh. Are they? Are prangs sheep?'

'I wouldn't know,' I say.

'Rams!' says Gaby. 'Prangs are rams. Sheep are baals. Of course. Of *course*. Baals,' she murmurs to herself, in the way I do to remind myself to buy milk. 'Baals.'

'Right. Do you think it's maybe a bit much, the tribute-wear? I mean, isn't it a bit like going to see Madonna wearing a conical bra? I don't know that it would *necessarily* encourage her to take you seriously. You know? It's like going to meet a judge wearing a judgey wig. You want him to take you seriously, after all.'

'I know what I'm doing,' Gaby says with dignity.

'Gabbro! You look *amazing*,' says Sky, who's just wandered in. 'Oh man. Grankhor ripyngo!'

'See?' says Gaby, turning to me triumphantly. 'Frippu, Massicot. Frippu.'

'Horlan,' says Sky.

'You are both *completely deranged*,' I say. 'I have no idea what you're saying. It's hurting my head.'

'They were at it for hours last night, when you were out,' says Jack, who's also come down to see us off. 'Speaking Lapidosan. Like, *for hours*. Laughing. Telling jokes. Even crying a bit.' He looks fondly at them both.

'I'd got a bit rusty,' says Gaby. 'I needed to practise, and it's so much more rewarding talking to someone who's fluent. Frippu for that, Massicot. Oh – sheep are baals, right? I got a bit confused just now.'

'Yeah,' says Sky. 'Definitely baals.'

I shake my head in disbelief: I don't know if it's the hangover or the lack of sleep, but I feel like I've slipped into some parallel universe.

'You're taking Maisy to school in the morning, remember?' I ask Jack, trying to get back to the normal world. 'Sam's going to collect her in the afternoon and then he'll come and stay here until we get back. Her uniform's on the chair in her room and look, here are her shoes. Try not to let her have a whole jar of Nutella for breakfast.'

'Yep, all cool,' says Jack.

'God,' says Sky. 'I so hope Dad's OK with all of this. I still don't know whether I should be coming with you.'

'I think you should be at home, getting on with your schoolwork,' I say. 'Revising. I have no doubt you'll see him very soon.'

'I wish there was a way of you letting me know how it's going,' Sky says, chewing her thumb.

'No Beakstrels on Muck,' says Gaby, hugging her. 'More's the pity. But remember what I said last night. It's all going to be fine, one way or another. Try not to worry.'

'We'll be back soon,' I say. 'Couple of days, maximum. It's the getting there and back that's going to take up most of the time.'

'Well, goodbye,' says Sky anxiously. 'And good luck. And thank you. Tell him gently, won't you?' she adds, chewing her thumb again. 'Can you text when you're on your way back, so we can make sure we're here?'

'Yes. Really, try not to worry,' says Gaby. 'It's going to be OK.' She opens her cloak and wraps Sky inside it for a moment, kissing the top of her head. The image is unexpectedly touching. 'Honestly, babe. It's all going to be fine.'

Which may perfectly well be true, but maybe not quite yet. Gaby's insane get-up, only partially concealed by her voluminous cloak – you can still see her crazy hair and her crazy socks and feet – garners more stares than I know what to do with, and causes intense merriment as we weave our way through Euston station. And this is London, where you'd think you could dress as a hippogriff and probably be completely ignored. But among the hilarity – at one point a group of children follow us, laughing, all the way from WH Smith to Costa – come three (I counted them) admiring glances and the same strange salutation that Sky and Gaby are in the habit of making at each other. Gaby graciously acknowledges these with a not-unimperious nod of the head. Later, once our train has been called and we're at the gate, a young man going in the opposite direction high-fives Gaby, calling out, 'The Matriarch! Man, that's so cool,' as they pass each other.

'Shall we go to the bar for a drink?' says Gaby once we've boarded the train.

'I'm still hung-over,' I say. 'And I've had enough of people staring at you for one day. Also – do you mind if I ask you a rude question?'

'Go ahead,' says Gaby good-naturedly. 'I know you think this is all very funny, but you don't understand. This – meeting Bernard – is literally the most exciting thing that's ever happened to me.'

'No, I get that,' I say. 'Kind of. It's just – you're so . . . well, so into the way you look. Normally, I mean – not tonight.

And this is so not the way you usually look. I mean, you're two inches away from being daubed in woad.'

'I know,' says Gaby happily. 'It's mental, right? Mentally great. It's so freeing. That was one of the reasons I started loving Men of Granite. It's a whole other world that he's created. You know? He takes everything we think of as normal and questions it, including how we think we're supposed to look.'

'You're a yoga teacher from LA,' I say. 'I mean . . . it's just so hard to compute.'

'It shouldn't be,' says Gaby. 'You've known me forever. You *know* I'm a nerd.'

'Yes, but it's so cunningly concealed. I mean, you couldn't have concealed it more, or better.'

'That's why I'm saying this is freeing,' says Gaby patiently. 'This is actually *who I am*.'

'Gaby. Get a grip. I'm actually a bit worried about you. You are not The Lady Gabbro.'

'No,' says Gaby. 'But I'm close. Inside, this is who I am. Outside . . . oh, I don't know. I sometimes think outside doesn't matter as much as I thought it did. Maybe Bernard Frossage gets it right, in those books.'

'It's a bloody weird way of finding out you don't need cosmetic surgery on your hands,' I say.

'I didn't say that,' says Gaby.

'What do you think will happen when you meet Bernard?' I ask. 'Really. I'm curious.'

'I don't know,' says Gaby, and blushes.

We are woken up at eight-thirty a.m. with a cup of tea. The scenery outside the window is spectacular, and my jaw actually drops open: we are on a single-track branch line going through the West Highlands at a stately pace, past lochs, hills with snow on their summits, brooks and, incredibly, deer. The sense that I am hallucinating – that I have now been hallucinating for twelve hours – doesn't leave me. We clickety-clack past the shores of Loch Treig, and I press my nose up against the window in wonderment. At one point after that, the train squeezes past a gorge, with a river below. It's like being inside a painting: one of the most breathtakingly beautiful things I've ever seen. Just before ten a.m., we arrive in Fort William, disembark, cross platforms and get on the train to Mallaig – the end of the line. This journey too is stunningly beautiful. Ben Nevis towers above Fort William as we pull out of the station. Soon we're going past Loch Eilt – we spy a tiny white church just past Lochailort station, or at least I do: Gaby is readjusting her forehead-braid at this stage. I am intensely moved by the beauty of our surroundings, in this new middle-aged way I have: ten years ago, I'd have glanced up, thought 'This is nice' to myself, and gone back to my book or my iPod. Now I am practically weeping at the beauty of the natural world: I feel like my heart is in my mouth. Some of the lochs have tiny islands on them, with bare trees. I'm reasonably well travelled, but honestly: I've never seen anything like this before. I make a mental note to never holiday anywhere other than remote Scotland, which strikes me forcefully as one of the wonders of the world.

The sea appears on our left-hand side, and then we're in Mallaig, where we get off and go wandering in search of the ferry. It is freezing cold and for one moment I rather envy Gaby's loony cloak: my parka is only keeping me warm from the thighs up. I eye the weather suspiciously and scan the harbour for MV *Lochnevis*, which is supposed to get us to Muck, but then realize it doesn't get in for an hour. I really, really hope no crossings are cancelled: we don't really have a plan B, and although I could easily while away an evening ensconced somewhere eating seafood, time is of the essence and we're not on holiday. I peer at the sea hesitantly: it doesn't look especially calm.

'Let's go and find some coffee,' I tell Gaby, who has perched herself on her wheely case and is gazing out dreamily, like a woolly, becloaked mermaid. She looks less peculiar in this context than she did in London: weather-appropriate and sensibly shod, Celtically ginger and Celtically pale. If she spoke Gaelic rather than Lapidosan, you'd take her for a mildly eccentric local who maybe had to dress like that in order to please the tourists – the Scottish equivalent of bare-breasted Africans with spears, who then go home to put their normal clothes on, make dinner and chat about current affairs.

Not that there are many – or indeed any – tourists other than us, as far as I can tell: you'd have to really have a liking for dramatic weather and intense cold to come this far in December. We leave our cases at the ticket office, where a nice lady (who also informs us that it'll be dark by three p.m.) points us in the direction of a café that will serve us bacon rolls and coffee. When we find it, both the coffee and the roll strike me as ambrosial, because they are hot.

And then, finally, we are on the ferry. We are on the ferry, puking like we've never puked before: the crossing is notoriously rough, even in clement weather – which this is not. The boat rides the waves like a roller coaster, so that you get that whooshing feeling in your stomach every time it crests a wave, and then – thump – down it comes, and up comes breakfast, until there's nothing left. The situation isn't helped by the all-pervading smell (even outside) of burgers and chips. Thank heavens Sky isn't here: she'd be throwing up in triplicate. We'd started off on the viewing platform – there are dolphins to be seen, we've been told, as well as whales and porpoises – but a combination of freezing cold and spray soon has us scuttling down to the relative safety of the coffee lounge, until the rolling motion of the ship sends us back up again to puke. Gaby's artfully constructed hairdo is in disarray. I have sick on my parka sleeve and have nothing to wipe it off with. We're both pale green. I had, comically, put on a slick of budge-proof lipstick earlier this morning, which Gaby now points and laughs at in between vomiting – 'Still glam,' she says, and then heaves.

Port Mór, the tiny harbour at Muck, is stunning, in a brutal way, though I imagine it is a great deal less bleak in summer. We disembark, the only two passengers to do so, and take a lonely walk up the stone jetty. Now what? There's a small settlement near the harbour. We have the name of Bernard's house, but there are no people around to ask for directions. Still, the island is tiny: if we walk for long enough, we'll find it, or at least find a person to point us the right way. There's wind gusting as we set off in no particular direction, pulling our wheely cases, past a field with very small ponies in it. Or maybe they're normal-sized ponies, or giant ponies. I can't tell any more. Everything is surreal. I start laughing at Gaby's Louis Vuitton case, which for some reason strikes me as the funniest thing I've ever seen, being pulled along by a madwoman in hooves through an insanely stark and beautiful landscape, in the howling wind, with neither of us really knowing where we're going, and not a soul about.

'Stop!' I tell Gaby. 'I have to take a picture.'

I get my phone out – zero signal, of course – and photograph her. When I examine the picture on my phone screen, I am struck yet again by the thought that, suitcase aside, in this particular context Gaby doesn't look that mad at all. In London: certifiable, like it would be a kindness to get her sectioned. Here: pretty much at home. This strikes me as highly comedic, and I start to laugh again.

'My turn,' says Gaby. 'It's not like you don't look hilarious in your cashmere and red lippy, and your blow-dry. Well, what's left of it.'

'At least I've got my Arctic parka,' I tell her. 'Four hundred quid well spent in one of Covent Garden's finest emporia.'

'Those are good boots too,' says Gaby.

'Thanks,' I say. 'Selfridges. Though I don't guarantee that this setting is quite what Kurt Geiger had in mind.'

'Kurt Geiger doesn't exist, you know,' Gaby shouts. The wind is rising, and fast. 'He's a made-up thing, like some of those "farms" in supermarkets.'

'Doesn't he? It seems an odd sort of name to make up if you want to convey shoe-glamour,' I yell back. 'Germanic. I'd have gone more for Italianate, or Frenchified.'

'I still don't think you can beat Manolo,' Gaby screams. 'Even after all this time. If it's luxe you're after, in a shoe.'

'What?' I can barely hear her, though she's only a few feet ahead. The wind is really whipping up. I'm not especially meteorologically on the ball, but I'd call this the beginning of a gale.

'Manolo Blahnik,' Gaby yells. 'MANOLO BLAHNIK. Oh, Clara! Look! Look! Over there! A person!'

And so there is, riding towards us on a quad bike with a trailer. I've never been so happy to see another human being. My hair is now completely vertical and my eyes are crying and stinging from the cold. My bottom half has gone beyond goosebumps and into a sort of cold-induced seizure.

'I HOPE HE DOESN'T WANT TO EAT US,' I yell at Gaby. 'THIS COULD ALL GO A BIT *DELIVERANCE*.'

'You're quite safe,' the man says, pulling up in front of us. 'I prefer langoustine.'

'Oh fuck,' I say. 'Sorry. I didn't realize you could hear. Stupid joke. Also, sorry for swearing.'

My Hebridean knowledge is limited, but I've suddenly remembered that a certain dour, hardcore Presbyterianism pervades some of the islands: they're not really the sort of place where you'd disport yourself in crotchless knickers while crying for strong drink. Thank goodness for Gaby's modest cloak, which hopefully atones for her pagan hair.

'Yes, sorry. We don't understand wind direction. We are from a city. Fàilte!' Gaby says.

'Technically I say Fàilte to you,' the man says. 'To welcome you. You say Hàlo, or Feasgar math.'

'Hàlo,' says Gaby, whose interest in languages is beginning to get on my nerves. 'I'm Gaby, and this is Clara.'

'Jim,' says Jim, holding out his hand. 'And I don't speak much Gaelic.'

'I love the Scottish accent,' says Gaby happily. 'It is redolent of ancient lands. Ancient wisdoms.'

'Thanks,' says Jim. 'What are you doing here, by the

way? Only, we don't get that many visitors in the middle of December.'

'We've come from London,' Gaby says, yelling again as the wind re-rises.

'I'd never have guessed,' says Jim. 'And – come from London for why?'

'Ah yes,' I say. 'Good question. We're looking for a Bernard Frossage. He's in a rented house somewhere. He writes books. We've come to find him. I don't suppose . . .'

'Bernard!' says Jim. 'I might have known. I'll take you to him. Here, put your cases in the trailer. Better get a move on: there's a storm on the way.'

He doesn't *look* terribly religious, but then it's so hard to tell, and my research didn't extend to which islands are violently devout and which aren't. I don't feel we should be taking any risks.

'God's wrath,' I say, gesturing at the sky, as if I would welcome nothing more than a really punishingly good storm. 'We are but miserable sinners,' I continue, warming to my theme. 'Craven *beasts*. Of, of, er, the field.'

'It's just a storm,' says Jim. His voice suggests amusement, but I can't really see his face, which is sensibly muffled against the elements. The sky has now gone completely dark, like granite.

'Come on, then, hop on,' Jim says. 'It'll be a squash but we're not going far.' He points to a dwelling in the near distance, but it's hard to see in the failing light. 'That's him, over there.'

'How do I look?' Gaby shouts into my ear as we chug along.

'Lovely,' I say. It's almost true. 'Windswept, but great.'

'I could pee,' Gaby says. 'With excitement. Boy, oh boy. Bernard Frossage!'

There doesn't seem to be any point in reminding Gaby that this is not, in fact, a date, but rather a pregnancy-related emergency. Within minutes, we have pulled up to a single-storey stone dwelling – just big stones, no discernible mortar – with what looks to be grass for a roof. There are two wooden window frames and a peeling blue door. It's not quite the dwelling that I had imagined – I'd been thinking more well-appointed former manse – but the light inside, glowing yellow, is the most welcoming thing I've seen all day.

'It's called a bothy,' says Jim. 'A shelter for travellers, you know,' he explains. 'But this one is privately owned and has been adapted for visitors, and is relatively comfortable. He's expecting you?' Jim asks as we climb off the quad and grapple with our suitcases. It has started raining horizontally.

'No,' I say. 'We couldn't get in touch. But it'll be fine.'

'Best check he's in before I peel off,' says Jim sensibly. 'Weather's come in.'

'Go on,' I tell Gaby. 'Knock on the door.'

You'd think this commotion, plus the sound of a bike, would have brought Bernard hurtling to the door, but we can barely hear each other speak.

'Oh no,' Gaby says. 'I couldn't. I don't even know him. You do it, Clara.'

I bang on the door with my fist. It is opened by a man whom I recognize from his author photograph: Bernard Frossage, large as life and twice as bearded.

'Hi,' I say. 'I'm Clara. Jack's mum. From London. Everything's OK.'

'Oh my good Christ,' says Bernard, blanching white.

200

'It can't be. Something must have happened for you to be here. Is Sky . . .?'

'She couldn't be better,' I say. 'She's absolutely fine.'

'Thank M'nork,' he says, exhaling. 'How do you do? I'm Bernard. But so . . . what brings you here? Ach, I'm forgetting my manners. Come in, come in. Fàilte. You're half drenched – I'll make some tea.' Only now that he's reassured about Sky does he look past me, to Jim. 'Thanks, Jim,' he says. 'See you tomorrow.'

'Will you want picking up?' asks Jim.

I don't know, is the answer to that.

'I'm afraid we haven't even thought that far ahead. I'm sure we can sort it out ourselves,' I say breezily. 'Thanks so much, though. And for all your help just now. We're really grateful.'

'We?' says Bernard. 'Who's we?'

'Oh,' I say, moving aside. 'Me and Gaby. This is Gaby, my friend. She lives with us. You've been corresponding.'

My standing aside has had the effect of pulling back the curtain on a stage: Gaby, soaked but beaming with pleasure, is revealed in all her glory. She stares at Bernard. Bernard stares at her. I can hear Jim's quad bike driving away. Time stands still for a second or two.

'Gabbro,' says Gaby. 'Morga balonkü, Bernard.' She holds out her hand.

'Gabbro. The Matriarch,' Bernard says in an awed whisper. 'Morga balonkü, Gabbro. It is an honour. I'm so glad you came. So glad,' he repeats, and ushers us in.

It's very snug inside Bernard's bothy, and there's a roaring fire. Half of the room is taken up with an ancient, highly waxed oak table, which is completely covered in paper-work – maps, diagrams, notes, Post-its, bits of paper with bullet points, typed-up material, A4 pads covered in hand-written scrawl. More paperwork is pinned to the back wall: what look like a dozen family trees, more drawings, arrows flying in every direction from one sheet to the next. I'm reminded of those whiteboards you see in police dramas, charting the course of the investigation. There's paper on the floor and paper on the sofa and, in one corner of the table, an old-fashioned typewriter with three spare spools of ribbon.

The other half of the room is taken up by a large, unPres-byterian bed, covered in what appear to be animal skins – seal skins, to be precise, or at least seal-shaped hides (you're sup-posed to think 'roar', but I just think of a strangulated 'ark ark', and of flippers flipping). There's a screen to the side of it, presumably shielding a small bathroom area, although it wouldn't remotely surprise me to learn that Bernard poos in a hole outside, digging his latrine merrily with an Iron Age spade. Back in the living area, there's a Baby Belling and a couple of free-standing cupboards, as well as a comfy-looking sofa. The floor is covered in old rugs. It's like a hobbit-hole, except for humans, and as the storm howls outside, it feels like the cosiest place on earth. Bernard makes three big mugs of sweet tea and digs around inside a tin, producing shortbread.

It takes me a while to realize that nobody is saying any-thing. Bernard is leaning against the big table, staring at Gaby like a meteor just landed at his feet. Gaby is smiling at Bernard, in her mad dress, which – I now see – was explicitly purchased for the effect it is now having on our host. I clear my throat. I have never felt more of a gooseberry in my life: my superfluity is actually palpable.

'Right,' I say. 'Well, first things first. You must be wondering what we're doing here. Well, what *I'm* doing here.'

'Yes,' says Bernard, seemingly shaking himself awake. 'Absolutely. Of course. But Sky's OK?'

I always think bluntness is the best solution: there seems so little point in shilly-shallying about, with announcements.

'She's terrific,' I say. 'She's wonderful. But she's pregnant.'

'What?' says Bernard.

'Pregnant. Up the duff. Three months gone. By my son. Jack's the father.'

'Good grief,' says Bernard, sitting down and, I note, speaking normal English.

'There's more,' I say. 'She says she wants to keep the baby. She's pretty adamant about it. I suppose we could raise the idea of adoption with them further down the line, but I haven't broached it yet.'

'I won't hear of it,' says Bernard loudly.

'Well,' I say. 'She's very determined and Jack is standing by her. You'll need to talk to them soon, obviously. But I thought it would be best to come and tell you in person.'

Bernard is leaning over the table, his massive head in his massive hands. He's built on an enormous scale, like a bear; his author photograph, taken from the waist up, gives no indication of his hugeness. When he looks up, he has tears in his eyes.

'My little girl,' he says. 'My little Sky,' and I have a lump in my throat.

'I'm so sorry,' I say, 'for breezing in and telling you all this out of the blue. We only found out three days ago. She was actually pregnant before she moved in.' This is a wholly self-serving and craven thing to say, but unfortunately the words are already out of my mouth.

'The world is wonderful,' Bernard says, sounding a bit distracted. 'The world is beautiful.'

This hardly seems like the time to enter into a spirited discussion of the beauty of the Small Isles, but people say strange things sometimes, when they're in shock.

So, 'Yes,' I say. 'It certainly is. This island strikes me as nothing short of magical, for example.'

'It is full of wonders,' says Bernard, like Shakespeare. 'But I meant it about Sky. Oh, I wish you'd brought her.'

'We thought about it,' I say, 'but we, er, we weren't quite sure of your reaction, and I thought it was maybe best to keep things normal, to continue with schoolwork and try and keep on an even keel. Exams, you know.' There is a pause. 'To be honest,' I say, 'I'm still not quite sure of your reaction, Bernard.'

'I'm shocked,' Bernard says, taking a sip of his tea.

'Well, yes,' I say. 'We all are.'

'Shocked and awed,' says Bernard. 'Shocked and delighted.'

'Oh!' I say, because I've clearly been reading the entire conversation wrong. 'Oh. Right.'

'Behold the great Gaia in her fecund glory,' Bernard says. 'Behold the blossom bearing fruit. Ah, fertility! She's young, of course. Very young – little more than a child. But she is a wise child, my Sky. She's had to be, in our circumstances. She's old beyond her years. And she's the age,' he adds, 'that her mother was when she bore her.' He pauses. 'In the

Chronicles, if the father falls, the clan takes in the Babeling. All Babelings are cared for. Tribe cares for tribe.'

'Nobody's going to be fatherless,' I point out.

'Tribe cares for tribe,' Bernard repeats, with a faraway look in his eyes.

'Well, that's a relief,' says Gaby. 'I've been holding my breath for five minutes. She was so worried you'd be angry. Oh, if only we had Beakstrels to let her know.'

'O marvellous Gabbro!' bellows Bernard, laughing heartily. '*If only we had Beakstrels* indeed. This calls for a drink, I think. I have some malt somewhere. Of course,' he says, rummaging around the bottom of a tower of paper, 'I won't hear of the child being adopted. Whatever help Sky needs, I will provide it. I'll adopt it myself.'

'That's a lovely idea,' I say.

'Yes,' says Bernard. 'Funnily enough, it's very like a scene in the third volume of my Chronicles, when Kyryn – the Komatiite, you know –'

'Son of Picrite,' Gaby says automatically.

'Quite, quite. When Kyryn adopts Little Scoria, a Babeling.'

'Despite her mare-like tail, for she has the mark of the Steed. Such a tender scene,' says Gaby, misty-eyed. 'And so profound.'

'The women propagate early in Lapidosa,' Bernard says. 'The wenches have meat on their haunches, and bodies built for birth.'

'Right,' I say. Is it my imagination, or is he looking at Gaby a tiny bit disappointedly as he says this?

'Do you have any more shortbread?' says Gaby, possibly coincidentally, or possibly not.

'Alack,' says Bernard. 'No more. But I have meats and roots, and tonight – tonight we feast like kings!'

'I need to think about getting back to the mainland,' I say. Aside from anything else, I don't think I can cope with any more peculiar linguistic tics: between them, Gaby and Bernard are making me feel like *I* talk funny. It's like listening to something in simultaneous translation: your brain is taxèd. Taxed, even.

'Too late, dear Clara,' says Bernard. There are only two crossings at this time of year, and you've missed the last one. Not that I imagine it set sail – not in this weather.'

'Oh,' I say, nonplussed. 'Right. Well, then, I suppose I'd better, er . . .'

'There's another bothy yonder way,' says Bernard, who is disconcertingly able to slip between speaking perfectly normally and speaking very oddly. 'But it's a tad basic.'

'It's December,' I point out, 'and there's a storm, and I'm from London.'

'Of course, of course. You'd be very welcome to stay. I've barely spoken to anyone for weeks. I'm enjoying the company, and you bring naught but good tidings. More malt?'

'I'd like to stay,' says Gaby, holding out her mug. 'And yes please.'

'Marvellous,' roars Bernard. 'Slàinte!'

I catch Gaby's eye and flick mine towards the bed – the only bed. She shrugs at me. There's always the sofa, I suppose.

Bernard turns out to be a most excellent cook. He makes us roast venison with shallots – God knows where he's got the shallots from – and roast 'roots', as he keeps calling them, 'roots' including potatoes, which it would seem

206

pedantic to point out are tubers. 'Nature's bounty!' he booms, setting the dishes down on the table, alongside a steaming jug of red-wine gravy.

'This is delicious, Bernard,' I say. 'I'm impressed. It can't have been that you were expecting guests.'

'I always have victuals,' Bernard says. 'Procuring them – foraging, where I can – is part of my routine here. I always make myself a cooked breakfast in the morning and a proper dinner at night. It gives shape to the day. And I love cooking,' he adds. 'Wasn't much of a cook when Diana – Sky's mother – first met me, but I became pretty good after she died. Out of necessity, you know. I can't countenance the idea of a life without good food and wine.'

'Me neither,' I say, helping myself to more parsnips.

'They're a celebration,' Bernard says, 'of nature and of beauty and of being alive. Adjuncts to happiness. I've been here for weeks and they have kept me sane. I'll take you both for a walk in the morning – you should see the island before you leave. Very fertile, as it happens. It's mostly run as a farm, you know. We want for nothing here.'

'I've brought my Kindle,' I say after dinner – the venison is followed by goat's cheese and crackers: he wasn't wrong when he said it was a feast. Gaby's washed up and the table is clear of dishes again. 'I know you and Gaby – er, Gabbro – are keen to discuss your book. Really, don't mind me. I'm going to curl up on the sofa and read. Or nap. I'm knackered – it must be the fresh air.'

'Wonderful place, isn't it?' Bernard says, gesticulating expansively. 'I could live here, in another lifetime. I can quite see why the publishers sent me here. The land . . . I am inspired by land, Clara, and the land here inspires me.'

'Jolly good,' I say. 'It inspires me too.' I can sort of see why Bernard is, as Jack so succinctly put it, a 'shagger'. He's very much not my cup of tea, but objectively he's not unattractive, if you like hugeness. He's at least six foot four, and wide rather than fat, with a big face, a big chest and big legs. The beard really does nothing for him. Beards seldom do, I find, and this is the full Cornish fisherman, a dark brown facial wilderness that swamps down well past his collarbones. He is rugged, if you like that kind of thing. Roughly hewn, like the staff of Bold Olivine, perhaps. It occurs to me that I have spent too long with Gaby and the Frossages.

'Shall we, Gabbro?' Bernard says.

'It would be my pleasure,' says Gaby.

'Before you start,' I say. 'Is there a loo?'

'The earth serves well enough,' says Bernard.

'Does that mean "outside"?'

'It does,' says Bernard. 'But I have plentiful supplies of lavatory paper – just to your right, behind the curtain.'

'Righty ho,' I say, remembering how only the other night I was complaining to myself about men standing up when you went to warm loos with lights and sinks and towels and mirrors. 'Well, I'll just, er, you know. Go. I'll just go.' I want to ask him what I'm supposed to do with the used loo paper, but it's too revolting. I'll think of something. I wander out, as dignifiedly as I can, clutching a jumbo roll of Andrex, grateful not to be expected to use a pile of leaves.

The storm has abated and the night is beautifully clear, if freezing. Thanks to my trusty torch app, I find a likely spot – though frankly the isolation and solitude are such that I could pee anywhere, which is freedom of a kind, I suppose. But I wish I *had* asked about what to do with the loo paper.

I can't just leave it there, but I don't really want to put it in my pocket either. Suddenly the solution strikes me, with the sort of clarity that descends after two tumblers of whisky and claret with dinner: I must bury the loo paper. I do up my trousers and remember I have no shovel, but never mind: I am at one with the land. I need no tools. Gaia provides, as does the body.

And so it comes to pass that I am digging the cold earth with my hands just as Jim appears out of nowhere, wheeling his quad bike. I am crouched, and very clearly – thanks to the beams of his lights – in the act of burying loo paper.

'I'm just doing my night run,' he says, not batting an eyelid. 'I drive round checking everything's as it should be.'

I pull myself up, my hands filthy with soil.

'Bernard's asked us to stay over,' I say, 'so I think we're going to do that.'

'Right you are,' says Jim.

'It's really kind of you to come over,' I tell him. 'I'm grateful. Also, I was burying wee-paper, not poo-paper.'

'Good to know,' says Jim with no discernible change of facial expression. 'There's a chemical toilet round the back, for future reference.'

'But Bernard said . . .'

'Bernard's ways are the ways of the land,' Jim says with what might be a wink. 'Well, goodnight. I'll drop by again in the morning with news of the ferry. It's clearing up – I think you'll be fine. Assuming you're going back tomorrow?'

'I am,' I tell him. 'We both are.'

Bernard and Gaby have the demeanour of two children caught doing something they shouldn't when I come back into the bothy – the air of two people who've only pulled apart seconds before. I smile at them and then disappear behind the curtain to wash my hands and put on my pyjamas, and head straight for the sofa when I re-emerge.

'Pelts!' Bernard cries. 'You need pelts, Clara. Heat-giving skins from the beasts of the sea.'

'I have this blanket,' I say, 'and it's still warm from the fire. I can always stick my parka on if I get cold.'

But Bernard is insistent, and crashes over with a pair of 'pelts', which smell funny and slightly creep me out. I must go to sleep.

'Goodnight,' I say, closing my eyes.

I feel exhausted, full from the dinner and warm from the fire, and tired from thinking about Sky's pregnancy for three days. For a little while I can hear snatches of conversation about sieges and quests and Horno, and the bloody Amphiboles, interspersed with cries of wonder and delight from Bernard and excited whispers from Gaby. But these soon grow distant, and I fall fast asleep.

Having slept surprisingly deeply, I am awoken by the smell of bacon frying. The sun is shining weakly in through the bothy's windows, and all seems well with the world. Bernard and Gaby don't appear to have gone to bed at all, judging by the number of coffee mugs scattered about the kitchen table. The drifts of paper have propagated in Lapidosan style: I can't actually see the surface of the table, which is entirely covered in scrawled and scribbled notes.

'Good morning, dear Clara,' Bernard booms.

'Morning!' Gaby trills.

'Have you not gone to bed?' I ask.

'Heh,' says Gaby, which I call ambiguous.

'Bed can wait,' says Bernard. 'I feel absolutely *elated*. Gabbro here turns out to be the solution! She is my muse. Well – no. She is far more.'

'I'm so pleased I was able to be useful,' says Gaby modestly. 'I loved talking to you about it.'

'Oh, so much more than useful,' says Bernard. 'I've been stuck for a year. A year! And you've unstuck me in one night. It's not just that, though,' he says, turning to me. 'It's that her input is so inventive, so creative. So intuitive. She is absolutely *steeped* in the ways and mores of Lapidosa . . . Our coming together, our union, has been nothing short of a miracle.'

'I invented a new character,' Gaby says proudly but in a quiet voice. She looks slightly shell-shocked by the admission. 'She's called Mica. She hooks up with Calcite . . .'

'Son of Horno, who has reached manhood,' I say, almost as a reflex.

'Mica, like Gabbro, is the solution,' says Bernard. 'And so I would like to propose . . .'

'Steady on,' I say. 'You've only just met.'

Nobody laughs at this, oddly.

'I would like,' says Bernard, 'to propose a collaboration.'

'How do you mean?' says Gaby.

'I would like you, Gabbro – O wondrous wench, O wisest maid – henceforth to write the Chronicles with me. To be my co-author. It is,' he says, raising his hand as Gaby's mouth opens into an 'O' of astonishment, 'not only the very least I can do, but what I'd like. What I'd love. It would renew me, and my work. It would be like drinking from a fountain of youth.'

'Like the one at Gneiss,' Gaby says robotically.

'Oh my God,' I say. 'That's so cool.'

Gaby is still looking post-traumatically stressed.

'I don't know what to say,' she says. She is pop-eyed and has gone very pale.

'Say yes, Gabbro,' says Bernard. 'Say yes!'

'I . . . I'm not a writer,' Gaby says. 'And that's the least of it.'

'I'm a writer,' says Bernard. 'The writing isn't the issue. The plot, the characters, the ingenuity of the storyline – those are the real concerns. And you have displayed a rare genius.'

'God,' says Gaby. 'M'nork.'

'M'nork be praised!' says Bernard. 'Please, dear, dearest Gabbro – please say you will. Or at least that you'll consider it.'

'Yes,' says Gabbro. 'I will consider it.' She stares rather wildly around the room. 'Really, Bernard – I'm so touched and so pleased and so proud and so, so . . . Oh man, I don't even know the words. I was so unhappy . . . Sorry, I shouldn't say this. But what the hell. I was so unhappy a year ago, and now . . .'

'Here,' I say, passing her a wad of loo roll. 'Blow.'

'Whuu,' says Gaby, crying. 'Whii, whii.'

'The world is beautiful,' says Bernard. 'And now, bacon. And eggs. And the finest black pudding known to man. And coffee, for the womenfolk are athirst.'

After a glorious early-morning walk, and a ferry, and two trains, and a taxi, we are back in London. (Travel really amazes me – this is another thing that's come with age. When I was

212

young, I'd think nothing of hopping on a plane and arriving in a whole new country seven hours later. Now, the idea that I woke up in an impossibly remote bothy – I didn't know what a bothy was until yesterday – and am now sitting in my kitchen absolutely blows my mind.)

Gaby is still in a state of shock, but never mind that now. Sky seems relieved that her dad knows and isn't angry. I tell her that her father is unblocked, that he's now writing up a storm, that he wanted to come back with us but that we persuaded him that staying for a bit longer wouldn't hurt if it meant that he could finish his book. I explain that he will call her tonight – any minute now, in fact – from the house of the neighbour who has a phone.

'He really wasn't crosss with me? Not even a little bit?' she asks.

'No. He was shocked, naturally. But then he was moved. In fact, he was pleased. He said that your mum . . .'

'Was seventeen too, yes,' says Sky. 'Anyway, how is he?'

'He's asked Gaby to collaborate with him on Men of Granite,' I say. 'Which is why she can't speak at the moment. She's barely said a word all day.'

'That's the coolest thing I've ever heard,' Sky said, going over to hug her.

'What?' says Gaby. 'Yes. No. Thanks. Sorry, I'm thinking. I'm really pleased that your dad is OK with the baby, Sky.'

'God, so am I,' says Sky.

'So am I,' says Jack.

'So am I,' I say.

The phone starts ringing. 'That'll be him,' I say. 'Take it upstairs. We don't all need to sit here listening.'

'Come on, Jack,' says Sky, grabbing the receiver. 'Let's go

to our room. Hello, Daddy,' she says into the receiver, and bursts into tears.

'What are you going to do?' I ask Gaby an hour later. We've opened a bottle of wine and are still at the kitchen table. 'You must be so pleased. It's amazing, right?'

'I can't put it into words,' says Gaby.

'Try. You've been practically mute all day.'

Gaby takes a deep sip of red wine, and then another.

'I am rethinking my entire life,' she says. 'I have been since breakfast time this morning. Well, late last night, if I'm being honest. I felt very . . . connected . . . from the moment we arrived.'

'I noticed,' I say. 'It was mutual.'

'OK, so tell me just this one thing,' says Gaby. 'I know you think it's all hilarious, but you do realize what a big deal he is, yes? What a big deal the books are?'

'Yes,' I say. 'Eighteen months at number one kind of thing. I read the papers.'

'Right,' says Gaby. 'And this is going to sound really lame, but if I say yes – if I agree to' – and here she laughs shrilly – 'co-author his books . . .'

'Yes?' I say. 'What?'

'Does that make me, like, Yoko Ono? Will the fans come at me with pitchforks?'

'Don't be ridiculous,' I say. 'Gaby! For God's sake. Is that what's been worrying you?'

'Well, one of the things,' Gaby says, sounding so small-voiced that I stand up to go and give her a hug.

'Thanks,' she says. 'You really don't think so?'

'No. All the fans care about is the books, and it sounds to

me like you and Bernard are two halves of the same brain when it comes to the books. So, no. It's not like you're going to force him to introduce talking pigs.'

'Hahaha! Oh, Clara! Of course not, no,' says Gaby, as if I'd suggested something absolutely insane. 'Hahaha,' she laughs again.

I don't see why talking pigs should be any odder than hornèd men or babies with tails.

'Haha. Let's not be absurd,' I say.

'No,' says Gaby. 'Let's not. Anyway. That's good to hear. But then of course there's all the other stuff.'

'Drink up,' I say. 'I get the feeling this is a two-bottle job.'

'Right,' says Gaby. 'Well, the first thing is – obviously – that I, I, I . . . I don't think I can see Ben any more.'

'OK,' I say. 'He's very nice. But he *is* twenty-nine.'

'And I am forty-nine,' says Gaby. She has not explicitly stated her age since she arrived. 'For another fortnight.'

'Yes. And I am forty-six.'

We catch each other's eye and smile.

'We're in our prime,' I say.

'You're going to be a GILF,' Gaby says. 'Or is it NILF?'

'Don't,' I say. 'I can't quite compute that part yet. Stay on topic, please.'

'I just . . . I really like Bernard,' she says, with some desperation.

'I know. And he really likes you. I'm a romantic. I believe completely in the coup de foudre. Which is exactly what happened. I saw it with my own eyes.'

'Do you really think so?'

'One hundred per cent yes,' I say, like an *X Factor* judge.

Gaby beams at this, then shakes her head and carries on.

'OK, so then: problem number two. Say we get together.'
She flushes at the idea, and again smiles to herself with
pleasure.

'Yes?'

'So we're together – I mean, God and M'nork willing,
I don't want to jinx anything, this is just wishful thinking.
But say. Assume. And then we work together too. And one
day something goes wrong.'

'Like what?'

'Oh, I don't know. Something. Either in our . . . personal
relationship or in our professional relationship. Then what,
Clara? It all goes to fuck, right?'

'This is not a way to think,' I say indignantly. 'This is the
opposite of a way to think. Why are you Voice of Dooming
yourself, like a freak?'

'Because I'm not you. I was married to the same person
for nine years.'

'Yes, I've been married too. So?'

'So I come to London and I think I like the idea of having
boyfriends that aren't serious. The novelty of it. I mean,
until Ben I hadn't shagged anyone other than Ham for a
decade and a half.'

'I understand,' I say. 'Your point is?'

'My point is that actually I *don't* like having boyfriends
that aren't serious. I liked Ben, obviously, and I fancied him
well enough, but – it made me feel anxious. Xanax has
become my friend, put it that way.'

'That's because you were pretending to be thirty-four,'
I say. 'It would take its toll on anyone.'

'No,' Gaby says. 'It's because I was unhappy and I didn't
love him and I thought it would be fun, and it wasn't as

much fun as I wanted it to be. It *was* fun, but not the right kind of fun. It wasn't the kind of fun that made me feel good about myself. Or the right kind of love. It was no kind of love, really.'

'You should have said that you were unhappy. When you arrived, I mean. I had no idea. In another life you could be an actress.'

'I want to be with someone who I love, and who loves me,' says Gaby. 'I want to be able to reference *Bagpuss* or *Mind Your Language* or Space Dust or, God, David Bowie on *Top of the Pops* and not be met with this . . . this blank wall of incomprehension. Plus then the wriggling out, the deception, the claiming I saw it on YouTube, because of course I was barely born at the time.'

'I understand,' I say. 'Who wouldn't want that?'

'And the drugs, you know. I mean, I'm all for them, every now and then. We're from that generation, aren't we? But, like, maybe twice a year. Not every sodding night. Do you remember when I took ketamine? I thought I was going to die.'

'I so wish you'd said,' I say, refilling our glasses. 'I honestly had no idea.'

'And while I'm at it,' says Gaby, 'I would have loved to have children. *Loved.* It makes me really sad that I couldn't. Four rounds of IVF, you know, but nothing happened. I mean, it's not the be-all and end-all. I'm over it. It's fine. But I'm sick of pretending – to myself, as much as to anyone else – that it was some kind of choice, and that making that choice means I have some kind of duty to behave in a certain way. Carefree. Up-for-it. Wholly without responsibilities. I mean, fuck's sake.'

'It's OK,' I say. I feel a bit like crying, so I add, 'Take mine, if you like. Or have a part share. The children, the responsibilities, the whole shebang.'

'God,' says Gaby. 'All this *stuff*. We all have so much stuff.'

'Do you want to know what I think?' I ask.

'Yes.'

'I'm with Bernard. Life is beautiful. And sad and dark and complex too, obviously. But mostly beautiful. I believe in love.'

'Oh, Clara. We all believe in love.'

'I'm talking about men, specifically. About relationships. What I'm saying is, I don't think it matters if you're with somebody for two weeks or twenty years, if you love them. I mean, it's everything. It's the world, for that fortnight or those two decades. That's not a thing you piss on.'

'I'm not pissing on it!'

'You are, though. You're saying, what if it goes wrong? What if we have a disagreement about those beak-thingies . . .'

'Beakstrels.'

'What if we have a disagreement about Beakstrels, what if he doesn't like my kids . . .'

'I don't have any kids,' says Gaby. 'Duh.'

'But you know what I mean.'

'Yes, I know what you mean,' she sighs. 'Sorry, you were saying? I interrupted.'

'Oh yes. Don't piss on it, I was saying. Don't piss on anything, but most of all don't piss on love. Especially at our age. You're unbelievably fortunate. You've met Bernard. You're forty-nine. He's, what, early fifties? Be happy. Don't sit there making lists of all the things that could go wrong.'

'I don't want to piss on love,' Gaby says dolefully.

'Well, then. Don't.'

'You're right,' says Gaby thoughtfully. 'Though, easier said than done. I'm a naturally anxious person.'

'It's hard to be anxious when you're really happy. Because you're really, wildly, totally in love with someone who is wildly in love with you.'

'And with whom you'll have great sex,' muses Gaby.

'Absolutely,' I say. 'With someone with whom you'll have mind-blowing sex. All the time.'

'God, I bet Bernard's going to be *amazing*,' says Gaby, to which there is really no reply.

'Mm,' I say.

'I'm going to say yes,' Gaby says. 'Yes to Bernard, yes to books, yes to love. Yes! I am!'

'You fucking rock, Gaby,' I tell her as we clink glasses. 'Everything is going to be fine.'

'He left me, you know,' Gaby says, almost as an afterthought. 'Ham. He left me for his twenty-six-year-old assistant, like in a miniseries. That was when I upped the work for a bit. Before that I was happy with' – she laughs – 'my massive facelift.'

'Don't knock the work,' I say. 'This isn't supposed to be some sort of Damascene conversion. The work is great and the work has served you well. I mean, look at you!'

'I would still have found Bernard without all this,' says Gaby with feeling.

'Yeah, maybe. The books, sure. The rest – who knows? Yes, probably, but I guess we'll never know. Look, I get that you were unhappy, and I get that it must have been horrible, and I get that having more and more cosmetic surgery, exercising more frantically, dieting more bizarrely are not healthy. But you look great. And now you feel great. So let's not get too sackcloth and ashes about it.'

'True,' says Gaby. 'True. I might leave it at that, though. At this.'

Epilogue

Six months later

'Does everyone have to be in here?' says the nurse. 'Only, it's very crowded. Mum barely has any room to breathe.'

'Absolutely,' says Kate. 'I'm hardly likely not to be present at the birth of my first great-grandchild.'

'Yes,' I say. 'It's my first grandchild too.'

'Yeah,' says Charlie. 'It's my niece or nephew, man.'

'Yes,' says Maisy. 'I am going to be an auntie.'

'Yes,' says Flo. 'I am to be a great-aunt.'

'As am I,' says Evie. 'Man, I'm so excited.'

'I'm the dad,' says Jack.

'I don't know what I am,' says the Man From The Connaught, whose name is James, 'but I wanted to be here with Clara.'

'I'm the grandfather,' says Robert. 'God, the horror. At my age, Jack!'

'Soz,' says Jack, grinning a huge grin.

'I don't mean it,' says Robert. 'Well, only half.'

'I'm the other grandfather,' says Bernard.

'And I'm the step-granny,' says Gaby. 'So, yes. We all need to be here.'

'Well, that's very nice, but I'm going to shoo you all away when she's ten centimetres dilated,' says the nurse. 'Apart from Dad,' she says, smiling at Jack.

'I think I can probably live with that,' says Robert, who is squeamish in the extreme.

'Are you scared, Sky?' asks Charlie.

'Only a bit.' Sky smiles. 'We've been going to pregnancy classes for ages.'

'It's not going to be a long labour,' says the nurse kindly, patting Sky's shoulder. 'At your age they usually shoot out. People tend to forget, but that's how bodies are made. You're just the right age to have a baby. Well,' she adds, 'biologically. Medically, I mean.'

'In all respects,' says Bernard proudly.

'She's lucky to have so many of you supporting her,' says the nurse.

'We love her,' says Kate briskly. 'So it's very simple. Sky, darling, do try to sit up straight. Bad posture really doesn't help anything.'

'It's time,' says the midwife. 'Everyone out please, except Dad.'

'Thank God,' says Robert. 'It's getting a bit grunty in here.'

'Um,' says Sky, 'and Gaby, please. She needs to stay. And my dad, if he'd like to.'

'The women of Lapidosa foal in the Wenches' Chamber,' says Bernard. 'With only other wenches witnessing the miracle of birth. I'll be outside, my darling girl.'

'And Gaby is?' says the midwife, as we all start traipsing out.

'My stepmum,' says Sky. 'And also this baby's mum. Well, this baby's other mum.'

'We're *all* going to be parents!' booms Bernard. 'And

grandparents at the same time. We are adopting our lovely daughter's baby.'

'We're all going to live together,' says Gaby. 'Me and Bernard, with Sky and Jack and the baby. Sort of a commune vibe, but not. More like a tribe.'

'Tribe cares for tribe,' says Bernard, sounding like a bassoon.

'And why not?' says the midwife cheerfully. 'Takes all sorts. Ah, here we go. Shallow breaths, darling.'

My grandson only took forty minutes to be born. He is beautiful, and he weighs eight pounds, and his name is Romeo. His second name is Stone. ('Obviously,' Sky, Bernard and Gaby said in unison. 'Obviously.') He pinged out, as the nurse said he would, and when we went back into the room, everybody was crying, except Romeo, who had a pleased little look on his face. Kate produced four bottles of champagne, and the toast was 'To love'.

My boyfriend is walking me to the bus stop, like a gent. I feel giddy every time I look at him.

'I wish they'd stop doing that,' he says as we pass number 33.

'Do what, darling?'

'Clara! You're supposed to be observant.'

'Huh?' I say. 'I have no idea what you're talking about.'

'Ogle,' he says. 'I don't like the way they *ogle*. Somebody should tell them it's the twenty-first century.'

'Really?' I say, astonished. 'What, ogle *me*?'

'Every time,' he says, laughing and pushing me up against

a tree to kiss me. 'I noticed as soon as I moved in. I can't say I blame them. But still.'

And across the blue sky of a perfect June morning it comes: the unmistakable whoop-whoop of a wolf whistle.

Acknowledgements

Vast debts of gratitude, as ever, to Georgia Garrett and Juliet Annan, and big thanks to Sali, Sophia and David. Thanks to everyone who talks to me on Twitter: it helps with sanity when you're in a book-hole. Apologies, as ever, to both the editorial and the production teams at Penguin, who must be wearying of me saying, 'But people put together *entire newspapers* overnight, where's the hurry?' Sorry. But here we are, so yay. Frippu, Penguin.